UNPUNISHED DEEDS

A PETER BLACK THRILLER

DAVID ARCHER

VINCE VOGEL

RIGHTHOUSE

ISBN-13: 978-1-63696-329-7

ISBN-10: 1-63696-329-3

Cover design by: Damonza

Printed in the United States of America

www.righthouse.com

www.instagram.com/righthousebooks

www.facebook.com/righthousebooks

twitter.com/righthousebooks

PRAISE FOR THE PETER BLACK SERIES

"A Twisting Tale of Murder, Revenge and Love."

AMAZON REVIEW

"I read the Orphan X series, the Reacher series, the Gray Man series, and many others. It's rare to find authors whose books grab you like this one did."

AMAZON REVIEW

"...the action is almost nonstop and you're not prepared for what happens on any given moment."

AMAZON REVIEW

"Ranks with the best of the genre: Flynn, Thor, Ludlum, Hagberg, etc..."

AMAZON REVIEW

PETER BLACK THRILLERS
Burden of the Assassin (Book 1)
The Man Without A Face (Book 2)
Unpunished Deeds (Book 3)
Hunter Killer (Book 4)
Silent Shadows (Book 5)
The Last Run (Book 6)
Dark Corners (Book 7)
Ghost Operative (Book 8)

ONE

OLENIVKA PRISON COLONY, EAST UKRAINE - RUSSIAN OCCUPIED TERRITORY

VASILY SAVELYEV SITS INSIDE A MIL MI-24 helicopter gunship staring out of the window at its ominous shadow gliding over an expanse of flat grassland. The scenery is relatively peaceful—for a war zone, at least. Along the horizon are low hills, beyond which are the Ukrainians, and the rapidly growing momentum of their counter offensive.

But Savelyev tries not to think about that. Instead he concentrates on the work ahead.

Vasily Savelyev is a commander in the Federal Security Service of the Russian Federation (FSB), the principal security service of Russia and main successor agency to the Soviet Union's KGB. With the Russian state essentially stretching into new territory, it means a widening of responsibilities for men like Savelyev. Chances to be a hero.

The prison colony comes into view. Tall fencing punctuated by gun towers surrounds a compound of rectangular concrete structures. They look like shoeboxes from a distance. Their walls are pitted with tiny, horizontal barred windows, mere slits in the stone. Very little sunlight reaches inside the dark chambers of Olenivka.

Before the war, this was where the Ukrainians would send their very worst. Now the Russians bring captured soldiers here.

The chopper lands at the far end of the compound. The relevant group of soldiers are there to greet Savelyev and check the legitimacy of his identification. All the men here are members of a Chechen unit already infamous in the war.

The one known as Scorpion Team.

Savelyev feels uneasy in their presence. In his early years, during the Second Chechen War, the FSB man had spent so long "disappearing" and torturing young Chechen men that he now felt uneasy around them. Like the ghosts of their ancestors hung from them. *Hell,* he would think whenever in their company, *I may well have once tortured one of these men's fathers or uncles.*

Nevertheless, time rolls over everything. Enemies become friends. Friends enemies.

"Take me to Tagirov," Savelyev says to the officer who hands back his papers.

The officer has gray in his beard and a sunbaked face. It wrinkles into a frown. "You mean the Colonel?"

"Yes."

The man guides him toward one of the concrete blocks. As they get closer, the sounds of men shouting, pleading, screaming, gets louder and louder until they are reaching the entrance to the cellblock and the cacophony rings in Savelyev's skull.

A soldier stands one side of the door. He salutes the officer and opens it for them.

The change in atmosphere is instant. Outside, the air was fresh, the world open. In here it is stifling and oppressive. The air thick with the stench of despairing horror: sweat, blood, feces.

Savelyev almost chokes on it.

"It takes some getting used to," the officer says, holding out a bottle of water.

Savelyev thanks him and takes the bottle, slugging a mouthful down, hoping to wash away the taste of this place. The worst of the screaming comes from behind a closed door at the very end of the corridor. The officer tells him it is where "the Colonel" is.

Of course it is, Savelyev thinks.

The officer leads on. They pass the barred walls of cells. Inside are men. They look barely alive, like the animals of some backwater traveling zoo. Some of them don't even look that good.

A soldier blocks the door. A few words are exchanged between him and the officer and it is opened for them. Savelyev steps into a small red brick chamber with a vaulted ceiling. The acoustics of the room amplify the insane screams to the point that the air shakes.

The door slams shut behind them, closing them in with it. Savelyev stands staring at a badly beaten man tied to an X-shaped rack. Splayed out across it as though he were frozen in the act of performing a jumping jack. His hands and feet are bound to the rack and he is naked except for the black hood over his head.

Two men occupy the room with him. Members of Team Scorpion. Tagirov stands before the hooded man like an artist in front of his work, running a hand down his thick beard.

"Colonel," the officer says to him.

The artist turns. Tagirov is just how Savelyev remembers him—crazy eyed, black bearded. Grinning, the Chechen shows off a set of yellow teeth.

"Savelyev," he hisses. "Long time no see, old friend."

The grin rides up the black hairs of his cheeks.

"Tagirov," Savelyev grunts back.

The two men don't shake hands. Don't hug. They aren't "old friends," despite the Chechen saying it. These men only meet for one reason, and one reason alone.

"The last time you came to see me," Tagirov says, "a lot of people ended up dead."

"They did."

"So what is it now?"

"Two things."

Tagirov goes to speak but Savelyev interrupts him.

"Outside," he says. "Away from your men."

Tagirov turns to the man in there with him. A dead-eyed subordinate with the look of death about him.

"You remember Khodov, don't you?"

The dead-eyed man nods respectfully at Savelyev.

"I do," the FSB commander says. "But I prefer to speak only to you."

"So be it." Tagirov turns to the officer. "Help Khodov with the interrogation."

"Yes, Colonel."

The two men leave the cell and the hooded man recommences with his screaming. When they exit the cellblock and enter sunlight, Savelyev feels himself able to breathe again. Tagirov, on the other hand, squints in it, bringing an arm over his face to protect his eyes. He looks as though he preferred the darkness.

"Wow," he says. "It's been a while since I was outside."

He takes a pair of shades from the breast pocket of his camo shirt and slips them on.

"That's better," he says before turning to Savelyev. "Now what is it you've come to ask?"

"This morning I got word that we are repositioning our defensive line eastwards."

Tagirov frowns. "Another retreat?"

"Not retreat. A strategic repositioning of battle lines."

"I'm sorry. I'm not Russian. I don't have your capacity for state-sponsored bullshit. It is a retreat."

"Call it what you want. In twenty-four hours the Ukrainians will be here. Before you and your unit move on, I need you to cover up what you've been doing in this place. The last thing we need are more pictures of atrocities in the hands of our enemies."

"And then what?"

"I have a new mission for you."

"What new mission?"

"A very important one. Easily the most important mission you've ever been on. One which will go down in history."

"History?"

"Yes. But before I brief you properly, I need you to get rid of this place."

"Count it done."

Tagirov turns to a subordinate and tells him in Chechen to evacuate all buildings of soldiers and to leave the prisoners chained in their cells. Then he asks the guy to get him an RPG-7 shoulder launcher and a crate of GSh-7VT anti-bunker warheads.

TWO

SORRENTO, ITALY

THE THRILL OF A GOOD ENGINE. THE ROAD rushing by a few inches below you, gliding on the air itself. The tremble of the wheel beneath your grip. The tiger's roar when you accelerate. The bucket seat surging you forwards.

This is what life is all about, Michael says to himself as he slides the black 1987 Ferrari Testarossa convertible along the sunbaked coast of southern Italy. The road follows the shore and every now and then they pass through little towns —Torre del Greco, Torre Annunciata, Castellammare— until, finally, they are approaching home: Sorrento.

From here on, the road is a narrow ridge cut into the side of the rock cliffs. Peter, who sits in the passenger seat, watches the villages down below at the water's edge slip by, the houses resembling breadcrumbs.

As the landscape rises into Sorrento, they come across a

bolder in the middle of the road that has broken away from the cliff.

Michael dodges it with a nonchalant swerve.

Houses line the rocks above them, straggling up the mountain, and below, the tile roofs of the lower buildings are silhouetted against the blue sea.

It is late afternoon when they arrive at the old stone city on the edge of the cliffs. Michael steers the Ferrari up zigzagging cobbled streets, toward home; a large two-story house with an iron gate that opens onto the road, and a terrace that projects over the cliff's edge, giving them the perfect view of the sea and surrounding streets.

As well as a good sniper's nest. If that is ever needed.

"What are you going to do when we get back?" Michael asks as he taxis through the narrow thoroughfares.

"Probably take another shower. I can still smell blood in my nostrils."

"Oh stop going on about it. I said I was sorry, didn't I?"

"You could try listening to me next time. I told you the M82 was too much. You should have stuck with the SSG 69 using .308 Winchester rounds like I told you."

"But would they have penetrated the glass?"

"Yes. They would have. And they certainly wouldn't have caused the guy's head to explode all over me."

"Yeah yeah yeah," the kid waves away as they reach their street. Then. "Who's that?"

A tall man in a black suit stands in front of their gate. Michael stops the Ferrari a few yards from him. Lays a hand on the grip of the pistol hidden beside his seat.

"It's okay," Peter says. "It's Salvatore."

The long-limbed Salvatore strolls up to Peter's side.

"Can we speak inside?" he asks in a deep voice.

"Sure."

———————

MICHAEL MAKES the coffee while Peter and Salvatore sit in the shade of the living-room. The Italian is sixty-three years of age with grayish skin and bloodshot eyes like a bloodhound.

Despite his washed-out look, the man is probably the most socially connected person in this part of the world. Sure, you won't find him attending Puccini operas with politicians or being asked his opinion on news items. He has no presence on social media, let alone a following. He's not an influencer.

But he is still very much connected. Because the circles that Salvatore spends his time in aren't the types to advertise themselves or their activities. The shadows are where men like Salvatore spend their time, and, like a spider with a web, the jaundiced Italian listens out for the vibrations of his people, and for a fee, sells what he finds out to those willing to pay.

Peter and Michael keep him on a retainer. Make sure that they are the first to find out if a hit has been placed on them or if a police investigation is getting to close.

"Two men have been asking around for you," he says once the coffee is served. "They are offering a huge price just for this address."

"Names?"

"No names and I cannot describe them because this information came to me secondhand. Only this morning one of my associates asked if I knew anything about Azrael living in Italy."

"How much are they offering?"

"A million just for this address."

Michael widens his eyes. "Wow." Turning to Peter, he asks him if he knows anyone that would be willing to pay such a high price.

"Many," is the answer he gives the kid.

"Look," Salvatore says, "I take my contract with you seriously. I never break an oath. But others know where you are. And they may be more willing to sell you out, so be careful, Azrael."

He finishes his coffee and leaves after that.

Michael and Peter watch him walk away from an upstairs window.

"What are you going to do?" Michael asks.

Peter takes a deep breath and then lets it out. "I don't know."

They watch Salvatore all the way until he disappears around the curve off the street.

"Come on," Peter then says. "It's your turn to cook."

"I'm not eating at home."

"Oh?"

"No. I'm eating out with Bianca."

"That little girl you've been dating?"

Michael knits his brows. "She's not a little girl. Anyway, there's a pizzeria that she's been raving about. Then, afterwards, we're off to a party."

Right on cue, a moped horn sounds down below in the street.

"That's her now," the kid adds. "Don't wait up."

Michael applies a couple of splashes of expensive eau de cologne and skips out of the house. Peter watches from the window as he climbs onto the back of the girl's scooter and they buzz off.

"So I'll be eating alone," he says to himself. "Again."

THREE

TYRRHENIAN SEA, ITALY

FOUR O'CLOCK THE NEXT MORNING, IN THE twilight just before dawn, Peter and Michael sail their small boat the *Mother-Magda* toward a set of tiny islands about eight miles off the Gulf of Naples. A collection of craggy rocks poke from the scalp of the sea and begin to emerge along the horizon with the sun.

Peter is in control of the craft. Michael too busy throwing up over the side.

"I take it you drunk beer at this party," the father says.

All Michael can do is hold a thumb up to him.

A few minutes later the kid comes away and flushes his mouth out with bottled water, washes the dregs from his chin. When he rejoins Peter at the cockpit, his father is holding out a stick of gum.

"Thanks," the kid mumbles as he takes it, before lumping himself down in a seat at the stern.

After a few cups of coffee from a thermos, Michael is more with it. "The wind's coming in from the east," he tells Peter. "If you want to hit the landing spot you need to steer into it. Otherwise we'll sail past and have to go around again."

When they initially bought the *Mother-Magda* Peter didn't have the first clue about sailing. A sailboat wasn't exactly the sort of thing you used in the world of espionage. It was a skill he had never required. If he needed to get around on water, he chose a motorboat every time. Didn't rely on the wind.

Michael, on the other hand, spent much of his summer vacations as a youngster with his stepfather Carl on their yacht. By ten he had learned to sail. Now he was passing that skill upwards to his father.

"How was the party?" Peter asks as he pitches the craft into the wind.

"It was good."

The kid is green.

"It looks it."

"The only reason I'm so ill," Michael attests in a somewhat bitter tone, "is because I'd only managed two hours sleep before my father came crashing into my room, telling me we'd be training today."

"We have to stay alert," Peter tells him. "Training sharpens the senses. Plus, it gives me a chance to hang out with you. You're always with your friends. I hardly see you anymore."

Michael grins. "You miss me?"

"You're my son. Of course I do."

The kid chuckles.

"You find that funny?"

"No," Michael assures him. "I find it sweet."

"Sweet?"

Peter has turned around to him.

"Yeah. That you miss me. Now pay attention or we won't make the spot. We wouldn't want you missing that, too."

———

FANG ISLAND IS a cluster of jagged, rocky islands that poke out the water and resemble teeth. Hence the name the locals have given it. Officially, Fang Island has never had a name, and only shipwrecked fishermen have ever called it home. Well, except for a brief period during World War II when the Nazis built a collection of fortifications on the three largest of the islands and placed armaments there in case the Allies ever invaded from the south. A series of concrete blocks that are partially buried in the excavated clifftops stand as the only testament of that time. The sea has greened much of them now through the perpetual crash of waves, but the bunkers themselves are still relatively intact.

They tie the boat up at the only place you can—a rickety jetty that sticks out from the sheer cliffs—then scale thirty meters of pure vertical rock wall, carrying 100lb loads on their backs.

Like Peter was at his age, Michael is now a sinewed machine adept at physical strain of any type, his body displaying perfect balance.

At the top, they find their usual gap in the barbwire

fencing, ignoring the futile keep-out signs, and make their way into the main hallway of the bunker.

The sounds of the sea echo in the vaulted space. Dawn is here and wedges of sunlight shine in through the horizontal gunner slots that line the walls.

Peter checks over his weapon; a Tavor CTAR-21 bullpup battle weapon. Once he's sure of its tip-top condition, he twists a custom-made suppressor on the end—being that he would prefer it if passing fishermen didn't hear them.

In the meantime, Michael tightens the straps on the body armor covering his torso.

"You know the drill," Peter says in a cool tone. "The flag is on the other side of the island. You have a five-minute head start. You have to get the flag, then double back and bring it here. Place it in that holder." He points to his left, where they've fixed a loop of rope to the wall. "Added to that," Peter says next, pulling back the cocking lever on the side of the Tavor's barrel, "we won't be using paintballs, because…"

"… it doesn't have the same psychological effect as knowing you could really die," Michael says over him. "Yeah yeah."

"There should be consequences," Peter says sternly. "Even in training."

"You're starting to sound like Mother."

"You want me to discipline like her?"

"No."

"Then make sure your helmet's on properly. I wouldn't want it slipping off and you taking one in the head."

The kid thinks about this. Then he asks, "What would you do if you did accidentally kill me?"

Peter spends a second or two pondering it. Then he

answers. "Probably bury you somewhere on the island, go back to the house, pack up what I can carry, leave."

"Cold."

"I keep telling you. It's the life of the assassin. Now run!"

———

FOUR HOURS later Michael commands the boat as Fang Island shrinks into the horizon behind them. His shoulder aches where Peter got a hit on his body armor, and from time to time he flexes the arm to relieve it a little. Peter doesn't allow him the use of pharmacological pain relief. Only meditation.

It's now nine o'clock in the morning and many of the other sailing boats are on the water, enjoying the bright and beautiful day.

"Why are we heading back to Sorrento?" Peter asks his son as the mainland looms into view. "I thought we were sailing out to Capri today."

"We are," the kid assures him. "But first we have to pick up Bianca."

Peter groans inwardly.

Fifteen minutes later they arrive at Sorrento harbor. There, at the end of a jetty, stands the pretty Bianca in shorts and polo shirt, a sash of red linen tied around her slender neck. Black hair flows down her back and big Dior sunglasses cover her eyes. A $350 gift from Michael for her birthday.

"Ah, bambino!" she shrieks when Michael jumps out of the boat and takes her in his arms.

It's left to Peter to tie the boat up.

With the help of Michael, who holds her delicate hand as though she were a princess, Bianca steps on board the thirty-foot craft.

"Ciao, Peter," she says with a smile.

"Good morning…"

She doesn't even wait for him to finish.

"… Bianca."

The girl has already turned to Michael, flipped her sunglasses up onto the top of her head, and, showing off her white teeth, throws herself into his arms, the teens necking almost straight away. Peter forced to avert his gaze. Then Michael grimaces when she squeezes his shoulder.

"Oh, baby," she coos, coming away from him. "Are you hurt?"

"It's nothing," he tells her bravely.

"Let me see."

He lets her lift his shirt and when she sees the bruising from the gunshot—purple and shaped like a fist—she cries out tenderly.

"My God! What happened, bambino?"

"I fell while we were rock climbing."

"Again?"

Bruises being a regular occurrence.

"Yes. But not too bad."

"Let me kiss it better."

This is too much for Peter. He has to leave them. Go somewhere else. But it's a small sailboat. All he can do is untie them from the jetty and pilot the *Mother-Magda* back out to sea, doing his best to avert his eyes.

———

During the journey to Capri, Peter does most of the sailing. The two teenagers spending the time giggling in the cabin. At one point, he decides to be facetious. In a loud voice, he asks Bianca how her father is. To which, Michael walks to the cabin doorway, eyeballs him from within, and unceremoniously closes the doors.

The day in Capri is much the same. The two teenagers practically ignore Peter as they stroll lazily around the narrow thoroughfares and market piazzas, the stalls and the shops. In the end, he leaves the lovebirds to it. Just peels off on his own, the two of them not even noticing his absence until he is long gone.

He simply sends Michael a text that he'll meet them back at the boat at five. To which he gets a thumbs up emoji as a reply.

For the rest of his lonely time on Capri, Peter sits people-watching from the café terraces. As for Michael, there's only one person he has any desire to watch.

Bianca.

The way she smiles with her teeth, eyes shining, the dimples on her cheeks showing, breathes light into him—makes everything taste better, look better, feel better. Not to mention the way anything can trigger that smile. Simple things like finding an ornament in some dusty tourist shop that she thinks quaint—or the low-ceilinged basement rooms at the bottom of an old bookshop that excite her.

There is such joy in her enthusiasm for life that she appears to hog all the light to herself. Like it is drawn to her and everything around her is cast in shadow.

Sometimes this includes Michael. And he can't help

worrying, during these moments, about how she would feel toward him if she knew what he was.

A killer.

The teens spend most of the day on the beach. Sunbathing and swimming. In the afternoon, they swim around the rocky coast to some caves they know. Inside is their own private place, and there they do what most teenagers do in such isolated settings. They make out.

Not that it makes it to sex.

On the occasions it ever gets that far, Bianca reminds Michael that she is Roman Catholic, not bothering to mention the part about sex before marriage, but definitely implying it.

Michael suspects the real reason has nothing to do with religion. That the truth is she's shy. Like Michael is shy. They're both virgins, and their inexperience shows. Each time they get close to the act, they back away. Bianca mentioning about being Roman Catholic, and Michael naturally disengaging, inwardly grateful, whilst at the same time wondering what would happen if she didn't stop him.

He can tell that it's getting close. That eventually the two of them will step over that line—that daunting, fascinating, exciting line. That they will take the plunge into the unknown.

Michael tries not to think of this as the two of them slip into the water and swim back to the beach.

———

"Do you think your papa likes me?" Bianca asks.

They are making their way to the harbor along a cobbled boulevard that runs past various little shops and cafés.

"Of course he does," Michael assures his girlfriend.

"But he never talks to me."

"Peter never talks, period. Don't take it personal."

She waits a little while. Then. "Mikey, why don't you respect your papa?"

"I do respect him."

"Then why do you call him Peter?"

"I told you. I had another father before."

"Yes. Carl. But Carl wasn't your real papa."

"I know. But when you've spent most of your life calling one man dad, it's hard to then call another man the same word."

"I guess. Ah! Gelato."

Bianco shows her teeth and draws in more light.

It makes Michael smile. Her attention so easily won.

And lost.

He buys them both ice cream and they walk off eating them.

"Michael?" Bianca says in the tone she uses when she is about to ask something personal.

"Bianca?" Michael replies in the same tone.

"I know you told me it is business. But what business is it that your papa is into?"

"I told you, he doesn't like me talking about it."

"But what is it?"

"It's a secret," he tells her before taking a lick of his gelato and winking.

She simpers at him. "Oh, Michael. You know how much I like secrets. Please tell me."

He grins at her. Opens his mouth. Looks like he's about to spill the beans. Then teases her with, "No. I can't."

She pouts, her bottom lip sticking out. "Michael, please," she whines. "If you love me, you would."

"You really want to know?"

She claps her hands together. "Yes. Yes."

In an ominous tone, looking left and right before he says it, Michael tells her, "He sells guns."

Her eyes are wide. "To banditos?"

"No no. He trades them legitimately to armed forces. Police. Things like that. We're in Italy because he's contracting for Beretta. Promoting their handguns."

"Really?"

"Yes. He doesn't like me to say because, well, you know, people don't always like guns. They get funny. Especially with those that trade and sell them."

"So your papa is an arms dealer?"

"No," he corrects. "Not an arms dealer. He's a legitimate salesperson working for Beretta."

"That sounds so much more boring."

"Would you prefer it if my father was an arms dealer?"

She smiles. Then her eyes brighten even more. "No. Better than that. I would prefer it if he was a hired killer. An assassin."

Michael blushes. Concentrates on the ice cream.

But then she shakes her head. "No. Not an assassin. Your papa could never be an assassin. He is too... boring."

She laughs loudly and Michael prods her on the nose with his ice cream.

"Michael?!" she squeals, wiping it off.

She goes to get him back, but he sidesteps it and her ice cream falls onto the floor.

"I'll get you!" she says, coming at him, and then tripping on a protruding cobble and falling into his arms, where he catches her and then pulls her up to him. "You saved me, Michael," she says.

"Then you owe me a kiss."

"I do," she says, showing off her white teeth.

FOUR

SORRENTO, ITALY

THE TRIP BACK FROM CAPRI IS RUINED BY A STORM that sweeps over the island from the west and follows them all the way back to Sorrento. The water, so tranquil in the morning, becomes rough and the *Mother-Magda* tips and bucks on the waves. Both Michael and Peter have to work together if they are to make their way back to the mainland.

As for Bianca, she spends the time in the cabin holding onto her knees. Every now and then her loud screams are enough to provoke Michael into leaving the cockpit for a moment to calm her down.

Serenity isn't something that father and son have to invoke, however; it flows through them naturally. Whether genes, training, or life experience, Peter and Michael never once panic that the boat may sink. So long as they do their jobs, the *Mother-Magda* will make it back to Sorrento. After all, they've sailed through worse. Much worse.

Back at the harbor Michael has to help a very shaken Bianca along the jetty, holding an umbrella over her to protect her beautiful hair from the thundering rain. She is so shaken she even refuses to remove the lifejacket until they are on the solid stone of the harbor wall.

"I don't... know... how you can be so calm," she says shakily as he guides her to the Ferrari.

Bianca lives about halfway to their place, up the sloping cobbled roads. She sits on Michael's lap while Peter drives, the rain drumming on the soft top of the convertible.

The entire journey, Peter has to listen to the teenagers kiss and cuddle literally inches from him. At a junction he almost runs down a crossing cyclist because he's in such a hurry to get the girl home.

When they reach her place, Peter taps an impatient foot up and down in the footwell while the kid says goodbye to his girlfriend.

"I love you more," Bianca says with sickly sweetness.

"No, I love you more," the kid replies in a similarly cloying tone.

"Noo. I love you more."

"Nope. It is I who love you more."

"No. I—"

"Okay!" Peter butts in. "Time Bianca got home. I'm sure her papa is waiting for her."

Both teens look at each other and sigh. Michael pops the door and Bianca finally squeezes herself out of the Ferrari.

"Arrivederci, Peter," she says, leaning back into the car.

"Arrivederci, Bianca," he replies coldly.

One last kiss and, finally, she is gone and they leave.

Storm clouds fill the sky and the air is black with rain.

Tendrils of lightning strike the sea in the distance, lighting up the bay in explosions of purple.

The deluge is so strong, Peter ekes the Ferrari up the wet stone toward their house. The roads are largely abandoned of people. A narrow street bisects this one. Instinctually, Peter gazes both ways as they slowly taxi past.

On the left is a truck with its engine idling, smoke and steam floating from the back. The colored light on a vape pen glows red in the darkness of the cab and he spots a set of eyes he vaguely recognizes.

A feeling begins to creep over Peter. Something feels off. He isn't sure what, but he definitely feels something. It could be paranoia, but the feeling makes him check his surroundings with added diligence.

His attention is back on the road in front. He has slowed the Ferrari to a crawl.

"What's up?" Michael asks, looking up from his phone.

"I'm not sure."

About forty yards through the rain, practically right outside their front gate, a man steps out into the road. He is tall and dressed in a black leather trench coat and flat-brimmed hat—and he is carrying an assault rifle.

"Get down!"

An asterisk of muzzle flash lights up the black air and the front of the Ferrari is battered with bullets. Thank goodness they spent the extra sixty thousand on armor proofing it. Even the soft top is lined with Kevlar.

Ducked down, practically in the footwell, Peter slams the car into reverse and heads backwards as bullets pound the UL 752 level-ten ballistic glass windshield, counting in his head the whole time and keeping an eye on the buildings they whip pass.

The truck makes its move, emerging into the road and blocking the way.

Peter doesn't go anywhere near it. Reaching the required number and the requisite house, he slams on the brakes and brings the Ferrari to a stop mere meters from the truck.

The cab door bursts open and a man identical to the first, both in dress and physiognomy, gets out. He too is holding an AR-15 assault rifle.

The two men open fire on the Ferrari, the windows shattering and misting, the bodywork dimpling under the merciless barrage, spent shell casings spitting out the ejection ports of the guns and tumbling onto the wet cobbles.

When their magazines are empty, they tug them out and snap in fresh ones. Before they resume firing, one of the men rolls a frag grenade underneath the Ferrari and they step back into cover.

It explodes, lifting the 1987 Testarossa off the ground by at least a foot. Every car alarm in a half-mile vicinity goes off and people come to their windows. The back of the car is on fire. The once beautiful Ferrari now a smoldering wreck.

The two men are cautious as they approach it. Using hand signals to communicate, they come around it from opposite sides. Wafting smoke out the way, they check the front seats.

The car is empty.

The men rip open the doors, the metal burning hot beneath their leather gloves. Leaning inside and waving more smoke away, they see the open hatches in the footwells. Large enough to escape through.

More hand signals.

Move it out the way.

The other nods. Shoulders his AR-15. Pushes the car from the front, where there are no flames. It rolls peacefully backwards.

Both men scowl.

There, in the middle of the street, is an open drain cover.

———

"MAN, YOU LOVE YOUR SEWERS," Michael points out.

Father and son are scurrying through a tight tunnel underneath the streets of Sorrento. The heavy rain has filled the drains and the putrid water flows around their ankles, the sound of it hissing in their ears.

"Sewers are good, Mikey. They link places together and keep you out of sight."

"Like a rat."

"Yes. You hardly ever see rats but they're always close by. Always beneath your feet. That's why I picked this particular neighborhood. A good sewer system."

They stop at a junction where fresh sewage flows down a narrow trench in the middle of the floor. Checking his smartphone, Peter chooses the tunnel on the western side.

"Who were those guys?"

"The Goldberg triplets," Peter replies.

"Triplets? But there were only two."

"There used to be three. Now there's only two."

"And I take it that's why they want you dead?"

"Yes. It is."

Michael groans. "This is the fourth time we've had to move safe house in the last year because of some vendetta."

"I did warn you that this life was hard, Mikey. I never lied."

Tepid daylight begins to reflect off all the slime and soon they are walking toward the gray sky. This particular tunnel is for drainage, the water flowing out of a grate about halfway up a cliff face, a great rusty stain running down the rocks.

The bars of the cover are already cut at the bottom—something they've done prior. The two of them easily bend the bars upwards, and then descend the cliff.

A two-person speedboat is moored on a little dock at the end of the small beach.

"You think these are the guys Salvatore was talking about?" Michael asks as they remove its cover.

"Probably," Peter replies as they fold the tarp up and tuck it into a storage container at the front of the boat.

"Who do you think sold us out?"

"I don't know. But I get a feeling Salvatore might."

Instinct causes them to glance backwards up the beach; at the cliffs, and more importantly the drain.

The glowing lights of two vape pens illuminate two faces. Sol and Eli Goldberg—missing a third: Abe.

"You should have boobytrapped the drain," Michael says as they climb into the speedboat.

"With explosives?"

"Yeah."

"And brought the whole cliff face down?"

"I guess."

Starting the speedboat, Peter is shaking his head at his

son. "So instead of having just the Goldbergs on us, you would add the whole of Italy and Interpol as well after we destroy half of Sorrento in a landslide?"

The kid says nothing.

"What did I teach you, Mikey?"

Mechanically the kid answers, "Quiet is the way to go."

"That's right," Peter says, pushing the throttle forwards. "Quiet is the way to go."

FIVE

BACOLI, ITALY

PETER AND MICHAEL TIE THE SPEEDBOAT UP AT A discarded stretch of beach close to Bacoli on the northern edge of Naples. A stone stairway zigzags upwards through gardens, taking them to the top of tall cliffs. Inside a dirt lot with only a few cars parked in it, they get into a black Fiat 500X. It is the most popular four-door in this part of the world, and much more discreet than a Ferrari.

"Where to now?" Michael asks as they drive away.

"I have no idea," comes Peter's reply. "Drive north, I guess. We need to at least get out of Italy before we can breathe."

"But go where this time?"

"Maybe we'll try the north. England?"

"Too much rain."

"Sweden?"

"Too much snow."

"Belgium?"

"Try harder."

"Okay, then. How about—?"

Peter is interrupted by his burner phone going off. The one connected to his work number. The fact of it ringing at this particular moment jars Peter and he instantly cancels the call.

"What did you do that for?" Michael asks.

"We're homeless, Mikey. We need another safe house before we take a job."

"It also takes money," the kid points out, "and what with having set up Sorrento not even four months ago, we only have sixty-three thousand euros."

Peter thinks about it.

"That's not enough," he says when he has.

"No, it isn't. Especially not enough to replace the military-grade weapons and safe room we just drove away from."

Peter attempts to speak when the phone goes off again, drawing their attention once more.

"Look, we need money," Michael points out. "So can't you just see who it is?"

Peter lets out a gentle groan. Answers it on speakerphone.

A male's voice. Russian accent. "I hear you and your son just had a near death encounter with a couple of twins who were once triplets."

Peter and Michael look at each other, then check the rearview mirrors. There's no one in them. Just empty road.

"How do you know that?"

"I have been keeping tabs on you for a very long time, Azrael."

Peter's eyes are pierced slits. "Who is this?"

"My name is Mikhail Gutseriev." He waits a while. "Do you know the name?"

"You're the third richest man in Russia," Peter replies in an automatic tone. "Fourth if you include your president."

"What else do you know about me?"

"You own Russia's largest bank. As well as its first online one. There's also shipping and property. Politically, there is your stint in the Duma, where you ended up as regional governor for North Ossetia during the early noughties. After that, you kind of disappeared from politics and have been pretty much out of the limelight ever since."

From his tone, the two can tell that Gutseriev is smiling.

"I am flattered you know so much about me."

"Don't flatter yourself," Peter says. "You were on a list of Russian targets I was once given. I had to research you."

"A list?" the oligarch mumbles in a trepidatious tone, his earlier cheerfulness gone.

"Yes. But don't worry. They pulled the job in the end. Stood us down."

"I'm glad to hear that."

"You should be. We wouldn't be talking if they hadn't. Now, enough chitchat. What is Mikhail Gutseriev calling me up for?"

"What do people usually call this number for?"

"So it's a job offer, then?"

"Yes. But I prefer to tell you the details in person."

"A meeting?"

"Yes."

"Where?"

"Unfortunately I am currently on certain sanctions lists

along with many of my fellow countrymen, so it will have to be here in Russia. I will pay your usual fee for nothing more than the honor of your visit. After that, it is up to you if you choose to take the job."

"I've had offers like that before," Peter tells him, "and they didn't turn out so well. People tend to have a hard time taking no for an answer."

"This is genuine. Five hundred thousand euros just to hear an old man out."

"How many targets?"

"I will only tell you in person."

Peter's teeth itch. They often do when he's not sure about things. It could be a trap—in fact, the more he thinks about it the more he's sure, his teeth burning into his gums.

"I'm afraid I can't," Peter says. "Thank you for the offer."

"No, wait..."

Peter puts the phone down.

SIX

GENOA, ITALY

GUTSERIEV TRIED TO CALL SEVERAL MORE TIMES after Peter hung up. It took a whole hour for him to finally give in.

On the eastern edge of Genoa, they park in hilly woodland. Inside the mildew-smelling shower block of a rundown campsite, having paid a fee to use the facilities, Peter dyes Michael's hair copper-red before cutting it shorter and curling it with electronic tongs.

It is three o'clock in the morning and no one else uses the building. Emanating from outside are the faint murmurs of people chatting around their camper vans and tents.

"Do you think Bianca will miss me?" the kid asks his father.

"Until the next boy comes along to take her mind off you."

"Ouch."

"It's the truth."

"But you don't have to be so brutal. You could at least pretend to care."

"I do. But I told you at the start..."

"I know. It's the life of an assassin."

Once Michael's hair is done, Peter shaves his own beard off. Then Michael dyes his father's hair blond, and afterwards, they place contact lenses in their eyes. Ones that match the pictures on their new passports.

Then they leave Italy and enter France.

"Merci," Peter says when the border guard hands him back their documents.

Eleven hours after escaping Sorrento with their lives, they arrive at the hotel Pan Deï Palais in San Tropez—a huge luxury townhouse with shuttered windows and a mansard roof. Using a forged Visa card—linked to one of the offshore accounts they pay their money into via a bank in Zurich—they shell out almost a thousand euros for the Prestige Suite.

The rooms are wonderful. All stone archways and antique French furniture, chaise longues and spindly-legged baroque tables. A balcony opens out onto the sunny morning and terracotta rooftops spread out all the way down to the beach.

"I'm hungry," the kid says.

He stands at the edge of the balcony, leaning over and gazing out across San Tropez.

"You would be," Peter says as he begins unpacking his luggage in one of the bedrooms. "You slept most of the way."

"Let's order room service," Michael says when he comes

back into the room. "Have breakfast on the balcony. Crois-sants and coffee."

Twenty minutes later they sit eating and admiring their splendid surroundings. The sea looks like it's made up of innumerable sapphires and sparkles in the morning sunshine.

"Was the Mediterranean as beautiful as this when you met Mom?" Michael asks.

"Yes, it was."

A pause. One in which Peter waits for the expected follow-up question.

"Do you miss her?"

"Of course I do."

Michael sighs. He takes a bite of his pain au raison, chews it, decides he needs a sip of café au lait to wash it down and says, in a sad tone, "You should have introduced yourself to us, you know. When you were living on the next street. Right on our doorstep. You should have come over. At least let us know you were there."

"I couldn't bring myself to break up what you all had with Carl."

"It didn't matter."

"Why?"

"Because it got broken anyway."

———

PETER SLEEPS MOST of the day. Then, in the evening, they go for a walk.

Dressed to impress in a loose-fitting sky blue Giorgio

Armani suit, Michael spends most of the stroll smiling at the young ladies that hang on the corners of the boutiques.

"You're such a creep," his father remarks.

"You're just jealous," Michael replies from the corner of his mouth as two girls walking the other way smile back at him.

They find a nice little café that overlooks the water, and order their evening meals.

"You think those brothers are still looking for us?" Michael asks as they gaze out across the cliffs.

"They won't stop until I'm dead," is Peter's answer. "You as well, most likely."

"Then we have to kill them."

"Another reason we can't take the Russian's job."

The food arrives, and, as they eat, the sun begins to dip below the sea, the shadows of the palm trees growing longer.

"You gonna switch the burner back on?" Michael asks.

"Not until we've dealt with the Goldbergs."

"More like the shit-bergs."

Peter frowns at the kid. "Don't be crass, Mikey."

It is then that the waiter approaches their table. Peter is about to tell him the food is excellent, thinking that is what he has come to ask, but doesn't when he spots the telephone in the man's hand.

"Monsieur, I am sorry for the inconvenience," the garçon says. "But I must ask if your name is Peter?"

"It is."

"Then I believe that there is a call for you."

He hands the telephone over.

"Hello?" Peter says when he places it to his ear.

"I am sorry to interrupt your dinner," Gutseriev says on the other end.

Peter becomes tense. He flicks his eyes about. Makes a hand signal at Michael. They both slowly get up from their chairs and leave the terrace, the waiter frowning as he watches them.

Inside the café, they take an alcove that is well out of the way of windows.

"Don't be alarmed at my interruption," the oligarch says. "I mean no harm. You see, I have been looking for you for a very long time."

"Why?"

"Because only you, Azrael, can achieve this job. Only you can give me peace at last. Please, just come speak with me. Five hundred thousand euros just for that. I can send a car for you immediately. What do you say?"

"I told you, I can't."

"Is it because you have other things to deal with? The Goldberg brothers, for instance?"

"How do you know these things?" Peter seethes into the telephone.

"I told you. I have been looking a long time. But that is not what matters. What does is that not only can I pay your fee, but should you take the job, no matter whether you succeed or fail, I will solve for you your problems with the Goldbergs."

Peter sighs. Thinks about it. Michael, having listened in on the call, makes a hand signal.

Take it.

"Okay," Peter says. "But just to talk."

SEVEN

BESLAN, NORTH OSSETIA, RUSSIAN FEDERATION

A GULFSTREAM G650 FLIES THEM IN LUXURY FROM San Tropez to the city of Vladikavkaz in North Ossetia, Russian Federation. From there they take a helicopter over sweeping low mountains to the town of Beslan.

A region in the northern Caucasus, North Ossetia borders Georgia. The landscape is rocky and hilly, covered in open valleys and vast forests. Built around the Terek River, the small town of Beslan covers a particularly flat stretch of lowland.

The chopper drops them at an airfield on the edge. The place looks like it was abandoned long ago. The corrugated iron roof of the hangar is half off, the rest flapping in the wind that cuts through the valley. Any aircraft sits rusted and broken down on the weed-ridden runway, their engines stripped for parts.

Two men are there to greet them on the cracked asphalt.

A short, thickset man with dark gray hair, a round face and sad eyes. And a tall man with a crooked nose and square face who stands with his arms folded over his chest.

The thickset man is Mikhail Gutseriev, the billionaire. The other is his bodyguard Alexei.

Gutseriev holds a plump hand out to them and wears a warm smile. "I hope your journey was comfortable," the Russian says as Peter shakes the hand.

"It was, thank you."

"It is not you who should be thankful, but me." The Russian turns his attention to Michael. "And this is your son?"

"Yes."

The kid steps forward and shakes his hand, noting that it is unreasonably cold.

Next, Gutseriev asks, "What do you think of Beslan?"

"It looks abandoned," Michael remarks.

Gutseriev smiles. "That's because it practically is. Twenty years ago nearly thirty thousand people lived here. Now there are barely five."

"What happened?"

"I will show you."

They get into a black Hummer. Alexei chauffeurs them, Gutseriev stuffs himself into the passenger seat, and the two guests sit in the back. They drive into town. Rectangular, concrete structures stick up out of the ground. Most of them are vacant and in disrepair. Their windows broken or boarded over, yards overgrown, roofs caved in.

Peter and Michael feel like they are passing through a ghost town.

"It didn't used to be like this," Gutseriev informs them.

"This place used to be filled with life. But the people deserted it."

Three tower blocks overshadow the valley. They drive by beneath them, down a lonely, abandoned road. At least two of the blocks look completely unlived in. The windows bust and the concrete facades flaking away in great lumps that reveal the inner structure. Like the partially flayed skin on a rotting animal.

"I was born in this town," the billionaire tells them as they pass the first sign of people—a few wretched examples slinking along the sidewalks, one man pushing a cart filled with junk, another two sitting on a bench, one passing the other a bottle.

"When I was elected the state's governor in 2000," Gutseriev goes on, "I moved my family to Beslan from St. Petersburg. I had already invested a lot of money in the area, and when I came back as governor, it was flourishing as a banking hub. Something that was especially impressive for somewhere so lost within the Caucasus."

It is as he says this that they arrive at the gates of a burned-out school. The words School Number One written on a soot-smeared plaque beside the entrance.

———

THE BUILDINGS ARE nothing more than smoke-damaged shells. An array of concrete structures with every window blown out and most of the roofs gone. In its heyday it would have housed over 800 students. Now it shelters nothing but rats and the occasional drunk.

Inside, Gutseriev's voice echoes off the crumbling walls

as a cool breeze whips through the cavernous wreck. The Russian leading them deeper inside the ruins.

"I made sure that they never tear it down," he tells them. "Paid the district to keep it like this. That way we would always remember what happened here."

They arrive at what was once a gymnasium. The roof is completely missing, not even the rafters have survived, and a huge hole in the main wall looks out onto surrounding apartment blocks. From the part of the wall still intact, a basketball hoop hangs, rusted and bent, and piles of weed-ridden building debris dot the floor.

Gutseriev takes a position in the center of the room and turns to them. "Twenty years ago," he says, his voice trembling with emotion, "this building was filled with parents and children celebrating the opening of the school year. A day we refer to here in Russia as Knowledge Day.

"Early in the morning, as they were celebrating the festivities, a group of heavily armed men left a forest encampment not far from here wearing green military camouflage and black balaclava masks. In some cases they also wore explosive belts.

"At nine o'clock, the terrorists arrived at School Number One in a military truck they themselves had brought. At first, some of the people gathered at the school mistook them for Russian special forces practicing a security drill. However, the terrorists soon began shooting into the air and forcing everyone from the school grounds into the building. That day, they took approximately 1,100 hostages. They gathered them here in this room. Herded them like cattle and ordered them to speak in Russian and only when first spoken to. When a father stood to calm people and repeat the rules in the local language of Ossetic, a gunman approached him, asked the man if he was done, and then shot him in the head."

He points out of the hole in the wall. A short field leads to a street and some four-story apartments.

"A security cordon was soon established around the school. It consisted of the police, Internal Troops, Army forces, Spetsnaz, including the elite Alpha unit of the FSB, and the OMON special units of the Russian Ministry of Internal Affairs. All our best men."

Peter observes a slight roll of the eyes when he says this.

Gutseriev points at the line of apartment buildings opposite the gym. Some of them are occupied. On one of the balconies a man with no shirt on sits smoking a cigarette, his pink torso glistening in the cold air.

"The Spetnaz evacuated those buildings and took over the flats. Almost every window and balcony had an armed man stationed on it. Makes you laugh when you consider that at the same time there was no fire engine anywhere near here and only two ambulances."

"Weren't you the governor?" Michael asks.

Peter gives his son a look.

"It's okay," Gutseriev says. "Your son is right. I should have been in charge." His face clouds over when he admits, "But I wasn't. Any authority that I may have had was taken from me almost immediately. As soon as the FSB turned up. But in truth, no one was really in charge. All those agencies were answering to different leadership. There was no one leader. No one plan. No one idea. Just competing voices trying to be heard."

"Did you ever get to speak with the terrorists?" Peter asks.

"Yes. At around eleven o'clock the first communications came in. The one they called the Colonel spoke to us via cell phone. He threatened to kill fifty hostages for every one of his own members killed by the police or military—and to kill twenty hostages for every one of his people injured. He also threatened to blow up the school if government forces attacked."

Gutseriev takes a handkerchief and pats his sweaty face. He looks fatigued, the story taking its toll. The bodyguard, Alexei, has spent the entire time of his boss's talk standing idly by in a corner of the room. Seeing him wobble on his feet he comes to his aid.

"You need to sit, Boss," the bodyguard tells him, taking Gutseriev by the elbow and guiding him to a pile of rubble. Concrete slabs fallen on top of each other to form a seat of sorts.

"It is tiring," Gutseriev says, taking the bottle of water Alexei hands him. "Ever since that day, this has been my obsession."

He drinks some water, pours a little onto his pale face.

"I must explain myself to you fully," he adds, fixing Peter with his eyes. "I ask you to do this not because I bore witness to the horror of that day. Not because what happened destroyed a place I care about. I ask you for personal, selfish reasons. Perhaps if it had been another way, I would have been able to leave that day alone..."

Tears fill Gutseriev's eyes.

Peter makes a guess. "Your own children were here, weren't they?"

The oligarch nods.

When he finally manages to speak, his voice is faltering. "Of the hundreds of children trapped in this room that day, my own two daughters Saskia and Dunya were among them."

Gutseriev looks much older than he did at the helipad. His words tremble from his lips as he tells them, "That day my soul was torn from my body. My girls," his voice becomes bitter, "were only eight and nine. They sat squashed in this room for three days. Their captors preventing them from eating and drinking. I had to do something. So on the second day, after paying a bribe to one of the FSB men for the leader's telephone number, I made contact with the terrorists myself. I spoke with the Colonel. I will never forget his voice. Devoid of any emotion, it was like the voice of a machine. In the background I could hear the children crying, pleading. All this pain and misery happening around him, and not a single drop of emotion in his voice."

He pauses to wipe a tear from the corner of an eye with the knuckle of his finger.

"The negotiations were all one way, of course," he goes on. "The Colonel refused to allow food, water or medicine to be taken to the hostages—or for the dead to be removed. All he wanted was to give me his demands. He demanded recognition of a formal independence for Chechnya. The release of some prisoners. The usual stuff. He refused to listen to anything I had to say and ended the call once he had finished speaking. Soon after, the man in charge of the FSB came to me and handed over a decree signed by the prime minister. It appointed him as head of operational headquarters, and I was essentially warned off with the threat of arrest for treason if I ever contacted the terrorists again. What followed was, therefore, completely out of my hands."

Her uses the handkerchief to mop his milk-white brow.

"On the third day," he goes on breathlessly, now in a hurry to finish, "at around one o'clock in the afternoon, the terrorists allowed four medical workers in two ambulances to come into the school grounds and remove twenty bodies. However, at around three minutes past one, when the paramedics approached the school, an explosion was heard from the gymnasium. Panicked, the terrorists opened fire on the emergency workers, killing two. The other two took cover behind their vehicle."

"An explosion?"

"Yes. One which happened outside of the gym. Then, seconds after that, there was another strange-sounding explosion. At five minutes past, a fire started on the roof of the gym, and soon the burning rafters and roofing fell onto the hostages below, until the entire roof collapsed, turning the room into an inferno. Whatever had happened, all hell broke loose. Everyone began discharging their weapons. Inside and out. People were killed in the crossfire. Some of them were part of the crowds on the streets. The terrorists began shooting hostages as they ran and the military fired back. By that stage the troops had no choice but to storm the building. In total 333 people died that day. 186 of them children—including my own. It destroyed the entire soul of a town. It was an issue between adults. The children had no part in it. They were innocent. But it is always the innocent who are punished. My wife, Olga, she couldn't cope with it —couldn't cope with the injustice of it all. The whole thing, those three days waiting for a breakthrough, for a glimmer of hope, they stretched her nerves to breaking point. When it ended the way it did, she couldn't go on. One year to the day after it happened she took an overdose, and I have been alone ever since."

And with that the old man breaks down into tears.

EIGHT

TEREK LAKE, BESLAN, RUSSIA

THE JOB OFFER COMES AFTER THEY LEAVE THE school.

Alexei drives them out to a large lake that sits at the foot of mountains. Gutseriev has a dacha on its banks. The small cottage is much more humble than the father and son had expected. After all, you presume a level of gaudy extravagance from a billionaire oligarch. Yet the four-room wood-slat lake house is plain and simple with decorative patterns of diamonds and hearts cut into the eaves.

The scenery is beautiful. Almost dusk when they arrive, the sun is practically gone. Its last wedge pokes out from the top of the foothills, shrouding them in golden light.

Two chaise longues have been dragged out onto a veranda that hangs over the tranquil water, the shadows of fish meandering around the large leaves of lilies. Gutseriev sits on one of the sofas while Peter and Michael take the other. The bodyguard Alexei stands in the background, arms folded over his chest.

"This was my parents'," Gutseriev tells them. "Back during the Soviet Union my father was an engineer, and because of his relatively high position at the nearby hydro dam, the party allowed him the use of this dacha in the summers. We'd all come out here and swim in the lake. When the regime finally fell in '91, I bought it off the state." In a sad tone, he adds, "I taught my two girls to swim in this lake."

"It's beautiful," Peter remarks. "But I'm guessing the scenery isn't why we're here."

Gutseriev sighs. Gets to it. "Of the thirty-three terrorists who entered that school, three of them escaped alive. At least two of them are still alive."

"And I take it," Michael interjects, "that you want that corrected."

Gutseriev smiles at the kid, then turns to Peter. "Your son is very frank."

"He is."

"It is a shame to hear such cynicism in the voice of a young man."

"Life experience will do that."

"It sure will," the old man agrees in a sad tone, before taking in a breath and continuing. "The man they called the Colonel—the one I spoke to—his name is Ruslan Tagirov. He was group leader that day. This is the last known photograph of him."

Gutseriev takes a smartphone out, finds the picture and shows it. On the screen is the portrait of a man. Two fierce eyes sticking out the top of a black beard. He is wearing a camouflaged baseball cap, and the beard covers most of him, but the penetrating eyes leave an impression—like staring into Nietzsche's abyss.

"Where is he now?" Peter asks, looking up from the phone.

"All in good time. Let me finish with the men first."

Gutseriev flicks a finger across the screen. Another bearded man. His eyes aren't so fierce. There's a dullness to them, in fact. Like he's drugged.

"This is Vladimir Khodov. Some of the survivors described him as the most frightening and aggressive of the militants. Khodov converted to Islam while in prison for rape. Before the attack, he was wanted for a series of bomb attacks in Vladikavkaz. He's always been seen as Tagirov's attack dog.

"As for the third man, I don't have a picture of him. All I know is what I have learned through the many private investigations I have initiated over the years. His name is Iznaur Zoyev."

Michael and Peter both note that Alexei has taken a step toward them and is now watching his master with a nervous look.

"An ethnic Chechen," Gutseriev says, "Zoyev was born in Moscow to migrant parents. From an early age he showed an athletic prowess in sport as well as fighting. But unlike the other two, he wasn't a terrorist. He was a member of the FSB, recruited during the Second Chechen War for undercover work amongst the various separatist groups."

Alexei interrupts. "Excuse me, sir," he says in Russian. "Can we talk—in private?"

"It is okay, Alexei," Gutseriev replies in the same

language. "I know what I'm doing." He turns from his bodyguard to Peter and goes on in English. "He worries for me. See, I've been warned to leave this alone by the Russian state. Threatened with imprisonment or worse if I dig too deep. My faithful bodyguard likes to protect me from such things. It is why I kept most of this from him until now. He thought I was only interested in the Chechens. But I'm not. I want to know the whole truth. Something happened that day. Somebody—who is hidden in the shadows—made decisions that cost my little girls their lives. I want to know why."

A bead of sweat navigates his pale cheek. The handkerchief is back out and he mops at his brow with it.

"Zoyev," he goes on, "was taking orders from someone. I want to know who that was. I understand that you are equipped at finding out such things. That you are trained in persuasive methods."

"That's a euphemism," Michael remarks dryly.

Peter nods at the oligarch. Then asks for a second time, "Where are these men now?"

Gutseriev gives a crooked smile. The handkerchief dabs at his forehead and cheeks.

"Believe me," he says, "when I tell you that I have spent almost as long looking for these men as I have grieved my family. But that only very recently did I find them for sure."

"So where are they?" Peter asks firmly. After all, it is the third time.

Gutseriev swallows. "Tagirov is running his own unit in the Chechen army. The Scorpion Team. Khodov is a member of the same unit. They are both currently in Ukraine, torturing and killing their way across the country like some Viking horde."

Peter and Michael look at each other. Frown.

"Now I know," Peter says, "why you wanted to ask me this in person. You want me to go into a combat zone to kill these men."

"Yes."

"Why don't you just let the war do its thing? I hear the Ukrainians have got the initiative."

"These men were born in war. They have lived it their entire lives. Always they have survived. Just like you, Azrael. Their luck is legendary. How else would they have escaped the school that day?"

"And the FSB double agent—this Zoyev. He might be dead already."

"If that is the case, so be it. But if he is alive, I want you to find him. I want to know exactly what happened that day."

"And all I have to do is walk into a war zone," Peter adds sardonically.

"It's dangerous, I know. But I will place you with a man who will guide you."

"Russian army?"

"No. He is part of Wagner."

"Great. Mercenaries."

"He is very skilled and knows his way around the Russian side. He will be your escort. He and you will travel with various units, avoiding the main fighting and treading carefully around the edges. As far away from the trouble as possible."

"But not out of range of the missiles and drones that are raining down on the place?"

"No. But you will be as safe as we can get you." The old man stares at him with an imploring expression.

Peter thinks about it. For a moment there is no other sound except the birds and the insects.

"So that's the job, then," Peter puts to the oligarch; "find these two men in the middle of a combat zone, torture them into revealing the whereabouts of Zoyev, and then find out from him the truth of who ordered the siege?"

Gutseriev leans forward. "I essentially want you to get me the answer to two questions." He counts them off on a pudgy finger. "One, I want to know the identity of Zoyev. And two, I want to know who exactly pulled the trigger on my little girls. See, they didn't die in the fire. They died from gunshot wounds. Somebody shot them."

He sits back before adding, "Get me the answer to those questions and I will not only make your problems with the Goldbergs go away, I will hand over a portfolio of investments which will pay you a one million annuity for the rest of both your lives. I offer you the chance to retire in style with all your enemies six feet beneath your feet. Peace of mind for the rest of your lives. So what do you say?" His eyes shine at them.

NINE

THEY HAVE A WEEK TO PREPARE, AND MUST SPEND the time wisely. A Wagner unit of six men are airlifted into Beslan. They're all ex-Russian Spetsnaz. Over the coming days Peter trains Michael on war zone tactics.

The ghost town of Beslan is a perfect training ground. On one edge the buildings are completely empty for a square mile, including two abandoned tower blocks. It is here that they practice urban warfare.

The Wagner men set up as snipers. Fake IEDs that only set off alarms are placed all around. Tripwires hidden throughout the buildings. They use an armored personal carrier (APC) to practice moving in a convoy.

Over that week Michael is pelted with paintballs shot from sniper nests, blown up repeatedly by the buzzing alarms, and gradually learns to listen to his father and the other men as they forge him into a soldier with sixteen-hour-a-day training sessions.

By the final day, the head of the Wagner unit tells Peter

that the kid is one of the best learners he's seen in all his years training men. A fine young soldier.

"But will he listen?" Peter had asked.

———

THAT NIGHT, as they pack, Alexei comes to see them at the dacha where they are staying—on the same lake as Gutseriev's place. The staccato beat of his shoes across the wooden decking alerts them. Soon, the tall, dark-eyed man is stepping through the open door of the lounge unannounced.

"So you're actually taking your own child out there," the bodyguard says.

He stands on the other side of the room watching them zip up the bags that line the seat cushions of a leather chesterfield.

"Yes," is all Peter says before turning back to his luggage.

"I know he says he'll keep you safe," Alexei goes on, "but nothing will save you if something goes wrong. What if all you get from this is to watch your son being shot?"

Michael zips his bag up and faces him. "I'm sure he'll deal with it," the kid says.

"What if it's your old man that bites it first?" the bodyguard then asks Michael.

"Then I guess I'm on my own. Cold world. Yah-de-yah-de-yaw."

Alexei grins. Widens his eyes. "A father and son hit man team. I never really thought of assassination as a family business."

Peter turns angrily to him. "Is there a reason you're here?"

"Yes," Alexei says. "You should leave Mikhail alone. If you are discovered by the wrong people and your purpose found out, it will come back on him. I don't want to see him compromised. Sending a man to kill the soldiers of his own country is treason. Let the war take care of these barbarians. Don't drag the old man into it. Just take your five hundred thousand euros and go home."

"I'm sorry," Peter says to this. "Me and my son need the money and protection your boss is offering."

"You mean this hassle with the brothers? He has asked me to settle it for you. I am willing to achieve this even if you walk away now."

"You really care that much about the old man?"

A sadness threatens to overwhelm the harsh look of the bodyguard. "More than you could believe," he says in an undertone.

"Then you should support him in his endeavors."

"Even if they will lead to his ruin?"

He and Peter lock eyes.

"Why are you so worried?"

"I have worked by Mikhail's side for eight years. I am all the family he has—and he is all I have. My own family are all gone. Just like his. When you share another's space for so long, you can't help but feel a deep compassion for them. I love Mikhail as a father and I hope he sees me as a son. I would lay down my life for him. It is why I beg you both not to endanger him."

"We won't," Peter says. "But that doesn't mean we're

going to let him down. We will act as quietly as we can. Draw as little attention as we can. But we are going to kill these men—and not just for your boss and his two daughters, but for all the people those men slaughtered that day."

TEN

SHAKHTY, ROSTOV, RUSSIAN FEDERATION

NEXT MORNING THEY ARE DELIVERED TO A military hangar in Shakhty, a city in the Rostov oblast, close to the border with Ukraine. There, they are introduced to their guide, Yevgeny Pavlov; a bald man with piercing eyes and an ugly burn scar mottling the left side of his face. The ear on that side is practically missing, as though it has been melted off.

The second thing Michael notices are the Wagner insignia covering his uniform: a white skull in red crosshairs. Dressed in full body armor, he has several Zs scrawled onto the armor's plating. When they are presented with their own Wagner uniforms, he advises them to do the same—paint Zs on the armor—but they refuse.

"It'll make you sink in," he tells them. "Make my job a little easier."

It doesn't convince them. No Zs on their uniforms.

Once they are dressed as a couple of Wagner mercenaries, they take seats in a far corner of the hangar. Pavlov stands before them, arms behind his back, chest puffed out, briefing them.

"We will primarily be moving with Wagner units," he tells them. "Whichever one is heading the way we need, we'll ride them."

Peter asks, "So we won't be moving with regular Russian army?"

"If we have to, I can arrange it. But, trust me, you're better off with Wagner guys—not the prisoners, though. Those guys are cannon fodder. No. We will be traveling with the best units. More skilled, better equipment, well organized—avoiding the army, especially conscripts. Now, to the job in hand.

"The Scorpion Team have gone dark recently. Gutseriev's people were tracking them by intercepting their communications. They had been chatting on regular army channels but ten days ago, they went silent."

"Any idea why?"

"We don't know. Probably a new mission that is sensitive."

"Can't you find out?" Michael asks. "After all, you are Russian army or whatever."

"Kid, if I was to go to the commanders in the Russian army and ask too many questions, do you think I will, A, get any answers, and, B, not be painted with a huge fucking target?"

He widens his eyes at Michael.

"I guess not," the kid mutters.

"You guess not. No, me neither. Not asking questions is

a good way to go if we are to survive this thing and get you to your targets. So instead of asking the generals, we will be liaising with Gutseriev's team who have recently tracked the Scorpions to Mariupol. Through regular army chatter they have discovered that the Chechens were in the city yesterday."

"You know what they were doing?"

"Our source said they were at the docks. Probably stocking up on supplies."

"They still in Mariupol?"

"I don't know. I hope. Because it's where we're going after here."

ELEVEN

MARIUPOL, UKRAINE

THEY ARRIVE AT MARIUPOL IN THE EARLY EVENING. It isn't yet dark, but the sun is barely visible above the flat blocks of the cityscape. Due to curfew, the dusk streets are largely empty except for military and police.

Sitting on the northern shore of the Sea of Azov, the city has a large harbor. At the base they land at, they take a rickety old UAZ-469 light utility vehicle and drive it to the dock. There they quickly find out who is in charge of the army stores—a certain colonel. The equivalent of a hundred dollars secures them passage to the man's office. In it, the colonel sits behind a desk. On the wall behind him is a framed portrait of the Russian president. Little Russian flags stick out of the corners of the desk. The man has a few strands of blond hair left to lace across his bare head, and with red cheeks and a mottled nose, it's clear he's a heavy drinker. As they step into his office, he watches them with a pair of lazy, reptilian eyes.

The equivalent of a thousand dollars gets the colonel to divulge what he knows. The first words out of his mouth lead to disappointment.

"The Chechens left this morning," he tells them in Russian, his breath stinking of vodka.

"You know where they went?" Peter asks.

"Izium was what I heard one of the men mention. I mean, everyone's heading there at the moment."

Pavlov asks, "What were they picking up?"

"Now that was the interesting part. The stuff they were picking up got shipped to us the day before yesterday. It came with no itinerary except a few signed papers and two FSB agents who accompanied the cargo. No one was allowed to touch the stuff, and it was the FSB who supervised the pickup. Wouldn't let anyone except the forklift driver anywhere near it."

"Didn't you at least see it?"

"I did."

"And what was it?"

"Whatever it was, it was packed inside a crate about the size of a refrigerator. What do you need these guys for, anyway?"

"It doesn't matter," Pavlov says. "You say one of them mentioned Izium?"

"Yeah."

Pavlov turns to Peter. "Then that's where we'll head next."

———

On their way back into the city they drive up to an army cordon blocking a wide boulevard overshadowed by a row of tall flat blocks. Before they get the chance to ask what is going on there is a loud explosion that rocks the seats beneath them.

A T-90 battle tank has just fired its 125mm smoothbore cannon at the building. A huge section of wall has been annihilated and the entire corner of the apartment block is crumbling away, falling into the street as an avalanche of bricks and concrete.

The inner rooms are exposed. Men appear at the edges, firing at the soldiers below. The cannon explodes a second time and another whole section of the building falls away.

Three more tanks arrive on the scene from the other end of the boulevard, joining the T-90, and the turrets on all four swivel to face the building. There is a pause in which the silence becomes almost oppressive with anticipation—and then their Kord-12.7mm heavy machine guns open fire, a cascade of bullets pelting the remains of the apartments, the tracer rounds lighting up the darkening air.

Pavlov gets the attention of one of the soldiers at the cordon. The man moseys up to the driver's window, and when Pavlov asks what's going on, the man explains that there are Ukrainians holed up inside. Saboteurs guilty of blowing up a checkpoint earlier that day which killed three Russian soldiers.

During a respite, probably due to the guns on the tanks overheating, someone begins shouting from the building.

"Surrender! Surrender!"

A white flag dangles out of a door on the bottom floor.

A soldier with a bullhorn calls for them to exit the

building with their hands up. Six men skulk out, looking worried. They are told to stand against the wall and each man takes his position, lining the outside of the apartment block.

It is then that the tank commander has his man open fire with the machine gun.

The huge bullets decimate the men, practically cutting them in half as the weapon fans across the wall, punching a jagged line of holes into the bricks.

With the dead lying on the ground in their own blood, the commander of the T-90 gets out and stands atop his tank. He makes a striking impression in the dusk, silhouetted by the low sun and surrounded by shadow.

He is wearing a Stetson and a pair of mirrored shades. With his chest puffed out, he looks like some crazy cavalry officer. He steps off his tank as if getting down from his stead, and approaches the dead men.

Another man, much shorter and less imposing, scuttles out of the tank after him like a beetle. The tank commander stands over the first of the dead and holds a hand out behind him without turning. The beetle comes up and hands a spray can into it.

The rest of the men slowly leave their tanks to watch. It looks like this is a common thing. The commander in the cowboy hat begins spraying red Zs on the bodies, the beetle following him and taking a picture of the graffitied dead man.

Once the picture has been taken, others move over and begin taking the bodies and loading them into the back of a truck that pulls up.

"Where are they taking them?" Pavlov asks the soldier.

"They string them up in the square. Remind people who's in charge."

The corpses are dragged to the truck. Halfway, a leg belonging to one of the "dead" moves. The soldier dragging the man instantly drops him, takes a pistol from his hip, and blasts the Ukrainian in the head.

Michael has never seen such utter disregard for human life. It seems almost industrial—like killing pigs at a slaughterhouse. As though to these men taking a life is as simple as working a production line. Just another job to do. Gotta earn a living.

"How come they're here in Mariupol?" Pavlov asks the soldier.

"They came here to pick up two new T-90s from the dock. They head over to Izium tomorrow."

PAVLOV DOES a deal with the cowboy. Commander of the Sixth Tank Brigade of the Russian Army.

He will be their guide to Izium.

To finalize the contract, they go for a little drink in a nearby municipal building that is now overtaken by Russian soldiers. There is a bar inside. A room with a long stretch of counter running along a wall. Some generic tables and chairs scattered about. Wood-paneled walls that are pretty barren except for the portraits of the president and the Russian tricolor. Other pictures show the de facto leaders of Mariupol. Only recently put in place.

They sit in a corner opposite the commander and the little guy who had handed him the paint out on the street and taken the pictures. The cowboy sits leaned back, fingers laced across his wide chest, shades off, his sharp little eyes sunk in the shadow of the wide-brimmed Stetson.

His men mill around them, all eyes on the three Wagner men. It feels intimidating. Like they're ready to rush them the second anyone says a word out of turn to their leader.

A blonde-haired woman with a black eye brings them their drinks. A round of vodkas and beers for everyone, including all his men. The commander assuring her that the "mercenaries" will pay.

The commander's name is Colonel Sergei Razamov, but his men call him Billy after Billy the Kid. It would appear he has a love of American culture.

"So," Billy says, "you men want to go up into the asshole of hell?"

"Not as far in as you," Pavlov says with a smirk. "We only need to reach the edge. From there we'll wait."

"For what?"

Billy has cocked an eye over his beer.

"Top secret, I'm afraid," Pavlov tells him.

"Whatever," the commander waves away. "So long as you get me the five hundred thousand rubles you promised, it doesn't matter." He suddenly turns his attention to Michael. "You not drinking, boy?"

Michael looks worried. He doesn't understood a word of what was just said.

"He doesn't speak Russian," Pavlov points out.

"You fucking mercenaries," Billy says with a shake of the head. "Where's he from?"

"Kindergarten," the beetle suggests.

The rest burst into laughter. Michael's cheeks go red, understanding that he is the butt of this particular joke.

In Russian, Peter says, "Can we get on with this?"

The cowboy cocks an eye at him. He's obviously recognized something in Peter's accent.

"Another foreigner?"

"Serbian."

"Don't sound Serbian. My father used to import busha from Belgrade. We used to go there to pick them up."

"I spent my childhood in the United States," Peter says.

The cowboy sits forward. "Where?"

"My father was a Serbian diplomat. We lived in New York, Washington, Virginia at one point."

"You ever go to Texas?"

"One time we took a trip to Dallas."

The cowboy is rocking in his chair. For the next hour they talk all things American. It is hard to get away in the end, but they manage it.

Back on the streets the place is now drenched in the soda glow of streetlights. The three of them separate. Pavlov has to update Gutseriev of their progress, as well as report to the local Wagner offices. Killing two birds with one stone, he decides to make the call on the satellite phone from the offices.

As for Peter and Michael, they head to a nearby hotel that is reserved for Wagner employees. It is where Pavlov will meet them once he is finished.

———

WAGNER HAVE TAKEN over a small office block on the edge of the docks. Inside is a hive of activity. Men and women move about behind desks, organizing the war effort from within the glow of strip lighting; the company constantly taking on more work from the regular army.

When Pavlov reports in, the woman behind the desk widens her eyes at his name.

"Lieutenant Yevgeny Pavlov?" she asks.

"Yes."

He hands over his ID and she checks it.

"The boss would like to see you."

"The boss?"

"Yes. Mr. Utkin."

"Dmitry Valerievich Utkin is here?"

Pavlov is incredulous.

"Yes, Lieutenant."

She picks a radio transmitter up from her desk and speaks into it. Tells them he's here. Gives Pavlov's exact name.

"Bring him here," crackles from the radio.

She looks up at Pavlov. "If you'd like to follow me."

She leaves her desk and leads him toward a door at the end of a narrow corridor. Pavlov can't stop worrying about why Lieutenant Colonel Dmitry Utkin, the head of Wagner, would want to see him. Had word gotten out that he'd deceived his superiors when he and Gutseriev had devised the contract?

The oligarch had come to him personally, without going through Wagner itself. Knowing that Pavlov liked to do his own dealings on the side. It had been Pavlov himself who'd then taken a version of the deal he'd agreed with Gutseriev to his superiors at the organization. On paper, and as far as they knew it, he was taking a couple of journalists working for *Novaya Gazeta* along the battle lines to report on the fighting. The Moscow newspaper was owned by one of the president's cronies, so no biggy.

Except if they found out it wasn't a couple of journalists but a couple of Americans—that would be a biggy.

Had someone tipped them off?

Yevgeny Pavlov is about to find out.

The woman opens the door and steps aside. She is smiling as he passes her on the way into the room. It is not a nice smile. It is a rather-you-than-me smile.

The pink marbled scar itches on the side of Pavlov's face.

Two men sit in there. One is Dmitry Utkin. The other is a man he doesn't recognize. A middle-aged man with light-colored hair and rattlesnake eyes. It is he who sits behind the desk. Utkin sits on the end of it with a laptop open on his thighs, the screen lighting up his completely hairless head.

"We heard you were in town," he croaks.

"Yes. I came down with…"

"Unit Seven. Yes," Utkin finishes for him. "Take a seat."

He gestures to a chair with a flick of his pink hand.

"This gentleman here," Utkin says, looking up from the laptop, "is Vasily Savelyev. Commander of the FSB."

The man behind the desk says nothing. Just sits there staring blankly at him.

Pavlov so badly wants to scratch the scar.

"How is your current job going?" Utkin asks.

As soon as he says it Savelyev chuckles, Pavlov glancing at him, then back at Utkin, who is now smiling.

"I'm sorry," Pavlov says, "but can I ask what this is about?"

The answer comes from Utkin. The big boss flips the laptop around so that the screen faces him, and Pavlov's heart sinks through his feet the instant he recognizes what is on the screen.

A live video feed from inside a car. The camera pointed at the house it is parked outside of. The lights on in the windows. The curtains open. In the kitchen a mother is helping a little girl cut out cookies. In another window a young boy plays on a games system while talking to friends on a headset.

"Do you recognize this house?" Utkin asks.

The scar is burning on the side of Pavlov's face.

"Well?"

It takes him a few seconds to get the words out of his dry throat. "It is my house."

"Yes. And those children?"

"My children."

"The woman?"

"My wife."

"Good. As you can see we have men situated outside of your home. With one word, they will leave their vehicle, go inside and murder them. Do you understand?"

"Yes."

"Good."

"What do you want from me?"

It is Savelyev who speaks. "We have received intelligence that the men you are traveling with aren't journalists. That this is a lie and that you are working your own job. What is your answer to this?"

Pavlov doesn't hesitate for a second. "They are not journalists."

"What are they?"

"Hit men."

"So it is true. You are helping them track down certain members of our own armed forces."

"Chechens," Pavlov says, like it makes all the difference.

"Still our own men," Utkin bawls. "Think of what it could do for the reputation of our organization if it was found out that we are taking contracts on our fellow soldiers."

"I am sorry."

"No you're not," Savelyev tells him. "You're greedy. But at least you do it for your family. Is that why you cut little deals yourself, Lieutenant?"

Pavlov looks at him, tries hard not to look immediately away, and says, "Yes, sir."

"Then do this for your family."

"Do what, sir?"

"Kill the Americans."

TWELVE

SUKHA KAM'YANKA, UKRAINE

THE SIXTH TANK BRIGADE REALLY ARE A BUNCH OF cowboys. The battalion is made up of thirty-one tanks, ranging from the incredible T-90 to the less incredible T-14 Armata, which make up the majority of the unit. As well as that, there are about twenty other combat vehicles, such as the BMP-1 infantry fighting vehicle (IFV). They all plod, like cattle, in a long, meandering line northwards across the country.

Colonel Razamov, or Billy, rides shotgun in his T-90M; the most advanced of the Russian tanks. Sometimes he rides atop the turret, a leg dangling either side of the main gun, his shirt off, showing a torso the color of canned ham, the Stetson stuck to his head as if by divine grace.

Over a thousand men move with them. The trip should take them less than half a day. But it's the next day before they're anywhere near Izium.

Why?

Because of the looting.

At every village, the men head in and begin picking through the abandoned buildings and streets like crows picking through carrion. Each time, Peter, Michael and Pavlov have to watch the men disperse from the vehicles and scatter off into the village like rats on the hunt. Then, they have to wait out the next hours till they all return. Many of them driving stolen cars they've loaded with loot.

It is the second day, as they approach the tiny village of Sukha about twenty miles south of Izium, that the convoy suddenly stops on the main road.

"Not more looting," Michael grumbles to Peter.

They are sat within the air-conditioned, yet extremely cramped, realms of a T-72 tank. Pavlov sits with them, very quiet. As a matter of fact, since he returned last night, he has been practically mute, constantly itching the scar on his face.

Peter asks the man in charge of the T-72 what's up and is informed that the checkpoint up ahead isn't responding.

"Looks like it's abandoned," eventually comes through the wire. "No, wait. I see blood."

Everyone becomes edgy. The air thickens inside the confined space of the compartment. The men begin to itch with sweat.

"This is Point Man speaking," eventually comes over the speaker.

It's Billy.

"I'd like the Wagner boys to come meet me up front."

Telling Michael to stay with the tank, Peter and Pavlov climb out through the cupola into the gray day. The place they are stopped at is a flat valley of farmland. A few trees add detail here and there, a couple of distant farms occupy the horizon, and a thin band of road bisects it. There really isn't much else. In the fields, the crops are all dead and overgrown with weeds.

Peter and Pavlov make their way along the line of vehicles. The occasional dull thud rattles the air from far away.

The men have begun creeping out of their vehicles, the hatches and cupolas flipping open, heads rising out of them like moles. At the very front, Billy stands proudly atop his T-90, one hand atop a knee as he leans forward. Someone must have fetched him a piece of long grass from the nearby fields, because he has a length of ryegrass hanging out his mouth.

"Billy?" one of his men says when he spots Peter and Pavlov.

The cowboy turns their way, spits on the ground, and jumps down from the tank. He holds a pair of field glasses out to Pavlov.

"Tell me what you think of that," he says.

Pavlov takes the binoculars and looks through the lenses.

"Well?"

The road is dead straight. About two hundred meters ahead is a temporary checkpoint set up by the Russians. The checkpoint is made up of a barrier blocking both sides of the road and a hut big enough for about four men. A Russian tricolor flaps from a pole beside it.

The barrier is down. The hut is empty.

"You see inside the hut?" Billy asks.

Pavlov does. Through the open window he spots blood spatter on the back wall. Not good.

No signs of the bodies. Until.

"There's more blood," he says. "On the grass besides the road. Leading out of the hut toward those trees."

About twenty feet to the left of the checkpoint is a copse of birch trees.

"Let me see," Billy asks, taking back the field glasses.

"You're right," he mutters when he's looking through them. "Okay," he adds, taking his eyes away and facing Pavlov. "You Wagner boys can help us out on this. I'm mostly a tank guy. Better at organizing bombardments and that sort of thing. You boys are foot soldiers: good in a fire-fight. How about one of you join us? See what's up in those trees."

Peter decides to speak. "I advise you to get back in your tanks."

Billy narrows his eyes at him. "There could be men still alive in there. In need of urgent medical treatment."

"It could also be a trap. We should just move on."

"You chicken?" the commander asks.

"No. Just not stupid. We leave these tanks, we lose our protection. Our advantage."

"I'd have to agree with my colleague," Pavlov puts in.

Billy stares at Peter. Chewing the piece of grass at the side of his mouth. "Then we'll go alone," he says. "But you Wagner boys can fucking walk from here."

"What?" Pavlov exclaims.

"You heard me."

"But we paid you."

"To get you close to Izium. Twenty miles is close enough in my estimates."

"Just because we won't walk into those trees with you to be shot at?"

"Yes. Because neither of you mercenaries will do anything unless someone pays you."

Pavlov goes to step forward, but Peter places a hand against his chest.

"Okay," he says to Billy. "I'll go with you."

The commander smiles. "Good man."

Peter tells Pavlov to stay with Michael. "Don't let him out of your sight."

The cowboy leads twenty men to the checkpoint. There, they loiter about. Several of them walk straight into the hut without thinking, no regard as to the possibility of there being some kind of tripwire.

Peter stands well back with his AK-74M held in front of him, covered by a tree. He doesn't like standing in the open. His eyes work their way to the copse, skirt along the fields.

"The blood leads right through the grass," someone calls out.

Without even checking, several infantrymen start following the dark trail.

"You coming?" Billy asks Peter.

"You should call in air support," Peter tells him.

"They're too busy in Izium. Now come on. We might get to see some action."

Trepidatiously, Peter follows.

The trail of blood is at least a day old. It has coagulated and gone black. Flies cover the air above it and are especially strong in the copse. The birch grow out of a divot in the land. The ground descends at the edge of the trees, so they don't see the bodies until they are standing within it.

At least now they know the whereabouts of the four men from the checkpoint. Each one has been nailed to a tree by their hands, their throats cut wide open. The black blood covering their fronts.

The men all clamor into the trees, quickly filling the copse as they stare at the dead. Peter stands at the very edge, using the trees as cover, gripping the AK firmly.

Billy marches up to the bodies. He looks as angry about it as if it was his own men hanging from those trees. Peter can't help thinking about the resistance men the battalion had mowed down in Mariupol. The way they'd taken the bodies away to hang in the square.

"Get them down!" Billy shouts.

Several men rush forward and grab ahold of one of the corpses. Instinct makes the hairs on Peter's back go up.

"No, don't!" he cries.

It is too late.

The body detonates, setting off a chain reaction, the copse coming alive with explosions. Peter is already face-down in the mud—dirt and body parts raining down on his back.

Infantrymen begin firing blindly out of the trees. Others run in panic, emerging from the copse into a field.

It's mined.

Peter watches as four men, one after the other, hit IEDs and are sent up into the air with an eruption of dirt.

That's when the sniper joins the party. Men begin getting hit by bullets as they race to their comrades at the road.

Peter crawls into the copse, sure that all the explosives have gone off. He hides within the smoke until he is certain where the shooter is.

Where would I be? he asks himself.

He quickly finds what he's looking for.

About five hundred yards across the road, on the other side of the convoy, is a row of wooden structures. Barns, probably. The sniper has set up on the top of one of them, Peter spotting something flash on its roof: the sun glinting off the man's optics.

As he lies there watching the sniper pick off the Russians, someone grabs Peter's foot. When he glances over his shoulder he sees it's Billy.

Both his legs are gone below the knees and his left eye hangs out of its socket. He's still wearing the Stetson, burnt down one side.

"Get me a radio," he croaks.

"Okay. Wait here," Peter tells him.

He isn't going to get him anything.

He crawls away from Colonel Sergei Razamov of the Sixth Tank Brigade, through the bracken, coming to a stop at the edge of the trees. Down on his front, he watches the road through the scope of his AK.

Peter knows what's coming next. The boobytrap was just an alert. The sniper and IEDs no more than show to confuse them while the Ukrainians ready the real attack. The one that's really going to put the shit up everyone present.

Before Peter can warn Michael through his comms, the sound of thunder rips through the valley. Except, it isn't thunder.

It comes from behind Peter and howls like the wind of a storm, a terrible scream that gets louder and louder, as if the sky is being ripped apart, and then—four Excalibur-guided artillery shells are bobbing and weaving in the air above, resembling racing birds as they head straight for the line of vehicles.

Peter holds his breath.

The explosions—a split second one-two-three-four—decimate at least eight vehicles and God-knows how many men. The ground trembles beneath Peter.

"Michael?" he shouts into his comms. "Michael?!"

There is a silence that seems to last forever.

Then.

"I'm here. Sorry. Had to give covering fire."

"Get away from the tanks."

"Already on it. Me and Pavlov are heading to that farm we saw about a mile back. The one with the red barn."

"I know it. I'll meet you there."

Drainage ditches divide the fields into acre squares. One of them lines the copse. Peter crawls down into it on his belly. Then, hidden by the overgrown ryegrass and weeds, he shuttles along brown, stagnant water that rises to his shins.

More Excalibur missiles race toward the battalion, causing two huge fireballs to spread across the road from both ends of the convoy. Peter guesses they must have several Howitzers set up. Probably about a mile away on either side.

Panic spreads through the remains of the battalion. The vehicles not yet hit begin breaking away from the others. Many of them head into the fields. Some go south along the road. Some head north toward the checkpoint. Anywhere but here. Others stay and fight, turning their turrets in the direction of the Howitzers, and begin bombarding whatever they can. Which turns out to be mostly thin air.

Amid the chaos, Peter concentrates on getting away. Rather than heading straight for the road, he takes a ditch that leads away from all those targets while still going in the direction of the farm. When he leaves it about three hundred yards up the road, he doesn't stop running until he reaches the farmhouse.

It lies at the end of a dirt lane; an old stone building with a wooden veranda. The curtains are all drawn. The front door wide open.

"Michael?" Peter whispers into the comms.

No reply.

Edging his way through the front door, he senses movement to his left and dives forwards across the hallway as shots are fired from the living-room. Scrambling to his feet, he takes cover on the other side of a narrow staircase. The living-room door is to the right of their bottom. Peter, at an angle to it, is unable to see directly into the room.

"Michael?" he calls out.

"He's here with me," comes Pavlov's voice. "Why don't you come and see?"

"I want to hear his voice first."

Peter waits for an answer.

"Hey, Peter," the kid calls to him from the other room.

"You okay?"

"Yeah. Well, except for the guy holding a gun to my head. I thought he was on our side."

"Evidently not. What's going on, Pavlov?"

"I am sorry about this," the Russian calls back. "But orders are orders."

"What orders?"

"They threatened my family."

"Who?"

"Someone tipped my superiors off. Told them why we're

really here. They want you dead—and they'll kill my family for it. I was going to wait until tonight, but it'll have to be now."

He's at the far end of the living-room. The kid standing a yard in front with his hands raised. Pavlov holding the pistol to the back of his head.

"Come on out," Pavlov says loudly. "Or I'll blow your boy's head off."

He cocks the hammer to make a point.

"Okay," Peter calls back. "Don't do anything drastic."

"Leave your weapons there."

Pavlov's heartbeat thumps in his head as a shadow creeps across the doorway, followed by a man.

Peter.

He has his hands up at shoulder height.

"Don't do anything stupid," he tells Pavlov calmly as he comes to a stop in the doorway.

"Stupid? Like what?"

Peter says nothing. Just stares at him.

Pavlov frowns. "Now you die."

He takes his aim away from Michael's head. This was the type of stupid Peter meant. The mercenary has underestimated the skill of the kid. Thinking him no more than a boy along for the ride. Before Pavlov gets the chance to fire, Michael has twisted around, taken him by the elbow with his right hand, and pushed his arm up, raising the aim. With his left, he then whips the knife from his belt and, all his weight behind it, pushes the blade through the chest plating of Pavlov's armor and deep into his heart.

The gun goes off. The bullet burying itself in the ceiling.

Yevgeny Pavlov lets out a final breath and is dead before he's finished sliding off the knife onto the floor.

"You let him take you?" Peter puts to the kid.

"I wasn't really paying attention to a double-cross," Michael replies, wiping the knife on the dead man's fatigues. "Not with all those bombs going off."

"Well you should have been paying attention."

"Really? You try..."

A whistling sound comes from outside, growing into a piercing scream.

"Get down!"

The sound is deafening. The mortar hitting upstairs. The house whining and groaning. Peter grabs ahold of Michael and pulls him up from the floor, dragging him through the collapsing house. Another mortar hits it the moment they are outside, the building falling in on itself behind them.

It is then that they spot the six Ukrainian soldiers standing at the end of the driveway—their guns trained on them.

Both stop sharp and raise their hands, the men shouting at them in Russian.

"Get down on your knees!"

They look incensed.

"Do as they say," Peter tells the kid.

They lower themselves slowly into kneeling positions. One of the men peels away from the group and marches up. The second he spots the Wagner logos on their uniforms, his eyes bulge from his head and he turns over his shoulder to the others.

"Mercenaries! Mercenaries!"

He comes right up to them.

"Just stay still," Peter whispers to his son.

The guy brings the barrel of his Malyuk battle weapon right up to Peter's temple. Poking it into his skull.

"Mercenary," he hisses at Peter.

He leans back with the gun, slides the charge handle back, gets ready to shoot, stops—

Peter has shouted something in English.

When the soldier asks him to repeat it, he says, "We're American."

THIRTEEN

TEREK LAKE, BESLAN, RUSSIA

MIKHAIL GUTSERIEV WILL BE SPENDING THE duration of Peter's mission in Beslan at the modest dacha by the lake. It is early evening and the sun is disappearing over the low mountains. A band of gold spreads across the jagged peaks, and the entire panorama reflects off the rippling water.

The oligarch is drinking tea and staring at the view. In his ears he can still hear the cries of excitement his daughters would make as they swam these very waters. Glancing along the curling shoreline, he can't ever see the nearby oak that leans over the water without imagining his girls swinging from it on the end of a rope and diving off into the water. He can even hear the splashes.

"Sir?"

Gutseriev turns in his chair to find Alexei standing beside him. His face is grave. This can't be good.

He informs Gutseriev that Peter and Michael have been attacked.

"Are they dead?"

"We're not sure. Lieutenant Pavlov hasn't been heard from since it happened. The tank battalion they were traveling with have lost half their vehicles. The rest are currently either lost or dispersed about the east. Their commander is dead. Apart from that, we know very little. The Ukrainians have taken the entire area."

Gutseriev is silent. He stares at the surface of the lake, the rippling mountains, golden sky.

"So they will get away with their lives once again," he mutters.

"You should just let the war eat them up, Mikhail."

Gutseriev stares into the abyss. Then mutters, "I should have paid the assassin to shoot me instead."

FOURTEEN

UKRAINIAN PRISONER OF WAR FACILITY, LVIV, UKRAINE

BOOTS, ARMY ISSUE COMBAT STYLE, TRAMP ALL THE way up to the cell door from the other side. The lock scrapes and the hinges creak and soon it is opening inwards. An officer of the Ukrainian army steps into the room, before closing the heavy metal door behind him.

The space is small. About four meters square. The only furniture is a metal table bolted to the middle of the room. Peter is currently chained to it by the wrists. Unable to move his hands more than a foot away from the table.

The officer takes a seat opposite. Stares pleasantly across. Introduces himself in English. His name is Lieutenant Igor Stepanenko.

"So," he adds once he's presented himself, "my first question is: what's an American doing fighting alongside Wagner?"

"Where is my son?"

Peter's cold eyes stare at him.

"Your boy is okay. Unlike the Russians, we don't kill children."

"Where is he?"

"Safe."

"I want to see him."

Stepanenko can't help cracking up a little.

"What's so funny?" Peter asks.

"It is ironic, don't you think? You seem so concerned for your boy, yet bring him all the way here to fight a war that has nothing to do with either of you."

"We weren't here to fight for the Russians."

"Then what were you doing with a Russian tank battalion dressed as Wagner mercenaries?"

Peter decides it's best to come clean. He explains to Lieutenant Stepanenko why they are there—the job. Then, he takes a gamble. He offers to fight for the Ukrainians. So long as they get them close to his targets.

Stepanenko thinks about this.

"It's a shame, really," he says once he has.

"Why's that?"

"We could do with the numbers, and I'm no lover of the Scorpions. I saw what those bastards left us in Svestopol. They're not human. They're animals."

"But I don't understand. You say it's a shame. What makes it a shame if I can help you kill them?"

"Because you won't get the chance. You're off to Kyiv. You and your boy. We just got word from the Americans."

"Wait, what?"

A wave of panic crashes through Peter.

"We sent your fingerprints to them. You're on some kind

of CIA wanted list. International terrorism. They're sending someone to meet you in the capital."

"They'll kill us," Peter pleads. "Don't hand me over. I can fight. My son can fight."

"I would love that. You're obviously high-level stuff to end up on this list. But with us relying so heavily on the United States for support, we can't really go denying them now, can we?"

"You'll be sending us to our deaths."

"I'm sorry," Lieutenant Stepanenko says, getting up from his chair and preparing to leave. "It is done. You leave for Kyiv in the morning."

———

After the visit from Stepanenko, two soldiers come and take Peter down several narrow corridors to another cell. When they shove him inside he finds Michael lying on a bunk at the far end.

The kid sits up as Peter comes over and takes a seat on the other end of the wooden board.

"How're they treating you?" Peter asks.

"They fed me," Michael replies. "Asked some questions. Weren't rough."

"What about escape?"

Michael goes through the possibilities he's thought of so far. It appears he's seen a little more of the place than Peter. But not that much more. Most of his already formulated escape plans lead to certain death. The most interesting involves him pretending to have a fit. Peter calling for help. Then rushing the guards as they come in. In the end, Peter dismisses it with a shake of the head.

"It won't work," he tells his son.

"No. Probably not," Michael agrees. "I suppose we'll just have to wait and see what they do with us."

"I already know."

"You do?"

"Yeah. We're being shipped to Kyiv in the morning. That's where we're being handed over to the CIA."

Michael's eyes expand in their sockets.

"So get some rest," Peter adds. "Because in the morning we face a whole new set of problems."

PETER IS right about facing new problems. Just not in the way he thinks.

It is late afternoon when they hear boots outside their cell. The mechanisms of the locks crunch, the door creaks open. Peter is already sitting up. Hands on his knees. Alert. Ready for whatever new problem they face. Michael is lying on his back staring at the ceiling. Thinking about Bianca.

A man in military uniform walks in. Peter recognizes the insignia on his scarlet-colored beret. He belongs to the Land Warfare Special Purpose Unit. The most elite Spetsnaz outfit of the entire Ukrainian Armed Forces. He is what you'd expect from special forces: formidable. He blocks the light from the corridor, drenching them in shadow. At least six-and-a-half feet tall, he is broad chested, but not in the steroid way. In the real way. Strength and muscle that's been worked for; that is unique to his body type. Hair the color of fire sticks out from under the beret and his square jaw looks as unbreakable as concrete.

Michael sits up.

"I apologize for the intrusion," the Spetnaz says in heavily accented English.

Neither Peter nor Michael say anything.

"I am Lieutenant Vitaly Mylenko, commander of Eagle Team. A small unit within the 8th Spetsnaz Regiment."

Michael talks for them. "And what does Lieutenant Vitaly Mylenko, commander of Eagle Team, want with us?"

"I would like to ask you some questions."

"Great. More questions."

Mylenko decides to get straight to the point. "Is it true you are here to hunt Tagirov and Khodov?"

"Yes," Peter says.

"Okay. So why are CIA after you?"

Peter looks at Michael. The kid makes hand signals.

Tell him.

Peter faces the special forces soldier. "Have you ever heard of the Fallen Angel program?"

"No. What is it?"

"It doesn't exist anymore. But it was a program run by the CIA that trained children to be unregistered killers for the United States."

"Assassins?"

"Yes."

"And you and he were a part of this program?"

Mylenko signals the kid with a nod of his substantial head.

"I was," Peter says. "He wasn't. He's my son. I've been training him myself."

"So what happened with CIA?"

"I was burned. When the CIA decided to pull the program and cover it all up, they sent our locations to the GRU. Most of us were killed by the Russians. Some by our own people. And those of us that survived are hunted down by CIA death squads."

"Seems unfair," Mylenko observes.

"It is."

"What about your job here? You were with Russians. Is that who you work for now?"

"I told Stepanenko earlier, the man I work for is Mikhail Gutseriev. I work for him alone. I have nothing to do with the Russian government. I am here to take out two targets, then return."

He doesn't mention the stuff about Zoyev.

"Still," Lieutenant Mylenko says, "a Russian. Former member of the Duma. Gutseriev bends the knee to the president. Has donated vast sums of his personal wealth to the Russian military. Paying for the bombs which now rain down on my people."

"Everyone in Russia has to bend the knee," Peter replies. "Unless they want to lose everything and see themselves thrown in jail. This is a personal job. Mikhail Gutseriev has no love for the war. All he wants is the deaths of the men who murdered his children."

Mylenko scratches the red stubble of his chin. "And these Wagner cronies were getting you close?"

"Yes."

"You were willing to fight if necessary?"

"Only to get to our targets," Peter assures him.

"Then how about now? Are you willing to fight Russians to get to these men?"

Peter and Michael look at each other.

"So?" Mylenko puts to them.

"Yes," they both say in unison.

"The men you hunt," the lieutenant says, "the Scorpion Team, are responsible for some of the worst atrocities in this war so far. We recently uncovered a series of mass graves in retaken territory which they had previously held. As well as this, they are responsible for the deaths of two hundred prisoners of war, killed in Olevnika when they bombed the prison with the men inside. Because of this, my commander has given my team a special mission. To hunt down and eliminate the Scorpion Team. Will you join us?"

"How many of you are there?" Peter asks.

"Four. We were six, but I recently lost two men in Izium, and we're a little short on Spetsnaz recruits. An ex-CIA assassin and his apprentice son may be just the thing we need."

"Good," Peter says. "I prefer small teams. I don't like working with too many people."

"So that is a yes?"

"It is. But how are you going to square this with the CIA?"

A grin works its way up Mylenko's face. "Lots of things get lost during wartime. Perhaps you and your boy will be another of these things."

FIFTEEN

MOSCOW, RUSSIA

IT IS A COMMONLY HELD BELIEF THAT TWINS, especially identical ones, share an inherent understanding of their co-twin's emotional state. They report experiences of enhanced emotional or physical connection, such as having a feeling of something being wrong when their twin is in crisis.

Often, one twin experiences a physical sensation of something that's happening to their co-twin, such as emotional distress or a heart attack. In one case reported in Italy a twin experienced inexplicable abdominal pains at the same time as her sister was going into premature labor.

The world is filled with anecdotes that appear to support the idea of some sort of twin telepathy. They may perform similar actions when they're apart, such as buying the same item, ordering the same meal in a restaurant, picking up the phone to call each other at the same time. Sometimes they appear to know the other's thoughts by speaking simultaneously or finishing each other's sentences.

Despite the lack of scientific proof, these individual personal experiences can't be denied. They do happen. Whether by coincidence or paranormal phenomenon, it is generally accepted that such incidents are signs of a deep emotional connection that produces an intense sense of empathy, strong enough to generate physical sensations. They can know each other so intimately that they can predict how their twin will speak or behave.

What, then, happens when one twin is killed while the other lives? Is it like losing a limb and still feeling it tickle?

Sol and Eli Goldberg felt the bullet that ripped through their brother Abe. They can still feel the beat of the dead man's heart. Abe is still with them in spirit. Egging them both on in their pursuit of Azrael.

It is what has brought them to Moscow. Following up on a phone call they received only the day before from a stranger inviting them to dinner.

The two former triplets are led through the tall rooms of the Café Pushkin by the head waiter. Their contact is in a private room at the back. The restaurant is set in the heart of the capital, in a baroque building on Tverskoj Boulevard that dates back centuries. Its interiors are like a stage set. Wood-paneled walls, coffered ceilings, chandeliers, high-backed chairs, polished dark wood surfaces, bookcases filled with leather-bound editions of famous Russian works, including those of the poet the place is named after.

The private room is small with a single four-person table. A skylight overhead breathes light into the room and ivy dangles from a latticed ceiling.

A man neither recognize stands up to greet them.

He is around six feet tall with thinning blond hair and terribly lifeless eyes.

"Sit," he says in English.

The Goldbergs, both dressed in wide-brimmed fedoras and trench coats they refused to take them off when entering the restaurant, take their places opposite while the waiter remains by the door.

"Something to drink?" the man asks his guests.

They both shake their heads. Eyes pinned to him.

Their host waves the waiter away and the man leaves, closing them all into the conservatory. Having retaken his seat, the man introduces himself. His name is Vasily Savelyev.

"I hear the both of you have taken a vow of silence," he says. "Not a word until Azrael is dead."

Neither of the brothers speaks.

"I'll take that as a yes."

Eli digs a hand into a pocket of his coat. When it emerges, it is holding a card up to Savelyev. There are words written in English.

You said you knew where Azrael is.

Savelyev narrows his eyes to read. Then. "I do."

Another card. *Where?*

"He was captured by Ukrainian forces two days ago."

The twins look at each other. Then back at Savelyev. Frown at him. *Explain.*

"He was on a job. A man is paying him to track down two men in the Russian army. Azrael was traveling with a unit of Russian soldiers when they were attacked and he was taken captive along with his son."

Abe places a card down, snaps the end of his pen and writes.

And what are we supposed to do about that?

Savelyev leans forward, staring into their eyes. "The Ukrainians were supposed to hand him over to the CIA. It would have solved all our troubles, as you know. However, I have received information that a group of Spetsnaz have secretly recruited both Azrael and his son. They are now continuing their mission. Hunting for the two targets with their new comrades. I need you to intercept them before they can complete their job."

How?

"Both of you were former Navy SEALs. You used to run covert missions before deciding to go private with your brother Abe. That is true, is it not?"

The brothers merely stare at him.

Savelyev goes on. "Do you want to find Azrael and kill him yourselves? Get your revenge?"

They both nod.

"Then I offer you a way in."

SIXTEEN

KHARKIV, UKRAINE

Taken straight from their cell and loaded into a Mil Mi-8 helicopter, Peter and Michael are flown to a military base on the edge of Kharkiv. Having only recently been retaken by the Ukrainians, along with Izium and most of its surrounding land, the sprawling compound they land at was in Russian hands only days ago. Having withdrawn in a hurry, most of their gear has been left behind.

All around Ukrainian soldiers gather up and record the thousands of items the invaders abandoned during their retreat. As Mylenko leads Peter and Michael through the rabble toward a single-story office building, they pass stacks of wooden crates filled with mortars, missiles and other ammunition. All of it laid out on the asphalt under floodlights.

"They're gathering it from all over the city," Mylenko explains. "The spoils of war."

More of it arrives in the backs of heavy equipment transporters and other improvised civilian vehicles. Fork-lifts unload it for counting, then move it into temporary storage sheds that have been erected one end of the base. A crowd of soldiers stand around a Russian T-72, the tank still in perfect operational order, the men taking it in turns to sit on the front or the turret to have their photograph taken.

"It must be Christmas," Michael quips.

They reach the offices. A flagpole sticks out of the roof showing the Ukrainian blue and yellow. The building appears to be lucky. None of the surrounding ones have been left standing, decimated by the Ukrainian artillery strikes, and not much more than broken parts of their former structures remain, the rest sunk into craters so deep they go beyond the utility pipes and sewers built underneath.

Men salute Mylenko and open the doors for them.

Peter and Michael obviously changed before leaving the prison. Got out of their Wagner uniforms. Switched into Ukrainian ones. The two assassins becoming the ultimate soldiers of fortune.

The rest of Eagle Team are standing in a gym on the other side of the offices. Two males and, surprisingly, a female. She's tall, athletic, with short blonde hair cut to half an inch. A thin scar runs down her face. Starting above her eyebrow and ending midway down the cheek below. She looks lucky to have kept the eye.

One of the men towers over his colleagues. He's almost seven feet tall and wide to boot. He looks like the front of a truck. Yet, despite his colossal size, there's something innocent about him as he stands there with an almost curious look on his wide-jawed face.

The third is a mousy-looking guy, much shorter than the others, with intelligent eyes.

Mylenko begins the introductions. "The huge bear of a guy is Yari."

The big man holds a paw up.

"The short dude is Andriy."

He nods at them.

"And the beautiful blonde is Anya."

She stares coldly. The compliment having meant nothing.

"This is Peter," Mylenko says, nodding sideways at Azrael. "And this is Michael."

"That one looks like a boy," Anya points out in Ukrainian.

"He's nineteen," Mylenko lies.

"He barely looks fifteen."

"Let's get down to business," Mylenko says, ignoring the statement. "Andriy, what have you got?"

Andriy is holding a tablet. He slides a finger across it and the screen lights up with a map of the surrounding area. Everyone, including Peter and Michael, crowds around.

"I'll speak in English," he says. "For our American friends."

Peter notices Anya roll her eyes.

"So the last contact we had with the Scorpions," Andriy tells them, "was in Lysychansk at the end of June."

He points to it on the map. The city is deep in occupied territory, close to Luhansk.

"They were involved in fighting there to secure the city

alongside separatists who'd taken it over in February. We fought hard to get close to them, but it was no good. The Russians took the city back and we had to retreat before we got our chance."

"Better to fight another day," Peter remarks.

"Exactly. Anyway, since then our intelligence had them at Olenivka Prison Colony. That was until ten days ago. Since then, tracking them has been more difficult. We know they headed south to Mariupol and we know they then turned up in Izium. But they were gone by the time we arrived."

"They weren't part of the fighting?" Peter asks.

"No. They were there for something else."

"What?"

"We don't know."

Michael is looking at Peter. "Tell them," the kid says.

"Tell us what?" Mylenko asks.

"Two days ago," Peter says, "we were in Mariupol. We'd tracked them there."

"What did you find out?"

"Not much. Just that they met up with some FSB drones and picked up several large wooden crates."

"Ammunition and weapons?"

"I don't know. Nobody really knew anything concrete down at the dock. All they said was that the Scorpions were due to head to Izium afterwards. You know where they went when they were there?"

"Yes," Andriy says. "Witness sightings claim they were at the prison the Russians were using to detain captured citizens."

"Then we should go there."

"Already one step ahead of you," Mlenko says. "We fly over to Izium tomorrow at first light. Speak with some of the prisoners. See what they say."

"Why can't we go now?" Peter asks.

"Soon it will be night," Mylenko tells him. "That's when the Russians send their drones and missiles. It is better to stay out of the sky during this time."

"Then dawn it is."

———

AFTERWARDS, Peter informs Mylenko that he has to call Gutseriev. Naturally, the leader of Eagle Team objects, but Peter is insistent. "I won't be revealing anything of substance," he promises. "I just need to let him know we're alive and still on the trail."

Andriy has given him an encrypted satellite phone. So, while the others enjoy a little R-and-R, Michael playing Yari and Andriy at video games, Peter slinks off to a quiet edge of the compound and makes the call.

Gutseriev answers immediately. "Who is this?"

"Azrael."

"Oh, thank God. I heard you'd been captured and were due to be handed over to the CIA. Is this still true?"

"No."

"Is that good or bad news? I'm sensing it's good because you're calling me."

"I can't tell you much."

"You've been recruited by the Ukrainians, I take it."

"Is that intel or a guess?"

"A guess."

"Does it bother you?"

"No. I said before, all I care about are the deaths of these men."

"There's something else," Peter says ominously.

"What?"

"Pavlov, the man you placed us with. He tried to kill us."

Gutseriev is silent while he thinks it over. Then. "Someone must have found out in Wagner."

"How?"

"Maybe Pavlov talked or they guessed."

"No one your end?"

Another silence. More thinking. "No. Nobody knows except myself and Alexei."

"What about Alexei?"

"No way."

"Why not?"

"Alexei has been with me a long time. As well as saving my life on three occasions, he has always been loyal. If I can trust him with my life, I can trust him with this."

"He practically begged me not to go," Peter points out.

"Only because he fears for my safety."

"Then it must have been someone in Wagner."

"Pavlov must have spoken to the wrong person," Gutseriev observes, "or perhaps they've been watching him."

"How did you find him?"

"He came recommended by a private detective I was employing. The man said Pavlov had been running side missions for years alongside his other Wagner duties."

"Then Wagner must have been watching him," Peter states. "What about any intel your end?"

"There I may have something. Though, I apologize beforehand for it being only a crumb of comfort."

"A crumb may do."

"My people have finally located which channel the Chechens are using to communicate. It is one of the FSB channels. However, it is highly encrypted and they have been unable to crack it. I am told it could take up to a week to be able to break through and listen in."

"Anything else?"

"That's it, I'm afraid."

"Then I'd better go. I'll stay in touch."

Peter attempts to end the call when Gutseriev says, "Peter?"

"What?"

"Keep your son safe. Okay?"

"I will."

And with that, Peter does end the call.

SEVENTEEN

IZIUM, UKRAINE

Dawn arrives at six. They travel the short distance to Izium in a Mil Mi-24 helicopter gunship; another present left behind by the Russians.

Earlier, they'd kitted up. Peter and Michael now wear the uniform of the Ukrainian Spetsnaz—essentially a normal uniform with different insignia. Body armor is added, as well as helmets with GPNVG-18 quad-lens night-vision goggles mounted to the fronts.

Mylenko told them both as they'd dressed that GPS trackers have been sewn into all the garments of their uniforms. He claimed that it was mostly for operational purposes, but Peter is sure that it is also because Mylenko doesn't want them running off.

As for arms, Michael chose the Malyuk battle weapon. Also known as the Vulcan or Vulcan-M, it is a development of the Soviet Kalashnikov assault rifle, reconfigured into a bullpup layout with the magazine in the stock.

Peter took a KRISS Vector submachine gun. It may not have the fire rate or sheer power of the Malyuk, but it does have greater precision. Using an unconventional delayed blowback system combined with in-line design to reduce perceived recoil and muzzle climb, it is able to shoot a rapid succession of 9mm rounds accurately on a single target with very little effect on aim.

They both carry Glock 17s. Standard sidearm for Ukrainian Spetsnaz.

Peter also grabbed himself a KS-23. The KS is a Soviet shotgun that he's heard a lot about but never used. Because it uses a rifled barrel, it is officially designated by the Russian military as a carbine. As a matter of fact, KS stands for Karabin Spetsialniy, "Special Carbine." Though looking at it, you'd think shotgun straight away—as it resembles a shortened pump action. Other than that, the KS is renowned for its large caliber. It fires a 23mm round, equating to 6.27 gauge, making it the largest-bore shotgun in use today.

Peter looks forward to firing it.

Izium is a small city containing barely forty-five thousand souls before the war. It sits on a wide stretch of the Donets River and is surrounded by low hills and woodland. The first thing they spot when they hit the city limits is the smoke. It billows up from last night's missile strikes. Some buildings still burn, the flames licking the gray sky.

A radio message comes in. A warning from the Ukrainian Air Defence Network. Russian drones seen in the vicinity they're headed for. It'll mean having to walk the last mile.

So the Mi-24 sets down in the courtyard of two huge monolithic flat blocks and they get out. Then, as the chopper ascends once more into the red sky, they gather around Mylenko.

"The place we're looking for," he tells them, "is about four blocks east from here. Stay alert, people. Remember this is a war zone."

They edge along the streets, moving around the craters that eat into the roads and sidewalks. Debris from the night-time blasts is spread about. At one point they pass a bathtub that's been blown out of a nearby apartment building and landed in the middle of the road intact. Most of the buildings in this section have been hit, either by the Ukrainian mortars during their offensive, or the Russian airstrikes that started almost immediately after their retreat.

Most of the city lies in ruins.

They reach Izium's School No.7. Walking under its sign, Peter and Michael can't help thinking about Beslan. It is a similar concrete structure, one surrounded by apartments. Troops stationed behind sandbags guard the doors with Kalashnikovs. Mylenko introduces Eagle Team, including the forged IDs of Peter and Michael, who are now Vitali and Ivan Assomov.

The man in charge comes to meet them. His name is Captain Litvenko. He is a tall, stringy man, but with a strong posture. His expression is hard, giving little away.

"Many of the former prisoners," he explains while guiding them through the interior of the school, "are unable to go home because there is none. Instead they stay here with us in their former prison, which we've now turned over as a refuge center. Perhaps one day it will again be a school," he adds dryly.

Every space of floor that isn't being consistently walked on is given over to a cot. In one classroom a family cooks stew on a paraffin stove, the smells of the gravy and meat spreading down the hallway.

"The former prisoners are in the gym," Litvenko tells them. "They've had it pretty tough. Subjected to torture."

Inside the gymnasium men and women mostly lie about in their cots. Some are asleep. Others awake, pacing the background, constantly smoking cigarettes. At least two appear to be in manic states, one nattering away to himself as he paces, another sitting in his cot rocking back and forth.

"These are the ones that have nowhere to go to," the captain tells them as they stand before the mass of damaged bodies. "They're all suffering from PTSD. They all need care. And what do they have? Us."

"It's so sad," Yari mutters with genuine sympathy.

"At least two men I know who have been returned to their families have killed themselves within days of their release."

Eagle Team decide to do things as sensitively as possible. They split up, go from cot to cot. Michael sticks with Peter. Azrael's Ukrainian is a little rusty but soon it is up and running, and he too questions the men and women loitering in the gym.

Most of them were brought in by the Russians for seemingly trumped-up charges. A lot of the men claim they were simply called Banderovets and carted away.

"All they wanted," one man explains to Anya, "was the

names of those who served in the police force, the Territorial Defense Forces, or were veterans of the 2014 fighting in the Donbas."

They would receive electric shocks or be beaten with hands, rifle butts, metal pipes, a rubber hose, and in one instance a stick with a bag of sand on the end. One woman they interviewed said soldiers slapped her, punched her in the stomach, and threatened to rape her during her day-long detention.

"But what about the Chechens?" Andriy asks another man as they sit on his cot.

"No. The men running this place, asking the questions, were all Russian."

"You want to know about the Chechens?" a man opposite asks.

Andriy turns his way. "Yes."

"They came to my cell," the man tells him. "Took the man who was in there with me."

"Are you sure they were Chechen?"

"Big black beards, harsh voices. Plus, they spoke to each other in Chechen. I used to work away in the Caucasus. I may not know the language to speak it, but I can understand a word or two."

"So they took your cell mate," Andriy says.

"Yes."

"And who was he?"

"His name was Davyd. But we never exchanged surnames. I guess stuff like that slips your mind in certain situations."

"Do you know if they were here specifically for him?'

"I think so. They never bothered with me."

"And what did they do to him?"

"They took him into another room." His face screws up. "Did what they always do. Tortured the poor bastard."

"You know why?"

"I couldn't make out the questions over the tops of the screams. I can only tell you that Davyd kept telling them he wasn't lying. 'I'm not lying,' he would shout and scream at them. 'I'm not lying.'"

"Is he here now?"

"No. They took him with them. It was the day before the Russians ran away with their tails between their legs."

He spits on the ground after saying this.

"Do you know what Davyd did for a job?"

"Some kind of engineer, I think. He wasn't from Izium, though."

"He wasn't?"

"No. They'd captured him somewhere in Zaporizhia and brought him here. I think they wanted him to help restore the power grid, but he refused."

"So he was, what? An electrical engineer?"

"Or at least something similar to that. He was very clever. In the week we were together we made our own chessboard on the floor of our cell. Made pieces out of the bread they fed us. I could never beat him."

Andriy comes back to the others with this information.

"An engineer?" Mylenko says as they all stand outside the gym in a corridor.

"Possibly electrical."

"I'll radio it in. See if there's any records of a Davyd being taken in Zaporizhia. Anyone else get something?"

Peter steps forward. "The Scorpions are heading to Kherson."

"How did you find this out?"

"A woman I spoke to was being interrogated by the Russian in charge. She was present when a subordinate informed him that the Scorpions were here. She says that papers were exchanged. After that, they took someone into a nearby room."

"Did she hear what was said?" Andriy asks.

"They wanted him for some sort of job."

"Any idea what type?" Anya asks.

"None. However, she did tell me that she heard clearly the man being hurt cry out that they needed another for the job. That it could only be done by himself and this other man. And that this other man is in Kherson."

EIGHTEEN

KHERSON, UKRAINE

They jump back into the Mi-24 and leave Izium. Travel southwest, staying on the northern side of the Dnieper, where the Ukrainians hold all the ground.

Kherson is in the midst of being retaken. The vast majority of the Russians and their ordnance have left the city, but several Special Forces units have been left behind to make themselves a nuisance for the newly arrived Ukrainian patrols.

Eagle Team lands at a temporary base that's been set up on the outskirts of the city. Kherson is much larger than Izium. The tower blocks are bigger and there are more of them.

The first thing they notice stepping off the chopper is the noise. Explosions thunder in the distant air, and gunfire breaks out every so often. It is the soundtrack of war.

A platoon of Naval Infantry, the 1st Marine Artillery

Battalion, are there to meet them. This will be their escort through the city.

Veterans of the Mariupol siege, the 1st were fortunate to escape. Several other battalions weren't so lucky and had become trapped at the site of a steel works. Many of them either died inside the factory or were taken prisoners to be used as political fodder by the Russians.

It had been the Scorpions, along with several other Chechen units, who had torn through the city with such fiery zeal, and who, when the Ukrainians were captured, had spent their time torturing them.

The 1st escaped. Now they wanted payback for their fallen brothers. It is why they eagerly volunteered to lead Eagle Team into what has already been nicknamed the "Hell Zone."

The 1st's leader is Lieutenant Rebrov. The burly man's hair is almost white with age, including the long beard which hangs from his chin and sways in the breeze. He looks at least fifty, and is clearly, to Peter, an example of a Ukrainian soldier who has come out of retirement to defend his country.

The eight-man team stand on the asphalt. Mylenko makes a beeline for Rebrov. The second they make contact, both men wrap their arms around the other and bearhug.

"Long time, Vitory," the leader of the 1st says.

"I had thought we would never again meet on the battlefield."

"Yet here we are. A couple of fucking granddads fighting a young man's war. Some younger than others," Rebrov adds, having caught sight of Michael.

"He's old enough," Mylenko says as they part.

"How old?"

"Nineteen."

"And he's in Spetsnaz?"

"What can I say?" Mylenko replies. "The kid's a fucking legend. Fast-tracked to me recently after we lost Usimov and Chenko."

"I heard you took some hits in Izium. At least you won the territory back."

"But we lost the Scorpions."

"Then maybe what I'm about to tell you will cheer you up."

Everyone draws around the two men to listen in. Rebrov speaks. "The Chechens are here. Three units. Including the Scorpions."

"So our intel was right," Mylenko says, looking across the huddle at Peter.

"Yes. They're currently occupying the Hell Zone."

Rebrovs nods at one of his men. The man in question comes forward with a tablet. He holds it out to them. Moves a finger across the screen to reveal a digital map. Kherson sits on the banks of the Dnieper River. The northern edge of the city is currently under Ukrainian control. But everything two miles north of the river is still in the hands of Russian units left behind.

"This is the Hell Zone," Rebrov explains, landing a finger on it. "For some reason, the Russians have left behind the Spetsnaz units to blockade us from coming into that part of the city."

"They're protecting the retreat?" Mylenko asks.

"No." He points to a stretch of land beneath the river. "Most of the Russians are well clear. And their new battle line is already complete here." He runs a finger along the south bank of the river.

"So then what are they protecting?"

"That's what we want to know. Because why retreat, right, if you're gonna still defend an area you no longer control?"

"It's the other man," Peter says.

Every eye turns to him.

Mylenko nods and turns back to Rebrov. "We did a little digging in Izium. Found out that the Scorpions captured an engineer there."

"Who?"

"We don't know. There was only a first name. But apparently they needed to fetch another from Kherson. Is there somewhere in the Hell Zone that the Russians have been keeping prisoners in?"

"Yes." Rebrov drops a finger on a part of the city close to the river—the hottest part of hell. "They were using this apartment building. It has a bunker underneath. They were keeping people there."

"Then that is where we have to go."

Rebrov lays his finger on a road that leads into the Hell Zone. "We'll take this route," he says. "Come in from the south on foot. Any vehicles from there on in will be noticed."

"What about flying in?" Mylenko asks.

"No way. The Russians have left behind enough air support to turn any chopper into a smoldering wreck."

"On foot it is, then."

———

THEY TAKE an armored personnel carrier (APC) to the border of the Hell Zone.

On arrival, Peter and Michael spill out the back of the carrier with the others and find themselves standing in the middle of a wide boulevard. Twenty-story tower blocks rise up over them on both sides. The only gaps in their continuous flow comes from intersecting roads.

The soldiers spread out, keep low and stick to the edges. The bottom floor of the tower blocks is recessed, the next floors overhanging a walkway that runs along a strip mall underneath. The alcove partially shields them.

The soldiers split into their separate teams. Eagle Team takes the block on the east side of the boulevard. The Marines take the west. All around, smashed-out windows and narrow balconies look down on them. It is hard not to get the impression that they are creeping past a colossal-sized creature with thousands of eyes covering its entire body, and if just one of those eyes spots them, all hell will break loose.

When they reach the place they want, they stop, stay back in the alcoves of the neighboring buildings, and watch the building through a haze of light rain.

The apartment that was being used by the Russians has a great big sheet hanging down the front of it. On it someone has painted a forty-foot-tall Z. Michael can't help thinking of the way the Nazis used to decorate the municipal buildings they'd taken over during WWII.

Apart from the improvised flag, there are no other signs of life in the tower block. The Marines send up a camera drone and search the outside of the building. After twenty minutes of seeing nothing suspicious on the video feed, they bring it back.

"We'll go in," Rebrov's voice comes over their comms. "Take a look."

"Okay," Mylenko says. "Keep your eyes peeled."

"Always do. Over and out."

Eagle Team stays ducked in the alcove across the boulevard, watching the Marines peel away from their positions and file into the building. The rain thrums a steady beat. In the background is sporadic gunfire. A grenade goes off about two blocks to the north, a low crump sound, and an RPG explodes somewhere further ahead. Even though it is a cool day, the sweat cuts clean trails down their dirty faces. Then, ten minutes into their wait, they get something through the comms. It's Rebrov.

"You gotta come see this."

———

MYLENKO GOES ALONE.

The plaque above the door reads Karl Marx House. Inside, it is deadly quiet, and the farther he ventures into the place, the more eerie it gets as the outside sound fades to nothing. He begins to miss the distant gunshots.

He's quickly swallowed up by darkness. The electricity is all out in this part of the city, the Russians having bombed most of the local power infrastructure before retreating. By the time he reaches the Marine guarding the stairwell, he's flipped down his GPNVG-18 quad-lens night-vision goggles, and everything is drenched in green.

"Down there," the Marine whispers. "Fourth room along on the next floor."

Karl Marx House is unique from all the other blocks

surrounding it. Up top it may look like the rest of its concrete herd, but underground it is something else. During the Cold War, the Soviets had multi-storey bomb shelters built under every fifth tower block throughout the city. Ready for when catastrophe hit. Karl Marx House covers this particular area and has an elaborate basement of interlocking rooms, sheer concrete walls, and low ceilings.

The place gives Mylenko the creeps.

The first room is a large dormitory lined with rusted bunkbeds. The next, a room full of empty desks. The Russians must have been using it as an office, because the desks have stickers attached to them with names printed across:

Alexander Lepkov, First Lieutenant, 76th Guards Air Assault Division.

Sergei Rostov, Officer of GRU.

Nikita Sharov, Unit Commander of FSB.

Reaching the end of the room, Mylenko begins to hear people. Men's voices. Not just the Marines. Other men with tired, desperate voices.

"Get us out of here," one man despairs.

"You need to stay calm," Rebrov is telling him.

Torchlight flickers from a doorway. Another Marine guards it. He doesn't says anything as Mylenko flips his quad-lens goggles up and enters a room that is bare except for the five badly beaten men lining the back wall.

Each man wears a metal collar around his neck, a chain hanging from a loop on the back of it—the chains then attached to a steel ring that sticks out of the concrete floor.

It's not so much the collars and chains that cause terror

in these abused men, however. No, it's the bomb jackets locked to their torsos.

Mylenko comes beside Rebrov.

"This is real bad," he says.

"I told you you had to see it," the Marine replies, his eyes never leaving the men.

"You able to get them out of those?"

"We can't even get them out of the chains. Gonna need bolt cutters—and the bolt cutters are back with the APC. And even if we could cut them out of there, they're more than likely boobytrapped. For all we know this whole place could go up at the slightest touch."

"Then you need to get your men out. Call it in from up top. Get the Bomb Squad down here."

"That's exactly my thoughts, Lieutenant," Rebrov says before stepping forward, whistling loudly and ordering his men back upstairs.

"You can't leave us!" the captives cry.

"I'll leave my medic," Rebrov says, before commanding the man to stay.

"I also have to stay a few minutes," Mylenko tells him as the Marine commander follows the rest of his men out the door. "I need to ask some questions."

"Don't be long," his old comrade says.

Mylenko directs his attention to the despairing faces gazing at him from the back of the room.

"Don't worry," he tells them. "Those men can't deactivate the bombs on you, anyway. They're calling in people who can."

"Can you?" one of the men asks.

"No."

"Then why don't you get clear with your friends?"

"Because I need to ask you some questions."

"Like what?"

"Who did this?"

A chubby guy with a cut lip and a bust nose answers. "Chechens," he says. "They came this morning."

"Do you know the exact time?"

"No. But I'd guess it to be about two hours ago."

The hunter in Mylenko goes cold. Only two hours separated them from their nemesis.

"They removed us from our cells and brought us here," the man adds. "Did this."

"Was that the only reason they were here?"

Another man speaks. He is nought but skin and bones and one of his eyes is completely blacked. "Not just that," he says. "I saw them when they first arrived. They were looking for someone."

"Who?"

"I don't know. But I think he had something to do with the university."

"The university?"

"Yes. Many of us were working at the university when the Russians came. They arrested those of us who wouldn't join them. Accused us of being fascists and brought us here."

"And you never heard a name?"

"No," he says with a shake of the head.

———

Up top, Mylenko meets with Rebrov. The Marine commander is standing outside the entrance, busy on the satellite phone.

"I'm gonna need medical, too," he is saying.

"Copy that. We'll be in your area ASAP."

"Okay. See you then. Over and out."

Rebrov turns to Mylenko.

"How long?" Mylenko asks.

"They can't say."

"Can't say?"

"Maybe half an hour. Maybe an hour."

Mylenko rolls his eyes and leaves him. When he crosses the boulevard, he does so with haste: ducked down and running, throwing himself into the alcove. The others immediately cluster around him as he explains things.

"Great!" Anya snuffs bitterly at the end.

"So they were here and now they're not," Andriy says.

"It's where they're going that's important," Yari pipes in.

"When did they leave?"

"Two hours ago."

"There's a good chance they're still in the city," Peter says.

Across the street Rebrov begins getting radio messages from the medic left inside the bunker.

"What's that?" Rebrov says into his comms. "Can you repeat? Over."

The line is fuzzy due to the twenty feet of lead-plated concrete separating the street from the basement.

"I said... -smitter... remo-... detonation."

"What?"

"...took a look... There's some sort... transmitter... think it is... controlled."

Sudden realization floods Rebrov. He realizes what the man is saying. There is some sort of transmitter on one of the bombs. It appears it can be remotely detonated.

"Get out of there!" Rebrov screams into his comms before turning to the rest. "Down! Down!"

"What's up with him?" Michael asks in English, pointing into the road.

Eagle Team all look. Rebrov is walking toward them from across the street. He is waving his arms and shouting. There is the crack of a round being fired. This one much closer than the others. Coming from a ten-story block at the end of the street.

The bullet enters the top right side of Rebrov's head at a forty-five degree angle and exits out the left side of his lower jaw. The power of the shot spins him around and he lands in a twisted heap in the middle of the road.

"Sniper!" the men call out.

Everyone in Eagle Team ducks in tight to the walls of the alcove. The Marines are out in the open, too far from the other flat blocks. So they duck back into the building with the bomb.

As Eagle Team watches, Mylenko switches channels to the Marines. "Marines?!" he shouts into his comms. "Marines, don't go back into that—!"

The explosion rips the words right out of his throat and shakes the whole street like an earthquake. Any windows with glass remaining burst. A great plume of white smoke coughs out of the entrance. Eagle Team watch as a crack runs down the front of the building. The great structure of stone and steel whines, groaning under the strain, like the tower block is crying out in pain.

Peter scans their immediate environment. The burned-out remains of a car about six yards away. One of the doors hangs off and another lies fully detached beside it on the road.

Two Marines run from the entrance of the building. One is on fire. They head straight for Eagle Team, but halfway across the boulevard the Marine on fire drops to the ground. The other one crouches over him, trying his hardest to bash out the flames with his bare hands.

Another crack. Same sniper. Same result.

The crouching man is hit in the neck. He grabs at his throat. Tries to stand. Falls. The Marine on fire thrashes and screams, the flames curling around his entire body. Then he just stops.

Michael stares at the guy. Unable to move.

"Hey!" It's Peter. He grabs ahold of Michael's arm and shakes him. "Stay alert," he shouts.

Michael nods and Peter turns his attention to Mylenko.

"Mylenko, you listening?" he says into his comms.

"Yeah. What?" comes back through his earpiece.

"The snipers are Scorpions, right?"

"So?"

"So if we catch one alive, we might be able to find out where the rest of their team is."

"Not a bad idea. But first we need to find out where they're firing from."

"Then we need to keep him shooting."

"How do you suppose we do that?"

"By giving him a target."

Peter shoulders the KRISS Vector and rushes straight for the burned-out car. He picks up the blown-off door with both hands and by the time the first shot comes his way the bullet is ricocheting off it.

"I saw him!" Michael cries out.

"Where?" Mylenko asks in English.

"In the flat block facing the road. Floor seven. Third window from the right."

Another shot hits the door as Peter zigzags down the boulevard toward the block.

"I see him!" Yari bawls.

"Then give him hell!"

Yari is wielding a PKP Pecheneg—a Russian-made general-purpose machine gun that is often fitted to light infantry vehicles. He steps from cover, holding it one-handed by the carrying handle, and rushes toward the end of the alcove, staying as low as his huge frame will allow.

A brick planter about a meter high gives him cover. All the flowers in it are dead. Flicking out the bipod at the end of the barrel, he rests the meaty PKP on the ledge of the planter, ducks down behind it, and begins pounding the flat block, spent shell casings spitting out of the ejector port like silver dollars at a casino.

The rest of Eagle Team begin hammering the sniper's position. All except Anya, who sneaks off to another brick planter, this one lining the edge of the sidewalk. Ducked down behind it, she rests the barrel of her Dragunov SVD marksman rifle on the ledge, shoves an eye to the scope, searches the flat block through the crosshairs.

The sniper is no longer at the same window. He has moved.

A shot slams the road so close to Peter's boot that he feels the vibrations through the sole. It came from the right of the building. Not the left like the others. Another shot almost gets him as he swings the door around to meet it. None of it matters, though. His hundred-meter dash is over. He makes it.

Throwing down the car door, Peter reaches the alcove of the sniper's building and heads for the main entrance. Sure that it's boobytrapped, he unshoulders the KS shotgun and fires a breaching round at the double doors. The hinges explode. The doors shudder inwards, tripping an IED and setting off a small explosion which would have maimed him had he been within its proximity.

Peter enters the flat block through smoke. An open door leads into a courtyard. He moves across it at a run, head down, bent at the waist. There is a children's mural on the wall—Snow White and the Seven Dwarfs. A lonely soccer ball sits idly on the paving slabs. He manages to cross without a single shot fired from the surrounding balconies, hits the stairwell, and begins ascending the steps as silently as he can, the Vector gripped in his hands, an eye lined with its sight.

He can hear more gunfire, some distant and some coming from inside the building. He can also hear that there's more than one shooter in there.

Peter exits the stairwell on the floor he wants, making sure to step over the crude tripwire set up there, and creeps along a hallway. A mortar rocket has recently hit the center of the building, caving in a large section. Peter uses the wreckage to his advantage, entering an apartment through a hole in the wall. He steps into a sitting room with patterned rugs on the floor, a leather couch, a bookcase now containing just a single lonely paperback, a coffee table tipped on its side. There is a tapestry of running horses on one wall.

Peter pauses, focuses his hearing.

He can make out the sounds of the snipers moving about. Scurrying from apartment to apartment. One of them has peeled away from the others to go looking for him. Peter can hear the man's military-issue boots crunching carefully along debris. Getting closer.

Azrael steps back as the Scorpion rounds a half-demolished wall at the other end of the sitting room. Slipping away into the hallway, he takes cover at the edge of the hole, shouldering his weapon and pressing his back to the concrete. Waiting at the edge, he takes a Czech Demon Knife and listens to the Scorpion move across the sitting room towards him.

Peter stops breathing. The air frozen in his lungs.

Closing his eyes, he listens hard.

The man is cautious, edging slowly toward him. But no matter how quiet he thinks he is, Peter can make out his every movement. He can hear the air whistling through the man's tight nostrils. His boots moving from the hardwood floor to the soft rug. He can hear the sounds of the clip rattling on the strap holding the man's AK to his shoulder. He can hear him step right out into the hallway not knowing that in just a few seconds, he will be dead.

Peter grabs the barrel of the AK before the man. Making sure to take the weapon out of the equation by pushing its aim up. Then, before the poor bastard can even fire, Peter plunges the knife straight into his throat, all the way to the spine, practically decapitating him. He rips the rifle out the man's weakened grasp and pushes him backwards into the room. Shoves him free of the knife.

The Scorpion lands on his back, coughs a few spluttered breathes and goes rigid.

Peter leaves him, resumes his journey to the sniper nest. He enters an apartment where sections of the roof are completely missing, everything illuminated by beams of sunlight that are almost solid with floating dust motes.

There are only two snipers left. The men at separate ends of the building. Peter hones in on the one closest, listens to him scuttle between three apartments, letting off his sniper rifle every so often.

He creeps closer. Slips into the apartment the man is currently shooting from. A half-demolished wall blocks his view of the guy, but he knows he's there, ducked down behind his rifle on the balcony.

Peter stays in the doorway, waiting for him to move. The Scorpion's only exit is coming around the broken wall straight toward him. When that happens, he'll shoot the guy in the legs and take it from there.

But Peter doesn't get the chance. He hears a gentle crunch in the hallway behind him. The other sniper. Creeping up on him from along the hallway.

Peter dives into the apartment as rapid fire cuts up the doorframe. He hears a click and realizes that his dive has triggered a tripwire. Another dive takes him through another doorway into a bedroom as the blast fills the apartment.

His skull ringing, Peter finds himself lying on his back on top of debris. Men are shouting in the background. No. Not the background. They're right there.

Get up!

Peter springs to his feet, runs to the end of the room, dives through the open window.

The Scorpion moves cautiously toward the bedroom, using a hand to wave away the smoke, gripping his AK-74M tightly with the other. His own ears ring incessantly but he ignores it as he enters the room, turns immediately right and gazes at the window. The other sniper has come away from his nest and is now in the hallway, asking what it was.

The Scorpion in the room turns to his comrade, opens his mouth—takes a round of buckshot from the KS straight in the face and chest. It throws him backwards like a hit from a bull and he drops instantly dead.

Peter climbs back through the window, having grabbed the ledge as he'd jumped through it. Hanging there and waiting for his moment.

He cocks the shotgun, dispensing the spent shell casing onto the floor, dodges around a bed covered in junk, shoves aside a pile of broken plasterboard that blocks his way, and gets into cover at the edge of the door. He listens out for the one remaining Scorpion, but is panting like a dog and can't hear so well.

Click.

The sound is faint but it is unmistakable.

Peter dives forwards onto his front as the .338 Lapua Magnum round punches a hole through the concrete wall right where his spine had been.

The Scorpion waits to see if he's hit his target or not.

Peter doesn't give him the chance. He runs for the window as the sniper sends two more rounds through the wall before he reaches it and jumps out like before, twisting in the air and grabbing the frame, the sunlight hitting him like a fist. At some point he loses the shotgun. Dropped in the commotion.

Fingers gripping the detail of the wall, toes rested on a concrete lip no wider than an inch, he shuffles toward the balcony. He expects to see another round punch through the outer wall, or at least the guy hang out of the window. But there's no more shooting.

Peter clambers over the railing and into the sniper's former nest. There are ammo cases littered about everywhere. It looks like they were planning on a long fight.

Peter reenters the apartment, back pressed to the wall. All he has left is the Glock. It's going to be hard to take the guy alive, but he'll try.

Entering the living room he senses movement.

The pistol is kicked out of his hand. Peter manages to grab the rifle as the guy attempts to wheel it round on him. They wrestle and the Scorpion gets the upper hand, pushes him backwards, smashing him into a wall. The wind is knocked right out of Peter. His lungs struggle for air, making him weak as his hands fight for purchase on the Scorpion.

The guy is tough. Real tough. He knows fighting. It is clear by the way he defends himself.

Pushing Peter away, the Scorpion drops the rifle and whips a pistol from his hip. Azreal gets to him just in time, grabbing the elbow, pushing the shot away. The gun goes off right against his temple and he feels the blood pound his eardrums. It shakes him. He feels dizzy and nauseous. Still, he must fight, mustn't lose his focus.

Peter manages to disarm him of the gun, but the Scorpion immediately grabs a knife from an ankle holster. Peter has to move quick to avoid it. He needs both hands to grab the wrist holding the knife. A hammer punch in the side of the head knocks him away.

It had been a full-on right hook. A sledgehammer right in the ear. He had felt it in his teeth and it had turned the room into two overlapping images.

He doesn't know which of the armed men to fight.

Both come at him with the knife. Peter practically acts on instinct alone. His head elsewhere, the defensive actions he takes to protect himself nothing more than muscle memory. Somewhere along the way the Scorpion gets Peter onto his back and is trying to drive the knife into his face. Azrael is losing. The concussion, the nausea, the weakness in his body, all of it work against him. The tip of the blade presses slowly into the flesh of his right cheek. He does his best to summon all his strength. Closes his eyes. Cries out. But the man on top has all the advantage and the blade begins to sink into him, until right at the moment he feels that he may give in, his attacker is suddenly dragged off.

Peter opens his eyes to see the guy staggering backwards as the heavy butt of a Dragunov rifle slams into his face with a sickening crunch and knocks him clean out.

Anya stands over the Scorpion, holding the rifle like a harpoon, daring the Chechen to get back up. But he doesn't. Lucky for him.

NINETEEN

KHARKIV, UKRAINE

THE UKRAINIAN ARMY CONTAINS MANY FOREIGN volunteer groups fighting within its regiments. Made up of various nationalities that have beef with the Russians for one reason or another, some estimates place the figure of foreign fighters at more than 20,000 from a total of fifty-two countries.

This is the "in" that Savelyev had mentioned to the Goldberg brothers in Moscow. In times of war vetting tends to be a little lax for new recruits. Especially foreigners offering their services. Of the many volunteer battalions within the Ukrainian army, one particular unit—named the Five-Five—has come under the command of a Georgian double-agent working for the FSB.

His name is Tamaz Kaladze. Not his birth name, but who cares. A former officer in the Georgian Army, Kaladze was recruited almost twenty years ago by the FSB, coming to the fore during the Russo-Georgia War in 2008. At that time he was a high-ranking colonel and Russia's best source of military intelligence on the Georgians.

Now in his early fifties, he welcomes the fifth-columnist unit's two newest members. Sol and Eli Goldberg.

They meet on a cold, cloudless afternoon in Kharkiv.

"You made it past the recruiters, then," he says to both in English as they stand on a street corner that straddles an empty park.

Neither of the brothers says anything.

"Of course," Kaladze adds, like he's just remembered. "I was told that neither of you speak. But I hear you're good with hand signals."

Both men make the signal for yes.

"And you are both ex-military?"

Another yes.

"Good. I will introduce you soon to the team. You are aware that not all of us are..."

He goes to say it but can't without glancing sideways at some soldiers lingering about the sidewalk on the other side of the street.

"It's best," Kaladze adds in a low voice, "if you don't speak too much with the others."

The brothers stare back like statues.

"But thankfully that won't be a problem. Now come on. Come meet the Five-Five."

He turns to lead them off but Sol grabs him by the shoulder.

"What's the matter?"

Eli gets a card out. Kaladze has to squint to read the writing.

Where is Azrael?

"I wanted to wait until we moved out to tell you."

Eli's lip curls. He taps the writing with a finger.

Where is Azrael?

Kaladze gives a furtive glance at his surroundings. He steps forwards so that he won't have to raise his voice above a whisper. A convoy of army trucks drive by just when he's about to speak and he holds off until they are gone.

"The Eagles are holed up in Kherson," the Georgian eventually hisses to the brothers. "We head there by chopper in one hour. Then we hit the city outskirts and make our way into it by foot. As far as the Ukrainians know, we're there to clear IEDs. Two of my men are expert bomb disposal men. That's our cover. It'll allow us entry into the city at nighttime. We'll have to move as quietly as possible and watch out for drone and missile strikes, but it's the best way to creep up on them."

TWENTY

KHERSON, UKRAINE

Eagle Team are camped in the Hell Zone, close to the northern bank of the Dnieper. Having found themselves an underground Metro station, they descended the frozen escalator and set themselves up along a platform. With the power out, the only light is provided by the flickering bonfires they've started.

An empty subway carriage fills the track. Its doors lay open. Discarded newspapers cover the seats and floor. The Scorpion is tied to a chair at the end of it. He's still out cold and Andriy is currently watching over him. Mylenko sits reading a book, Yari takes a nap, his entire length stretched out close to one of the fires, and Anya sits cross-legged, cleaning her Dragunov. Peter sits not far from her, while Michael is fast asleep, curled up and looking like nothing more than a boy.

Anya looks up from the disassembled rifle and gazes at

him. "I can't believe you'd bring your own son somewhere like this," she says.

"He insisted," Peter replies.

Anya goes to speak when Andriy leans out of the open doorway of the carriage and says, "The prisoner is awake."

It is like a bell going off. A shiver runs through the air. Michael and Yari stir, their eyelids opening. Everyone else stares at Andriy.

Peter turns to Michael, the kid looking straight at him.

"What's up?" he asks while yawning.

"The guy's awake."

The Scorpion sits in the middle of the carriage. Snapped ChemLights lie around his feet, giving the scene an eerie green glow. Zip-ties run all along the guy's forearms, securing them to the arms of the chair. Something similar has been done to fix his legs. His face is a mess, his forehead scraped and cut. One of his eyes is completely closed over and the gash above it oozes blood. It was one hell of a hit from Anya.

His good eye shimmers at them.

Mylenko asks him his name, speaking Russian, but the man just looks at him like he doesn't understand.

"I know a little Chechen," Peter says.

"Then be my guest." Mylenko steps aside.

"What's your name, soldier?" Peter asks in Chechen.

The Scorpion pierces his eyes at him. Weighs things up. Decides it's just a name.

"Khamzat," he says.

"I'm Peter."

The prisoner's eyes are slits. "You're not Ukrainian."

"That isn't important."

"Then what is?"

"I am looking for the men who are in command of your unit."

Peter expects him to want to know why. But instead all the Chechen does is ask for a cigarette.

Peter asks Andriy and the Ukrainian gets his pack out, places a smoke in the guy's cut lips and lights it for him.

"How do you know our language?" the Scorpion asks Peter in between puffs.

"I once had to track down a Chechen inside your country for three months. In order to sink in, I had to learn your language."

"Why were you tracking a Chechen?"

"He owed a Russian arms dealer over two million dollars. A big price was put on him. I took up the offer."

"You are a mercenary?"

"You could say that."

"You must be a very clever man to learn our language."

"Not that clever. I wouldn't be here if I was."

"And neither would I," the Chechen sighs. "My father told me not to join this war. His generation still sees the Russians as the enemy."

"You're a proud people."

"We are mountain people. The mountains molded us. And like them, we are tough and demanding of both ourselves and of each other."

"Then why did you join this fight?"

"I am a soldier. A good one. The best way to keep my family secure back in Grozny is with Russian pay."

"How old are you?"

"Twenty-seven."

"Twenty-seven," Peter repeats. "So you would have been a child during the Second Chechen War."

Khamzat's eyes go dark. "I grew up through it," he says. "Three of my older brothers were killed fighting the Russians."

"It was during this time," Peter goes on, "that I was in Chechnya looking for my target. One day, I witnessed a bus of civilians being pulled over by Russian soldiers at a check-point. I remember them getting into an argument with the driver before turning their AKs on him and everyone onboard."

Khamzat has gritted his teeth. "That is nothing," he spits. "Those people had an easy death. My uncles and cousins were shepherds. The Russians came. Cut off their ears. Removed their teeth. Gouged out their eyes. All before shooting them in the head. The farmers had it the worst. They would shoot all the livestock. Destroy our farm equipment. So that we would starve."

"A lot like what they're trying to do here," Peter points out.

"It is because the hungry are easy to control. The Russians would starve us and then come in at the last moment with humanitarian aid. In the end it was our stomachs that dictated our surrender."

"So you don't agree with this alliance between your president and theirs?"

The Scorpion's eyes are once more narrowed at Peter. "I know what you are doing," he says in a dry tone.

"Having a discussion," Peter suggests innocently.

"You are trying to make me give up the positions of my brothers."

"You know what two of your brothers have done?"

"This is war."

"Not now. Before. What they did to children."

Khamzat closes his eyes and breathes in. Then. "I cannot betray my brothers." And with that, his head slumps between his shoulders and muttered words slip from his broken mouth. "I believe in the words of the Prophet," he mumbles. "I believe that the holy war will be fought in blood. That the infidels must be cut from the earth like poisoned crops... Allah Akbar!"

The Scorpion repeats this over and over.

"What's he saying?" Mylenko asks.

"It doesn't matter," Peter says. "It's no good. Not even torture will make him give them up."

A general sigh goes around Eagle Team.

"Then all we can do," Anya says, "is hand him over to Army Police and keep searching."

"I have another idea," Peter says. "The satellite phone you have." He's looking at Andriy.

"What about it?"

"I can use it to call Mikhail Gutseriev in Russia, right?"

"Of course."

"No way," Mylenko says.

"He's tracking the Scorpions," Peter tells him. "He might know where they are."

"He's Russian," Mylenko says. "A personal friend of the president. He might even be under the watch of the FSB like a lot of the president's personal acquaintances. They could get our position from the signal."

"Then I'll make the call away from here to be safe."

Eagle Team look at each other. Then Mylenko gives in.

"Okay," he says. "Go northeast two blocks. That sector should be clear."

"The StarLink can be glitchy," Andriy tells Peter outside on the platform as he digs into his pack for the satellite phone. "You'll need to get high to get a good line, so you'll have to do it from a roof or balcony."

He hands the bulky handset over. Peter stashes it in his camouflage canvas rucksack before shouldering the bag, the KRISS Vector tucked underneath the straps at his shoulders like the crossbeam of a crucifix.

Michael wants to go with him.

"No," Peter tells him. "Only one of us needs to go."

"But who'll have your back?"

"I'm only making a telephone call."

"What if you come across Russians?"

"Then it'll make sense to go on my own. Less likely to be spotted if there's only one of me."

"But..."

Peter lays a hand on his shoulder and makes a face. "Come on, Mikey," he says. "Don't argue. I won't be long."

Michael gives in and Peter says goodbye to Eagle Team.

As he begins ascending the frozen escalator, Mylenko turns to Anya. "Go with him," he whispers to her. "Make sure he doesn't give too much away to the Russian."

She nods at her superior, grabs her recently reassembled Dragunov, and follows Peter up the metal steps.

TWENTY-ONE

A HARD RAIN BEATS AT THE CITY. THERE IS NO light except the faint glow of distant fires. All over Kherson, buildings burn as the waves of Iranian-supplied Shahed-136 kamikaze drones bombard the place, the Russians hoping to wash Kherson off the map.

Peter and Anya choose an apartment building far from a power supply. Hoping that this will make it less likely to be hit. At the top of the ten-story block, they have a good view of the damage.

Buildings burn like pyres all over the city. Black smoke joins black sky, enveloping everything in darkness. Seeker rounds light it up as the Ukrainians attempt to knock the drones out of the air.

"Make this quick," Anya whispers to Peter in Ukrainian.

He unshoulders his kit and pulls the phone out. Ducked down away from the edge of the roof, he makes the call. Anya, in the meantime, unshoulders the Dragunov and uses its thermal scope to scan their surroundings.

Mikhail Gutseriev answers immediately.

"Is it you?"

"Hello, Mikhail."

"Thank God," the oligarch breathes. "You are alive. And your boy?"

"He is well."

"Where are you now?"

Peter turns to Anya. She is glaring at him over her shoulder.

"I cannot say," Peter tells the Russian. "Now listen. I don't have much time. I was close to the Scorpion Team, but I've lost the scent."

"Then it is lucky you called. My people have today successfully broken into the Russians communication channel. I have new information on Tagirov's unit."

Anticipation livens Peter up. "What information?"

"It appears they are aware of your presence. My people intercepted a communication between Tagirov and his second Khodov. The Scorpion Team has split in two. Khodov is staying in Kherson with his half for the sole purpose of engaging you and the rest of your group. And he mentioned you by your codename Azrael. It appears he's eager to meet you."

"Wagner must have tipped them off. What about Tagirov?"

"He and the remaining half of the Scorpions are currently camped out at Sahy. It is a small village on the southern bank of the river. About twenty kilometers from Kherson. They leave in the morning for Zaporizhzhia."

Peter asks, "Did your people pick up anything about

what they're up to or the identities of the two men they've taken?"

"I'm afraid not. But they clearly don't want you following. So be careful."

As they talk, Anya spots a shadow gliding through the air. It keeps a constant forty-five degree incline, moving smoothly toward a nearby flat block. Through the thermal camera, it is only a speck of yellow heat—until it reaches the flat block and explodes in rapidly blooming red.

The building rocks beneath their feet.

"We need to go!" Anya cries out.

She is standing up and pointing.

Peter follows the gesture.

There are waves and waves of the ominous shadows gliding toward them.

Gutseriev is still speaking when Peter abruptly cancels the call, throws the phone into his kit and shoves it over his shoulder.

They run, heads down, to the open door of the bulkhead, reaching it right at the moment more drones slam into the surrounding buildings. As the concrete steps move beneath their feet, the two of them throw themselves down the stairwell. Another impact close by causes everything to lurch. Anya slips on the stairs, almost loses her footing, but Peter grabs her arm and keeps her upright, practically dragging her down the last few flights and out the door of the apartment.

The whole street looks like it's on fire. Flames reflect off the wet surfaces.

"Look!"

Peter wheels around. Anya is pointing at the building

next to them. It is hit right at the moment he spots the drone. The explosion rocks the entire street. The burst of light is almost blinding. It is a critical hit and the twenty-story block begins to crumble immediately. Cracks race across its facade. It starts to keel into the street, the front wall of the building peeling away like a sheet of loose skin.

Anya stands frozen. Peter grabs her wrist and tugs her across the street, toward a forty feet long CargoMAX flatbed semi-trailer; the heavy-duty types that carry cranes. Both their legs pump to get there before—

They dive into a skid, sliding under the trailer, into the three-feet cavity below, right at the moment several tons of bricks and mortar and debris come raining down on the flatbed, smothering them in darkness and silence.

TWENTY-TWO

THE FIVE-FIVE TRAVEL DOWN TO KHERSON IN TWO pickups. The lead vehicle contains the Goldberg brothers, the two of them stuffed in the front with Kaladze, the unit commander driving.

The journey takes them all night and they arrive in Kherson at the crack of dawn; at the same military base that Peter, Michael and Eagle Team landed at the day before.

The men unpack themselves from the pickups and Kaladze speaks with the commanding officer. The Five-Five are assigned clearance detail, something that Kaladze has organized ahead of their arrival. It will take them to the same sector the Eagles are in.

As they prepare to head out, Kaladze asks the CO discreetly about Eagle Team.

"They went out yesterday with a battalion of Marines," the officer tells the Georgian. "I heard they got ambushed. Only one of the Marines that was with them survived."

"Anyone from Eagle Team get hit?"

"No. Just the Marines."

"Did they come back to base?"

"No. They camped out in the Hell Zone all night. I heard a rumor that they're tracking a band of Russian special forces across the river."

"Yeah?" Kaladze acts all coy.

"I can't see any other reason why they'd stay in the city at night. I mean, it's a mess in there. The whole east side of the sector was destroyed by drones last night. The place is rubble."

"The Eagles?"

"I don't know. I guess they're still in there."

Kaladze taps the guy on the shoulder. Thanks him. Rejoins the others.

Furtively checking his surroundings with sideways glances, he tells the brothers in English, his voice low and conspiratorial, "They're still in there. Spent the night."

TWENTY-THREE

"Anya, come in," Mylenko breathes into his radio. "Anya, give me a sign. Please, Anya."

He's been at it all morning.

They're about to hit topside. The four of them spread out in cover at the edges of the Metro exits—the wet street laid out before them, the pinks and golds of the morning sky reflecting off the surfaces, a strong scent of smoke in the air.

"You stay close to me, kid."

Michael turns sideways.

Yari is standing behind the next pillar. A benevolent expression on his round, big-jawed face.

Andriy's voice comes over their comms. "I got their GPS."

He is checking the screen of a tablet device. Michael notes that he is wearing a grave expression.

"It's in blue sector," Andriy adds. "Where most of the bombing happened last night."

They are speaking English for Michael's benefit.

"Then we need to go there," he says into his comms.

"Don't worry, kid," Mylenko replies. "We're not about to leave one of our own behind. Andriy, you have a fix on the location?"

"Yes."

"Then we move out."

———

PETER LIES DEADLY STILL, listening closely to the movement of the rubble above them, taking in short, calm breaths in an attempt to reserve what remains of the dusty air.

The weight of the collision caused the trailer to burst its tires and sink down; turning the meter gap into a foot. That was when Anya got hit in the head, the blow knocking her out. She lies unconscious, pressed to his front, the two spooning in the limited space of the cavity.

She begins to move.

Opening her eyes onto compete darkness, she panics, screams, begins thrashing. Peter tries to contain the movement, whispering softly into her ear.

She freezes. Realizing for the first time that he's right behind her.

Her breaths jerk into her. "I, huh, don't, huh, like, huh, closed spaces."

"It won't be long," he assures her. "We're both fitted with GPS. They'll find us soon. Just stay calm."

"I can't, huh, breathe."

"Just calm down."

"I, huh, can't move."

"We're pinned under here, but it shouldn't take long for them to dig us out. All we have to do is reserve our oxygen."

"I can't, huh, see. I, huh, don't want to, huh, die under here."

"You won't. But you have to stay calm."

"I, huh, can't."

"Sing."

"Sing?"

"Yes. Sing with me." Peter breaks into Irving Berlin: "What'll I do, when you are far away, and I am blue? What'll I do?"

She knows the song. On the next verse, she joins him.

"What'll I do, huh, when I am wondering who, huh, is kissing you? Huh, what'll I do?"

By the fifth verse her breathing is much better.

"When I'm alone, with only dreams of you, that won't come true, what'll I do?"

———

RAINDROPS HISS ON THE FIRES. Eagle Team climb a landslide of crushed debris that blocks an entire street. At the top, they enter the remains of an apartment block. Step straight into what is left of someone's living room. Water runs down the walls in a sheet, a burst water main somewhere. It looks like the walls are moving.

The next apartment block is nothing but a rolling valley of rubble, and they enter a trench that used to be a ground floor corridor. Its walls are eaten away from about three feet up and mounds of rubble rise above them on all sides.

Andriy is in front, checking the tablet every so often.

"How far now, Andriy?" Mylenko asks.

"Not far. About half a mile."

"ETA?"

"What am I, psychic? We don't even know how much..."

Andriy stops talking. Stops moving.

He freezes and holds a hand up. Then, he has just enough time to turn around to them and give an apologetic look. That's when the others spot the steel-tripwire sagging against one of his boots.

The explosion blows him into the air. He somersaults within a cloud of debris, lands at the feet of Michael and immediately begins thrashing and screaming. His legs are gone from about halfway down his thighs. Nothing remains of his lower left arm except strings of flesh and a shard of bone poking from the elbow, the half limbs flailing about leaking blood.

Yari rushes to him, grabs ahold of his remaining arm, tries to settle him. Turns to the kid and shouts, "We need to stop the bleeding. I need you to tourniquet the wounds while I hold him down."

In the background Mylenko shouts into the radio. "We need medical evac ASAP. Man down in blue sector."

To Michael, everything is white noise. All he can do is stare at Andriy as he screams, his remaining hand grabbing ahold of Yari's armor, begging in Ukrainian, "Please, stop the pain, Yari, please, stop it, stop it, please, the pain!"

Yari turns over his shoulder. "Come on, kid! Wake up! Help me hold him down."

Michael shakes himself out of it, nods, and runs over.

ABOUT THIRTY MINUTES ago there had been movement in the rubble above them. A loose chunk of it had fallen away from the edge of the trailer, uncovering an opening about the size of a head.

A ray of tepid sunlight now half illuminates the dust. It helps to calm Anya. A little more air and a little more light, even if the gap is too far to reach and too tight to crawl out of.

More relaxed, she is telling Peter about her husband and daughter. Perhaps their close proximity to death has made her open up.

"Like me, Roman," that was the husband's name, "didn't think that the Russians would invade. That it was only Putin playing mind games with the West. But we were wrong."

"Did your husband join the fight?"

She grins. "No. Roman was a schoolteacher. He spent his military service peeling potatoes with the catering corp. He wasn't a fighter. I guess that's what I loved about him. He was so caring. Not just for me and our little girl but for others, too. He could speak four languages. It was he who taught me English. He had a PhD in world history and could have taught anywhere, but instead he chose to teach in some of the poorest areas here in Ukraine."

"He sounds noble."

"He was," she breathes. "I was the military one. The marksman. It was why when the war broke out, the decision was easy: I would join the military and he would take care of our daughter. Get her out of Kharkiv and to our relatives in Kiev. It was supposed to be me going into danger. Not them."

She lets out a withered sigh.

"I thought they would be safe," she goes on. "The last I spoke to them they were at the train station about to board. I was on my way to the recruitment center. I told them I loved them and that I would speak to them as soon as I could." She pauses, breathes in deeply, then adds, "I never got the chance. The first I knew that something was wrong was when I reached the center. There was a television set showing the news. Everyone was gathered around it. On it I saw the Kharkiv Train Station. What was left of it was on fire, including all the carriages along the platform. The Russians had bombed it. Had bombed people trying to escape their invasion."

Her body, pressed to his, is trembling. He doesn't say anything.

"After that," she adds, "I took a week off to bury their remains. I don't even know if it was really them. The coffins were sealed. By the end of the week I'd joined the fighting." She pauses. Then. "I've been fighting ever since."

———

NOT FAR FROM where they'd triggered the IED is an abandoned parking garage. On the second floor of the four-story building, away from the edges, they wait for an Mi-2 AM-1 medical helicopter to come take Andriy away.

He's currently out of it on morphine, barely conscious, face as pale as a week old corpse's. Where his feet, shins and knees used to be he has pressure bandages on the stumps. Blood already shows through the gauze. He's damaged his face, too. His left cheek is torn open and the eye above it is bleeding and all crooked in its socket.

No one has mentioned whether he'll make it. The question burns inside of Michael, but the kid holds his tongue, realizing that it would be deeply inappropriate to discuss a man's mortality while he lies there almost dead.

Seconds after it had happened, they'd pulled the medical kit from Andriy's back, found the morphine capsules and jammed several of them into his mouth, Yari holding his jaw to make sure he chewed them. He'd been delirious from pain when they'd done it, and, thankfully, it hadn't taken long for the drugs to work. Then, while Michael and Yari held him, Mylenko placed tourniquets around the remains of his maimed limbs, Yari tightening the straps as much as they'd go, thick, coagulated blood oozing from the bloodied stumps. Following that, Mylenko had cleaned and dressed the wounds, and they'd carried him here to the garage.

"We still need to find them," Michael whispers to Mylenko.

They stand in the shadows while Yari sits in the background with Andriy, holding a bag of fluid above him, an IV line feeding into the patient's wrist.

"Don't worry, kid," Mylenko says, laying a hand on his shoulder. "Only one of us needs to wait here. You and me are gonna go find them."

He gets the tablet out and shows him the two GPS signals.

"Look," Mylenko says, "I didn't want to show you this earlier and upset you."

Straight away Michael knows why. Both signals are right on top of each other. Like two bodies.

"Have they moved?" the kid asks.

Mylenko breathes in, slips the tablet into the pocket of his fatigues, and squeezes the shoulder. "I'm afraid not."

Michael goes cold all over. He has never really contemplated Peter's mortality. They have been together now for three years and in all that time, he'd thought of the man as immortal. He'd watched other men die as easily as if their lives were no more than the flame of a candle in the breeze of a cave—one strong gust, and they're gone. But Peter, he always lived. Michael never feared that he would be killed, and it was this feeling of immortality that had rubbed off on himself. The kid, too, felt a nonchalance when facing death —one based on his own father's.

This latest evidence tested it all. And Michael suddenly felt very cold indeed. Like only now had he realized that he was in a war zone surrounded by enemies—his life in the balance.

"Come on," Mylenko says, waking the kid out of his stupor. "Just follow my lead and do as I say. We'll find them."

Michael and Mylenko kit up. They say farewell to Yari, promising to be back soon with the others. The big man wishes them well and they leave him nursing Andriy until evac arrives.

———

"WHAT DO you think you'll do after the war?" Peter asks Anya.

She admits that she hasn't really thought about it.

"My family was my life," she tells him.

"But you have other family, right?"

"My mother and sister in Kiev. Roman's parents in Kharkiv. A few uncles and aunts. All of them have their own lives and their own families."

"Then what about you?"

"I don't know. If I survive, I guess I'll go back to Israel. Get my old job back in armed security. It pays well and at least keeps me on my toes."

"Maybe you'll meet someone else."

Anya trembles. "You can't just replace them."

"I guess. Kate was the only person I ever wanted to be with. I haven't really ever looked at another woman."

"Maybe *you'll* meet someone else."

Peter smiles. "Maybe."

"And, anyway," Anya adds, "the way this war is going, I can see myself being a soldier for the next..."

They both freeze.

A shadow has just crossed the hole.

"You think it's them?" Anya whispers cautiously.

"Could be. But let's wait."

The shadow returns. Stays there. They can't make out its face, but whoever it is turns over their shoulder and speaks. Their voice too muffled to understand.

There is sudden movement above them. The rubble starts shifting. A giant piece of masonry, the bottom of a window frame still attached to it, is lifted to the side and suddenly hands are reaching in and pulling Anya out into the sunlight and the second the gun is pressed into the back of her neck and she is pushed down onto her knees and ordered to raise her hands, she knows this isn't good.

Peter sees the gun at the last second. As a hand reaches in

and grasps his left arm, he reaches his right back and grabs ahold of the KRISS Vector that was strapped to his back when they'd slipped under the trailer last night.

As a pistol comes toward him from the back and he is making it to his feet, Peter whips the submachine gun around.

The men back off, their guns trained on him. There are at least twelve of them, armed with AKs and pistols. All of them bearded, and on their body armor they have stenciled their team's insignia: a red scorpion.

Their commander steps forward and Peter instantly recognizes the beady little eyes sticking out of a face of black hairs. It is Vladimir Khodov. Tagirov's attack dog and one of the targets.

Khodov appears easy with the gun pointed at him. Unlike his men, who grip their assault rifles with intention, he has his hands behind his back like some wise sage.

"Throw the gun down," he advises.

Peter glances to his left.

Anya is on her knees with her hands raised in a surrender pose. The only gun that isn't aimed at him is pointed at the back of her head.

Khodov gets impatient. Turns to the man behind Anya.

"Kill the girl." He says it in English to make sure Peter understands.

Before the Scorpion can pull the trigger, Peter tosses the gun onto the ground. Khodov holds a hand up to the would-be executioner as the man cocks the weapon and Anya gets to keep her life.

Turning to another of his Scorpions, Khodov orders,

"Put them both in shackles. And I want a gun aimed at him at all times."

———

MICHAEL AND MYLENKO are watching the scene through the optics of their battle weapons, the two of them tucked behind a ridge of broken brickwork about a hundred yards away.

They'd spotted the twelve-man team the second they'd gotten there. Far too many to ambush, they stayed back as the Scorpions had uncovered Peter and Anya and dragged them out.

At first Michael was relieved to see his father alive. But the relief lasted less than a second when he realized that his father was now at the mercy of the very men they'd been sent there to kill.

"We should attack," Michael whispers.

Mylenko turns to him and gently shakes his head, before turning back to the scene.

"But they're going to shoot them."

"They might not."

"But they also might."

"They will definitely shoot them if we start shooting. So stay tight. Give them a chance to live another day."

Michael can't help feeling the tension of his trigger. The crosshairs aimed at the leader, Khodov. An inner voice willing the kid to take the guy's head off.

But he holds back.

Especially when they bind Peter and Anya's hands behind their backs with prison shackles and march them off.

"See, kid," Mylenko whispers. "Now we can use them to lead us to the rest of their team. Organize a real ambush. Come on. We need to get back to Yari. A new unit has been assigned to us for escort."

"More Marines?"

"Infantry this time. They should be with us soon. We'll go after the Scorpions with their help. Even up the numbers."

Assured once more of his father's immortality, Michael relaxes and agrees. They peel away from the lip of masonry and creep quickly back to the multi-story parking garage.

When they reach it, the Mi-2 AM-1 medical helicopter is taking off from the roof. Just in time, too, because the sun is sinking and soon the Russian drones and mortars will begin raining down on the city.

Inside the lot, they find Yari with the eleven-man unit that's been sent to them. The big man looks worried as they stroll up.

"What happened?" he asks.

"They're alive," Mylenko replies. "But they're now prisoners."

"Scorpions?"

Mylenko nods.

"Then it's lucky these guys arrived," Yari tells him, gesturing the soldiers with a hand. "Mylenko, this is the Five-Five."

Their commander steps forwards and offers a hand.

"My name is Tamaz Kaladze," he says as they shake.

"Georgian?"

"You guessed."

"Yes. I fought alongside a Georgian named early on in the fighting. He fought well. I hope you do too."

"We like to think we give better than we receive," Kaladze says with a smile. "Anyway, your man, Yari, was just telling us that two of your people are missing."

"Yes. One of them is a foreign fighter like you."

"Ah. I see. And where is he?"

"He's been taken by the enemy along with one of our own. I was hoping you and your men could help us get them back."

While they talk, Michael can't help staring at the two members of the Five-Five who stand aloof from the rest of the group. They are identical twins.

TWENTY-FOUR

ST. PETERSBURG, RUSSIA

THE ALEXANDER NEVSKY MONASTERY IS ST. Petersburg's largest monastery. Its burial grounds house the composer Pyotr Tchaikovsky and the writer Fyodor Dostoevsky, among others, and costs Mikhail Gutseriev a pretty penny to house his fallen family here.

In the dark days that followed the siege, there were hundreds of funerals—many of them on the same day, often at the same time. The only two burials that didn't take place in Beslan itself were those of Saskia and Dunya Gutseriev.

Their mother, Olga, was from St. Petersburg and wouldn't hear of them being buried in the town in which they were slain. Gutseriev had a family plot in a cemetery right on the edge of Beslan, but Olga insisted, falling into a fit of anger and despair when he suggested burying his daughters amongst his own dead family.

In the end he had given up and allowed it. Was even

passive when she began fantasizing about burying them amongst some of Russia's finest, and when the fantasy became a full-blown mania, the doctors advised him to do all he could to bring it about, believing that perhaps it might cure her if her wishes were met.

The donation he had had to give to the monastery rose into the seven figures. Those old monks milked him for every penny they could get, and not even a year later, they milked him again for the privilege of a third plot in their precious graveyard for his wife.

The hope of Olga finding catharsis through her daughters being buried among the stars, as it went, was wrong. She waited a whole year on tranquilizers and anti-psychotics before hanging herself on the first anniversary of the siege—when all the newspapers and TV programs were full of it.

Gutseriev considered joining them. Except, he always was the proactive type. Doing everything he could to find justice was much more his thing.

The three tombstones are surrounded on three sides by thick conifer hedges, as though inhabiting the end of a hedge maze. It is getting dark and the stones are lit by an electric lantern that hangs from a post on the corner of a stone pathway.

Gutseriev kneels in the wet grass before them, saying a silent prayer, eyes closed, hands together. Making the sign of the cross, he goes to rise but stumbles.

Alexei rushes to his aid, catching his boss by the elbow as the old man almost goes down. Gutseriev smiles at him, the bodyguard helping him all the way onto his feet, before leading him to a small wrought-iron bench, where the two sit down together.

"I never should have entered politics and left this city," the old man says as his eyes stare at the tombstones. "If I had stayed out of the Duma, and therefore Beslan, they would still be alive. But I was told to do my duty."

"We often have to do things we don't want to for the greater good, sir."

"The greater good? Huh! Whose greater good, is the real question. While boys are thrown into the meat grinder of war—whole generations lost—our president spends his days sitting peacefully in his bunker reading history books about greater men and more justified wars."

"He is the leader of our country, sir."

"He is," Gutseriev says bitterly, then smiles. "Have I ever told you about the first time I met our president?"

"Yes, sir. Many times."

The old man furrows his brows. "What the hell. I'm getting old and I like telling it."

"Then tell it, sir," the bodyguard says.

"Putin was only a subordinate in Yeltsin's government at the time. I'd known Boris a long while by then. We'd both been keen to see an end to communism and had helped each other out with a few things. It was at a fundraising party for his 1996 reelection campaign that he introduced this little pip-squeak as his new head of campaign headquarters in St. Petersburg. This softly spoken little man straight away offers me his sweaty hand and wants to be my friend. He begins talking about his big plans to create a political party that will dominate Russia. I said, we only just got rid of one party and you want to create another. And then he came straight out and asked me to be a donor. I just looked at him for a moment and said, 'You'll go far, Mr. Putin. And I hope to hell you stay there.' And with that, I turned my back on him and continued talking to someone else."

His grin is as wide as ever by the story's end and his cheeks have taken on a rosy hue. Then his eyes go dark.

"I should have guessed it then," he says. "The future belonged to men like him. Men with nothing but ambition."

Gutseriev sighs and refaces the gravestones of his family. He places a hand on Alexei's shoulder and squeezes.

"When this is done," the old man says, "I will be glad to join them."

TWENTY-FIVE

SOMEWHERE SOUTH OF THE DNIEPER RIVER, UKRAINE

A single thought runs through Peter's head as he sits in the back of the Scorpion's APC:

Why are we still alive?

Khodov sits opposite. "I guess you're wondering why we haven't killed you yet?" he says in Russian.

Peter says nothing.

"All in good time, Azrael. All in good time."

A grin shows off his crooked teeth. In the red light of the carrier, it looks like they're coated in blood.

Anya sits next to Peter. He doesn't like the way the men all look at her; all lascivious smirks behind their beards. Some of them wink, others blow kisses, the worst stick their tongues out at her.

Khodov leans forward and whispers, "Do you know how long my men have been without their wives?"

Peter's gray eyes burn into Khodov. He sums up the

odds. Takes in the positions and postures of all nine men sitting in the carrier with them. Their proximity to their weapons. Though his hands are shackled behind his back, the rest of his body is free. But Peter's not dumb. Tallying up, he realizes it's not enough. Not against nine armed men with their hands free. It takes Peter less than four seconds to come to the conclusion that he'd be dead long before he managed to kill more than one of them with nothing except his head, knees, feet and teeth.

Instead Peter decides to play it cool. Do a little small talk.

"How'd you find me?" he asks Khodov.

Another smirk. The Scorpion chuckling inwardly. "Good intel," he says.

"Wagner?"

"You guessed it."

There is a slight twitch that runs up the side of Khodov's face. He's lying.

"Wagner couldn't have guided you to my GPS," Peter says.

Khodov stops chuckling. His eyes go dead and he pulls his best poker face.

"So you're getting intel elsewhere," Azrael suggests. "Or Wagner is, at least."

Khodov's eyes narrow. Then another of those ugly big grins raises the wiry hairs of his cheeks, showing those dirty red teeth.

He leans forward and says, "No more talking."

His eyes shift sideways.

Before Peter can do anything the man to his right is jamming the taser into his ribs between the gap in his body armor. The prongs burn. The burst of cramping sends him sideways onto Anya's lap, every muscle clenching, including his heart. He expects the guy to give in or for Khodov to call him off, but it seems endless, and Peter is proud that he hasn't defecated himself when it finally does end, Anya's voice echoing in the background:

"That's enough! That's enough!"

A hand grabs him and lifts him up. The next Peter knows he is facing Khodov again. Lumps of sweat slide down his face, his heart races, guts screwed up tight.

"No more talking, American," the Scorpion says. "We have plans for you." Looking sideways at Anya, he adds, "We have plans for her, too."

The men burst into laughing, but it's cut short when the inside of the carrier lurches, the vehicle braking hard. A radio message comes through. It appears something is blocking their progress.

Khodov and his men climb out the carrier. Two of them stay behind with the prisoners. The man watching Peter holding a pistol on him.

The back door is left open so they can see out.

They're part of a huge convoy of Russian troops and equipment, having joined them on the south bank of the river after leaving Kherson. There's several tanks among them, a couple of APCs, some smaller fighting units.

The troops mill about outside the vehicles, stretching their legs or smoking cigarettes. Looking bored and uninterested.

Peter turns to Anya and whispers, "This must be the tail end of the retreat."

"Hey!" one of the men says. "No talking."

They're on a three-lane highway that straddles the river.

It means they're heading northeast. Peter wonders whether they're going back to Luhansk, where the Russians are still relatively safe.

The men return and begin unpacking the APC.

"What's going on?" Peter asks Khodov as the commander gives his men instructions.

"The fucking bridge has been blown."

"The Ukrainians?"

Khodov looks pissed. "No. Fucking Russians. They blew it to stop the Ukrainians from following. No one told them to wait for us. Now get your shit together. We spend tonight in the woods."

———

IT ISN'T QUITE dark yet. There's still enough illumination to see the outline of things. They travel without headlights. Hoping to go unseen as they follow the convoy from about four miles back.

"They still haven't moved," Mylenko says, gazing down at the screen of the tablet.

He, Michael, Yari and the Five-Five Foreign Volunteer Unit had returned to base and retrieved vehicles. Then they'd taken a military cargo barge across the Dnieper, the Russians having blown all the bridges.

Yari drives, Mylenko in the passenger seat, the kid in the back.

Kaladze comes over the radio into the cab.

"They moved yet?" the Georgian asks.

Mylenko places the receiver to his lips. "Yeah. Looks like they've been moved to a nearby forest."

"You think they're staying the night?"

"Looks like it."

"There's a village not far from here. The next left leads to it."

"Yeah," Mylenko says, gazing down at the tablet. "I see it. Zelene."

"That's the one. It's close to their position. We should head there. Use it as a base. Go out there on foot and see what's up."

Mylenko agrees.

The tiny village is on open ground. The area flat with only occasional hills. Most of the single-story cottages are long abandoned. But some of the hundred and fifty villagers have stayed behind.

Night is upon them when they arrive. Those that still inhabit the bungalows, stand about in their yards under the glow of battery lights, all eyes focused on the three pickups that move slowly through town.

"These people don't look happy," Yari remarks.

"You think they'll let us stay?" Michael asks from the back seat.

"They're tired of the war is all," Mylenko replies. "I'm sure once they realize we're friendlies, they'll…"

They've all seen it.

About forty yards ahead, a group of people block the road. Yari puts the headlight beams on low. There are at least twenty of them. A man steps forwards from their center and Yari brings the pickup to a gentle stop.

"Trouble?" comes Kaladze's voice over the radio.

"Hold tight," Mylenko says into the receiver.

He next jumps out the pickup, telling Yari and Michael

to stay put, and meets the villager. From the back seat Michael watches him talk with the man.

The villager is old and lacking any front teeth. Wearing a threadbare suit jacket over a dirty gray T-shirt.

It is a brief exchange, and soon Mylenko is getting back in.

"What did he say?" Yari asks.

"He was warning me about the Russians camped in the nearby forest. He said there's hundreds of them there. The Scorpions must've linked up with a bunch more units."

"What's up, group leader?" Kaladze's voice rings from the radio.

Mylenko tells him.

"Then it looks like we'll have to rethink our strategy," the Georgian replies. "If there's hundreds, we cannot be going in heavy. It'll have to be quiet."

"The guy's got a place nearby. He says we can stay there tonight. They've got a rabbit stew on the stove. They'll feed us and give us a clean bed. Plus, the guy knows a trail. Says he can get us close to the camp without being seen."

"Rabbit stew and secret trails. Sounds good."

———

HAVING MARCHED the prisoners into the woods, the Scorpions placed a chain around the thick trunk of a spruce and manacled them to it by their wrists, forcing them to stay sat at the tree's base at all times, unable to leave it.

The Scorpions have taken up an entire corner of the woods, away from the others. Fires burn everywhere except for here. Khodov is clever enough to allow the rest of the

Russian units to light themselves up like a big ol' sign and take all the attention should any of the Ukrainian units be brave enough to venture this far south of the river.

Soldiers linger about amongst the trees. A stereo plays somewhere far off. Men shout and laugh and stumble around the tents and campfires. Most are drinking. Some eat.

Neither Peter nor Anya have been fed, and none of the fires are close enough to provide any warmth. A chill wind bristles through the creaking trees and both are cold.

But it could be worse.

Through the brush, they can hear the Scorpions talking. Earlier on, Peter got to hear Tagirov's voice for the first time. He was speaking to Khodov via radio. They mentioned a meeting. That people were waiting for Azrael. Peter didn't catch any names but he definitely gathered that they were talking about some kind of handover in the city of Donetsk.

Peter had wondered whether it was the CIA. Surely not. Maybe someone with a vendetta like the Goldbergs.

Probably.

"What do you think they plan to do to us?" Anya asks him.

It is the first she has spoken since they were chained to the tree.

"I think," Peter replies, "they're going to hand me over to someone. As for you, I don't know."

Anya shivers a breath in. When she exhales, he senses the quiver of a sob. Her voice is trembling when she speaks next.

"Why am I still alive, Peter?"

"Honestly?"

"Yes. Honestly."

He considers his reply. But in the end he just can't do it.

"I don't know," he lies.

"I think I do."

They get little time to contemplate this. The noise of someone approaching through the thick scrub takes their attention. The two men guarding them stand up and salute as Khodov arrives.

He salutes both men back. Then he comes before the prisoners and squats down to meet their eyes—his own as lifeless as a stone gargoyle's. His men follow him out of the scrub and linger in the background.

Khodov doesn't say a word. Instead, he twists around and nods at the guards. One of them retrieves a key from his pocket and both men make their way to Anya. Rough hands grab her by the shoulders and lean her forwards. While one begins unlocking her shackles from the chain, the other keeps her there.

The second Anya is off the chain, she struggles. Both men handle her forcibly, lifting her up from the ground, and gripping her upper arms, her wrists still shackled behind her back. She tries to twist away from them when one of the men lands a vicious sucker punch to her abdomen and Anya lets out a shriek of air and goes limp between them.

That's when the rest of them join in and the men carry her away into the scrub.

Khodov now stares solely at Peter.

"Don't do this," Peter says to him.

"Who am I to stop it?"

Within the shadows, beyond Peter's sight, Anya cries out as the men grab her and begin tossing her from man to man, playing a game with her, chasing her about the trees as she screams—and they laugh.

"This is wrong," Peter tells Khodov. "Think of your prophet."

Anger wrinkles Khodov's brow.

He leans forwards and takes ahold of Peter by the throat. Begins choking him like a boa.

"Who are you to talk about my prophet?" he snarls. "Some kaffir infidel wants to tell me what is right and wrong in my religion?"

He slowly shakes his head at Peter.

Azrael doesn't move a muscle. Just faces him with those cold gray eyes and concentrates on conserving what oxygen he's got held in his lungs. He can hold his breath for quite some time, and though the pain in his neck is starting to burn, he just pushes it to the corners along with everything else.

All the while the men chase and manhandle Anya in the background. Tiring her out for the rape.

Khodov brings his purple lips to Peter's ear and hisses, "You came here to hunt me. So surely like any good hunter you know about your quarry. And in your research you should know the things that I have done. So don't waste your breath on her. My men will have their way— and then, if she is still alive, we shall drag her into the woods and put her out of her misery with a bullet to the head."

He lets go of Peter. The throat marked by his fingers. Then stands. A loud scream from Anya and an even louder cheer from his men make him turn to the woods.

"Looks like they caught her," he remarks.

Khodov turns to grin one last time at Peter when the assassin asks, "Do you have a computer?"

Khodov frowns. "What?"

"Do you have a computer with access to the internet?"

"Why?"

"Give me a phone and a computer and the details of any bank account you want and I can have ten thousand US dollars placed in it within five minutes."

The frown begins to turn into a pensive expression.

"I have money," Peter goes on. "And you can have it. But only if she isn't hurt. In fact, I will pay you ten thousand dollars every day she isn't hurt. All I need to do is call my bank in Zurich and go online to access my account."

As Khodov thinks it over, Anya manages to get the first man off her and is back on her feet making a run for the open woods. Unfortunately, like before, she is easily caught and hauled back to the camp.

Tugging gently on the end of his beard, Khodov agrees. "Okay."

He marches off and soon returns dragging Anya by the arm. The men follow with expressions of dubious disappointment.

The two guards lock her back to the tree.

"You better not be lying," Khodov tells Peter as one of the soldiers runs off to fetch the computer. "Because if you are, I will have my men do it in front of you."

———

You can hear the Russians from at least half a mile away.

Six men line thick scrub about a hundred meters from

the edge of the camp. Michael, Yari and Mylenko from Eagle Team. Kaladze and the twins from the Five-Five.

There are at least a hundred men milling about those woods—going on further than their eyes can see.

They get up from their bellies and move along the edge of the camp, all the way until they find Peter and Anya.

They are deep in the woods, far from the edge. Tents block the way to them and two men sit opposite keeping guard. They take some pictures and do a little more reconnaissance, then leave.

No one speaks until they are back at tonight's shelter.

As it turned out, the guy who met them in the road is the caretaker of the local kindergarten. He's allowing them to sleep on the floor of the gymnasium.

"Why do you think they're still alive?" Kaladze says as they enter the school.

The Georgian seems genuinely confused about it.

"I don't know," Mylenko says.

He turns to Michael and asks the same question.

"I've been thinking about that all the way back," the kid says.

"And what did you come up with?"

"My father has many enemies. Many many enemies. Right before we came here we were attacked by some."

The Goldbergs look on with blank, glazed expressions.

"Some of those enemies have money," Michael adds.

"So what?" Yari says. "You think the Scorpions are gonna hand him over to someone for money?"

Michael nods. "That's all I can think of."

"Well, whatever it is it gives us a chance," Yari says.

"What chance?" Kaladze puts to him.

"A chance to wait for the right opportunity. Wait for the Scorpions to split from the rest of the Russians."

The Georgian is looking at him with wide eyes. "Are you seriously thinking of following them further into Russian territory?"

"Why not?" the big man puts to him.

"Because it'll be suicide."

Mylenko steps forward. "Then go back," he tells the leader of the Five-Five.

The Georgian turns sideways to the brothers.

The looks they wear tell him that's not an option.

Swallowing, Kaladze says, "Then we should sleep. Get some rest for the journey."

———

KHODOV SITS a few yards from Peter watching the screen of a laptop. More importantly, he is watching the balance page of his bank account reload.

Peter has just gotten off the phone to his private banker in Zurich—getting past the voice recognition software that is required for all major transactions. With everything in order from a security standpoint, the Swiss banker has transferred ten thousand US dollars into the account Khodov had earlier supplied Peter the details of.

A huge smile opens up on Khodov's face as the money shows in the account. In the garish light of the computer screen, he looks even more ghoulish than normal. He snaps the laptop shut and stands up. Turning to his men, who like normal linger in the background, he tells them in Chechen that they are all a little wealthier thanks to their kind friend Azrael.

"You'll receive," Peter then tells him, "another ten thousand tomorrow night at the same time. But only if Anya remains unhurt."

"You know," Khodov says, "I could just have my men force you into giving up the entire amount."

Peter looks at him with a cold stare. "You talk about knowing those you hunt," he says. "Well, surely you must know a little about me."

Khodov's eyes narrow. "What sort of thing should I know?"

"That I am trained to withstand torture. Especially the types of crude torture you and your friends enjoy. Because one thing you should know about me is that I'm a stubborn son-of-a-bitch. I'd rather die knowing you failed to get anything out of me than give you a single dime of that money. And, anyway, you're forgetting."

"Forgetting what?"

"That you're supposed to be delivering me to someone unharmed. Isn't that the deal?"

Khodov's eyes go blank. He lunges at Peter with a kick. Puts everything into it.

The boot almost shatters Peter's jaw and knocks him sideways. Sitting back up, he feels the inside of his mouth with his tongue. Several molars appear to be loose.

"*Alive*," Khodov says. "Nothing was said about you being unharmed."

He and his men leave after that.

When they have, Anya leans her head on Peter's shoulder. "Thank you," she breathes.

He can feel the tears on his skin.

"For what?"

"You know what."

Peter says nothing as she begins to cry.

————

MICHAEL IS awoken by someone gently shaking his shoulder. Opening his eyes, he finds one of the Goldberg brothers crouching at the side of his cot with a finger over his lips.

The twin slips him a piece of paper.

You wanna try and bust your old man out?

Michael's eyes brighten. "Yeah," he whispers.

Eli smiles. As does his brother Sol who stands behind him.

"We'll take Yari and Mylenko," Michael adds in a hushed voice.

The two of them are fast asleep on the other side of the gymnasium.

Eli and Sol Goldberg shake their heads.

Eli has another card.

Just the three of us. Better that way. More quiet.

TWENTY-SIX

PETER IS SHAKEN AWAKE. ANYA MOVING NEXT to him.

No.

Anya is being moved.

Wild, clumsy hands pull her forwards. The first thing Peter sees is the handkerchief tied around her mouth. The second thing: her wide, frightened eyes.

Peter goes to speak but can't. Stopped by the hand that comes across his mouth. He goes to move but can't. Stopped by the blade that comes across his throat.

When Peter looks up, the man holding it shakes his head.

The two men guarding them are gone. These men aren't the guards. They're not even Scorpions. These are drunk men. They stink of alcohol. Khodov had warned his own people against joining in the supposed festivities. Drinking would not be tolerated amongst his men.

No. These aren't Scorpions. The men who crowd

around them now are a bunch of drunks that have peeled off from the rest of their regiment. Having obviously heard about the woman staying here.

One of them swears under his breath as he tries to pick the lock of her manacles with a hairpin while his buddy holds Anya by the shoulders. The pin is constantly dropped and they have to use the light of a phone to find it again on the forest floor.

As well as the two dealing with Anya and the one holding Peter's mouth and the knife, there are another three watching from the sidelines like hungry dogs.

Peter wonders where the guards are. Whether some ruse from the drunks caught their attention, or if this is just a lucky break.

"Got it!" the drunk hisses in Russian.

The shackles pop open from her wrists, but they've made a mistake. A terrible one. They should have unlocked her from the chain, not the cuffs. They should have kept her arms manacled behind her back until a more convenient time. They should have planned this rape better. This latest mistake is one of a string. The first has been to think that the blonde with the big tits is merely some defenseless chick and not someone who is a master of the Israeli martial art Krav Maga.

These drunk rapists have no idea what is coming.

The second she is free, Anya is like a coiled spring. She whips into action, launches herself upwards from her feet, hits the nearest guy under the chin with such force that it splits the lower mandible right through the middle. It makes a sickening crack.

The next guy staggers at Anya and she sees a window.

In a swift, single movement, she sends a kick right between his unsteady legs and hits his balls like she means to reach his heart. The blow splits one of his testicles and the guy flat-out screams like some cheerleader in a horror movie.

There are four men left. To Peter, they are too drunk to fight, and they haven't brought their guns.

They really should have brought their guns.

"Get her!" the one holding the knife to Peter's throat snaps at his cohorts.

In Krav Maga, the student is taught that the best way to finish a fight is as quickly and aggressively as possible. Attacks are aimed at the most vulnerable parts of the body.

The Russians come at Anya one after the other.

The first makes a clumsy grab for her. Not good.

Anya counters. Skips back on her feet, lets him lose his balance, then pushes forwards from her toes and sends the hardest part of her palm arrowing into his larynx.

The sound of it cracking shoots out of his mouth along with a gasping shriek.

Proponents of Krav Maga believe that physical aggression is the most important component in a fight. Anya is burning on adrenalin. They haven't eaten in over twenty-four hours. They've had minimal fluids. Have hardly slept because of the cold. Yet still, after all that, she is a ball of kinetic fury.

The next guy steps right into her reach. He's had way too much to drink. He throws out a right jab, which she steps inside of, and comes at him with a knee thrust.

It doesn't reach.

The third guy has grabbed ahold of her from behind.

Halfway through the thrust, she's standing on one leg, stretched out. The Russian tips her off balance and tosses her into a tree.

Anya strikes her head on the rough bark. Cuts open her eye. Manages to regain her balance. Stay on her feet as one of the guys rushes at her, almost catches hold of her, Anya scrambling away like a cat.

She's back in stance. Eyes shining in the moonlight. Blood throbbing from the wound. The two men round on her. The others are in the dirt or creeping away.

Except for the guy at Peter's throat.

All at once the men explode at her. One of them swings a punch while the larger of the two goes low for a tackle.

She avoids the punch. Takes the tackle.

The blow to her midriff winds her. The guy lifts her off her feet, Anya sagging over his shoulder like a tackle bag. He drives her into the tree, pushing what's left of the air out of her lungs.

Peter isn't so sure she's gonna win this one anymore.

The guy, at least six and a half feet tall and two hundred and fifty pounds, pins her by the chest to the tree with one hand. Cocks a fist with the other. Hammers her with a sickening punch.

It sends her head whipping back, completely dazing her. His fist has left a bloody mark in the middle of her face. She goes to move and this time he hits her above the right eye, exactly where the cut is, opening it up.

Peter watches the brush. Praying for the return of the Scorpions.

Anya looks half out of it. Her eyes flicker like dying lightbulbs. Screwing her lips up at the guy, she smiles—blood running down her teeth, dripping from her chin.

The guy goes to throw another punch. One that will break her face. Doesn't make it.

Anya has stolen the knife from his belt. It is now in his guts at the belly button.

His body blocks the view for his pals. From behind, they don't see the knife, let alone spot her push it all the way up his torso with every bit of strength left in her—not stopping until the blade is resting against the bottom of his sternum. Opening him up like a pig.

She wrenches the knife out and a large portion of his intestines comes with it.

His pal standing a few yards away doesn't realize what's going on until the big man is on his knees trying to reel his guts back inside of him.

By then it's too late: Anya has already thrown the knife.

The guy just stands there.

But the knife isn't for him. No.

It flips through the air right past his ear and lands in the forehead of the man crouched beside Peter.

First the hand, then the blade come away as the guy falls backwards into the brush. The handle of the knife sticking out of his face like a horn.

The one remaining drunk stands there, piss running down the leg of his fatigues. He is very drunk and very scared. Holding his hands up, he repeats over and over in Russian that he is sorry.

Anya doesn't care.

She marches up to him and palm strikes him straight in

the nose. The blow obliterates his nasal column and knocks him out cold.

That done, she rushes to Peter. The soldier has left the twisted hairpin on the ground. Feeling about the ground with her hands, she quickly locates it. Then she begins fiddling with the lock on Peter's shackles. Right at the moment they hear sounds coming from the Scorpion's camp.

IT's three a.m. and the camp is dead. Only sporadic groups of soldiers are still awake. Either wandering aimlessly amongst the trees or sitting about smoldering fires, their low muttering reaching the ears of the three men watching from across a field.

Michael and the Goldberg brothers lie on their fronts, hidden in brush. The kid is holding a pair of night-vision field glasses to his eyes and scanning the camp.

The Russians have put perimeter guards in place but most of them are missing or asleep. The camp is essentially open.

Nevertheless, in their Ukrainian uniforms, the three of them are gonna stick out to the odd eye that is still on watch.

"Those three," Michael whispers, handing the field glasses to Eli Goldberg.

Many of the men don't have tents. Instead, they lie amongst the trees in sleeping bags or in holes they've dug. Three men at the edge, probably placed on guard, lie in a triangle, an extinguished fire in their middle.

Eli nods. Gives the kid a thumbs up.

The three emerge from the brush in crouched positions. The field is covered in tall rye that should have been harvested weeks ago. It hides them. Three sharks coming up on three seals.

The brothers split off left and right from Michael, who heads straight. When they emerge from the rye, their shadows cut out the moonlight over each man. All three lie in fetal positions as though they've been returned to the womb.

The assassins already have their knives drawn. And, unlike the Georgians, they make no mistake. The soldiers never know what's hit them. Each man dies in his sleep. An easy death when all things are considered in war.

None of the sleepers struggle any more than a few pathetic kicks. Dead without a single harsh sound escaping far enough to alert anyone.

They undress the men quickly. The clothes are a little tight on the brothers and a little loose on Michael, but none of it matters. They look like Russian soldiers and with so many units, most of them alien to each other, there's not a chance that someone will figure that these three guys aren't Russian.

They zip the men up in their sleeping bags before dragging them into the rye field.

As they emerge from hiding the bodies an alarm goes off.

Men begin emerging from tents. Scratching their heads and wiping sleep from their eyes. An officer comes through the trees and begins barking orders.

His eyes shoot in the direction of the three soldiers standing at the edge of the rye.

"You!" he shouts in Russian. "Get your rifles! We've had two prisoners escape!"

And with that, the officer dashes off to shout at more people. Most of the soldiers simply frown at him, then retract their heads back into their tents and return to bed.

———

Khodov bursts into the center of his men. They all stand around the empty tree. Two dead men litter the ground around it. Those that survived have limped away to lick their wounds elsewhere.

"What happened?" Khodov snarls at the two who were supposed to be guarding the prisoners.

"We were tricked, sir," one of them tells him in Chechen. "An officer from an infantry regiment told us we were needed on the other side of the camp for sentry duty. He said all the units were offering up men for it and that our superior officer, you, had volunteered us."

"And you believed him?"

"He was an officer, sir. A lieutenant."

"And where is he now?"

The men look at the corpse lying on the ground with the knife hole in its head.

"He is there, sir."

Khodov looks down at the dead lieutenant.

"Looks like he and his men came for the woman. It is unfortunate no one told him she is Spetsnaz. It has cost him his life. Now," Khodov's eyes darken on the two guards, "you need to make this up to me."

"Anything, sir."

"You can start by finding them. All of you!"

The men disperse and Khodov is left alone to contemplate events. He lights a cigarette, closes his eyes, takes in a long lungful of smoke.

He's not going to radio Tagirov yet. He's hoping he won't have to.

Think, man, he says to himself.

His eyes snap open.

Of course, the GPS trackers. The same way they found them in Kherson.

The tablet is in the tent. He marches off.

Doesn't get far.

A figure drops from the tree, landing right behind the Scorpion. Khodov only knows he's there when the cold blade is touching his throat.

"I think it's time we talked," Peter hisses into his ear. "Don't you?"

———

BEFORE GOING TO BED, Yari had, like usual, placed his flask beside his cot, often needing to take a drink in the middle of the night.

Setting it a few inches away is what saves his life.

Because when a clumsy boot knocks it over, it wakes the big man up.

Someone is standing over him.

With a knife. That comes rushing down.

Whipping an arm up, Yari blocks the strike at the wrist.

A quick glance in the direction of Mylenko.

Another figure is creeping over to him.

"Vitory!" Yari shouts. "Vitory, wake up! Wake up!"

The knife is coming down as Mylenko's eyes snap open. Instant reactions, he sends a hand up with lightning speed to grab the forearm and block the lunge.

Two more figures lie in wait within the shadows of the school gymnasium. One of them attempts to help his struggling pal with Yari, but the big man spots him in the corner of his eye and sends a kick out, his foot hitting the guy's chest and pushing him away.

Mylenko, meanwhile, struggles with his own life-an-death situation. The guy on top presses down on him with all his weight. Trying to force the hunting knife into Mylenko's throat. Mylenko trying to push upwards with everything he has, his muscles creaking from the effort.

Yari controls his guy one-handed. The killer has to place both hands around the knife, the big Ukrainian's arm as immovable as stone. With his free hand, Yari grabs ahold of the guy by the neck.

There is a sickening crack as he snaps the head to the side at a crooked angle, one of the cervical vertebrae poking out the skin. The killer goes limp and Yari is able to move off the cot right at the moment the next man is coming at him with another knife.

Unlike Yari, Mylenko isn't built like a bear. He can't just go one-handed and snap a neck. He has to stay strong until an opportunity opens up.

One does.

The guy makes a fatal mistake when he turns to the others, taking his eyes off Mylenko, and gets halfway through calling for help when Mylenko twists his body, slipping out from underneath him and off the bed.

His wannabe killer falls forwards onto the cot, the knife digging into the pillow.

Mylenko springs to his feet and whips out the Kershaw double-edged boot knife holstered to his ankle. As his attacker tries to get up off the bed, he comes around the back of him, straddles his torso at the hips, grabs him by the hair, cocks the head back, and saws into the throat.

There is a gurgling cry as a spray of crimson fans across the air.

In the corner of his eye, Mylenko sees the next man pulling a pistol from his belt. He has little time to burst at him, snatch the wrist holding it, and force its aim upwards as the shooter lets off three rounds into the ceiling of the gym.

On the other side of the room Yari is face-to-face with his man, and only now does the Ukrainian recognize him.

Frowning, he says, "Five-Five?"

The Georgian thrusts at him with a knife. Yari catches it in his wide forearm. The blade sinking into the muscle.

It is a painful tactic. But one which takes the knife out of the equation.

Though he's not a student of Krav Maga, Yari still knows that the best way to end a fight is as quickly as possible. If that means taking an injury to achieve this, then so be it.

With his free hand, Yari rips the guy off the knife and tosses him into the wall like he weighs less than his clothes. Then, before the Georgian can get up, he is plucking the knife from his arm, coming over him, and stabbing the would-be assassin repeatedly in the head, neck and chest.

The guy lets out a wheezing death rattle, and Yari doesn't stop until he no longer moves.

A huge pool of blood is spreading out across the parquet of the gymnasium.

Mylenko is still wrestling over the gun. The guy he fights is strong. He tries to kick Mylenko's feet from under him. Gets one. Not the other. Mylenko nearly loses balance. The guy uses it to get over him, push down on the pistol, bring the barrel slowly in line with Mylenko's fore—Yari tears the guy off him, grips the wrist of the hand holding the gun, picks him up and drives him into a wall. There are clothes pegs lining it at head height. The guy's head is in Yari's other hand, being pushed toward them.

"No," the guy pleads. "No, please."

Yari pushes him onto the peg, the guy using every bit of strength to stop it. But once the peg is a couple of inches into his ear, he gives in and goes limp. Yari pushing the whole head onto the peg to make sure. So that the guy is hanging from it when he lets go.

"What the fuck just happened, Vitory?" he says, turning to Mylenko. "Why would our own people attack us?"

Mylenko is bent double, trying to get his breath back. He's almost fifty. He really shouldn't still be doing this shit.

"Where's, huh, Kaladze and the others?"

"More importantly," Yari says. "Where's the kid?"

Mylenko's eyes widen and he glances about the room. The kid's bed is empty.

"Our weapons are gone, too," Yari points out next.

It is then that the sound of an idling engine reaches their ears.

They dart to the window, pull the curtains aside and peek out.

One of the Five-Five's pickups is filled with the rest of

the men. Kaladze leans against the hood smoking a cigarette. Waiting for the return of his assassins.

Mylenko and Yari make their way out of the school. They find their guns in a classroom next to the main entrance. Mylenko checks over his AS Shaft Special Automatic. Snaps a fresh magazine into it.

Yari grabs the big heavy PKP like it weighs no more than a pool cue. He makes sure that it is ready to fire and then the two of them exit the school, marching across loose gravel to the pickup.

Kaladze looks surprised to see them. His eyes bulge and the cigarette drops from his bottom lip. Observing the blood on them, he swallows down a dry lump.

Mylenko swings the AS at him the second the Georgian is within range, chinning him with the stock. It splits the skin and sends Kaladze sprawling backwards onto the hood.

Coming over him, Mylnko grabs him by the scruff and pulls his face up to his. The four Georgians sitting in the pickup go to leave, but Yari points the PKP right at them and gently shakes his head.

That would be a bad idea.

So the Georgians stay put inside the vehicle.

"Why did your men just try to kill us?" Mylenko sneers.

"W-W-What?" Kaladze snivels.

"Where is the kid?" Yari adds.

Kaladze looks paralyzed with fear.

"So?" Mylenko snaps.

"I-I can explain."

"Then explain. Where is the kid and why did your men try to kill us?"

"The brothers took him."

Mylenko glances into the pickup. Notices that they aren't there. Turning back to Kaladze he asks, "Why?"

The slimy double agent lies.

"They've gone to rescue the father."

"Rescue him?" Mylenko is frowning. "Then why did your men just try to kill us?"

Kaladze tries to look innocent. "I don't know. They were supposed to be waking you up."

Mylenko stares into him. "With knives?"

He drops the Georgian on the hood and walks away. Yari marches up with the PKP raised high and swings the heavy stock into the guy's face before he can avoid it. The blow sends Kaladze into an unconscious heap on the ground.

———

"WHERE IS TAGIROV?" Peter demands in Chechen. "Where are the rest of the Scorpions?"

Khodov smiles those ugly yellow teeth at him. He sits tied to a folding field chair, arms stretched out along the rests, hands duct-taped to the ends, legs the same way.

With every Scorpion out searching for Peter and Anya, the two of them had dragged the commander back to his deserted camp and all three of them are now in Khodov's tent.

It is a decent-sized space with enough room for them to stand over him.

"If you'd really wanted to know where Tagirov and the others are," Khodov tells him, "you should have stayed chained to that tree. After all, I was taking you to him. As a matter of fact, we'd all be together now if it wasn't for those fucking idiot Russians blowing up the bridge before we could cross."

Anya steps into the ring. Grabs Khodov by the beard and yanks his chin up so that their eyes meet.

"What mission are you on?" the Eagle wants to know.

Khodov just smiles.

She tries another question. "Who are the men you took from Izium and Kherson?"

The smile widens.

"What was the equipment you took from Mariupol?"

Those disgusting yellow teeth.

Anya glances sideways at Peter. Nods.

She lets go of the beard and takes a step back.

Azrael has his hands behind his back. He brings them out front. A clear plastic bag dangles from one of them.

Khodov swallows. He knows what's coming. Has done it to many men himself. Done it to the point of death.

The wide-eyed look they have at the end fills his mind.

Grabbing ahold of Khodov by the top of the head, Peter brings the bag over him.

Pauses.

"One last chance," he whispers. "Where are they?"

This time Khodov doesn't smile. He merely gives Peter a defeated look. *Just do it.*

The bag is downed over his head. Peter gathers it in his fist at the back of the Scorpion's neck. Khodov holds his breath at first. But all he's doing is delaying the inevitable. He knows it. Peter knows it. But, still, he offers up this small token of defiance.

It doesn't last. He's not much of an underwater

swimmer by the looks of things. He can't hold his breath for that long. Less than a minute, as it turns out.

Khodov's mouth opens wide. So do his eyes. He sucks in a big mouthful of bag, his lungs ordering him to bring them oxygen. Peter lets go a little. Lets him take some into his throat. Khodov begins choking on it. Peter gathers it in a little to stop him from gagging. Something that can lead to him blocking his airways with vomit.

Peter stares at his wristwatch. Counts down the seconds. Waits for the feet to begin pounding the ground in panic.

The bag is removed. Choking, coughing, gasping. Khodov needs some time. Peter gives it to him. Sure that the Scorpions will be away a while yet. After all, they still haven't found them.

"Not so good when you're on the other end," Peter says once the Chechen has his breath back.

"You may, huh, as well, huh, stop wasting your time," Khodov pants. "Better get this over and done with."

"You'd die to keep Tagirov safe?"

Khodov looks up at him with an expression of complete conviction. "Tagirov is my brother. I am alive because of him. Allah, He looks after men like Tagirov, and men like Tagirov look after men like Khodov. So you tell me—do I defy my God and my brother? Or do I defy you?"

His eyes burn at Peter.

"What about Zoyev?"

Khodov looks genuinely stunned. "Why do you ask me this?"

"Don't you know why I've come after you and Tagirov?"

"Beslan."

"That's right. So if you won't give up Tagirov. Maybe you'll give up Zoyev."

"Zoyev is dead."

Peter watches the twitch. The lie showing itself.

"No he's not. Where is he?"

"Looks like you'll have to shove that bag back over my head. I promise not to hold my breath this time. I see now that it is time to go to paradise."

"You're not going to paradise," Anya tells him. "The only place you're going is hell."

Peter is about to bring the bag back over his head when the sound of someone approaching the tent makes them freeze.

They turn toward it. Khodov goes to cry out, but Anya is quick enough to get her hand over his mouth in time.

There are no guns at hand. They only have a knife.

All they can do is wait as a shadow approaches, reaches the opening, and begins unzipping it. Anya stays with her hand clasped over Khodov's mouth. Peter takes up a position at the edge of the opening as the zip moves slowly down.

The canvas is pulled to the side and a boot steps in.

Peter throws an arm around the intruder, wrapping him up and pulling him into him. Before whoever it is can do anything the knife is already at his throat.

But there is something familiar about the young soldier in the badly-fitting uniform.

"Michael?"

"Peter?"

He lets go. The kid spins around and the two embrace. When they part, Peter is wearing a stern expression.

"You shouldn't let yourself be so easily taken," he scolds. "How many times have I told you? Never walk into a room without considering there could be someone at the edge of the door."

Michael rolls his eyes. "Thanks for the tip."

"Where are the others?" Anya asks.

"They're still at the village."

"You came alone?"

"No. I came with my two buddies. They helped me get into the camp. Now come on. They're waiting for us at the river."

———

YARI AND MYLENKO left the Five-Five at the school. Tying them up on the floor of the gymnasium.

Yari and Mylenko find the Russian camp in disarray. Flashlight beams streak the trees. Groups of soldiers are outside of the woods, searching the fields of rye, sweeping truncheons across it.

Submerged in tall grass at the edge of the field, the two Eagles watch the woods through a pair of night-vision field glasses.

"What is going on, Vitory?"

"Looks like they escaped."

Yari grins behind the painted-on teeth of his ski mask. "The kid did say his old man would."

"It's not just him, though, is it? He's got Anya with him."

"You think the kid's with them—and the other two?"

Mylenko takes the tablet from his kit and checks the

positions of the GPS signals once more. The two markers representing Peter and Anya are moving.

"They're not far," Mylenko says. "Moving north towards the river. We'll go around and rendezvous with them on the other side. If the kid and the others are with them, we might just make it in time."

———

PETER HOLDS ON TO KHODOV, keeping the knife at his throat, the Scorpion's arms bound behind his back with duct-tape.

Along with Anya and Michael they hide behind a tent. All four of them stooped down, Peter peeking from an edge as men amble past.

Once the Russians have disappeared, their muttering voices fading, they leave their cover and move away from the last of the tents. The forest floor dips down as it approaches the river. Its noise begins to filter into their ears, first as a gentle hiss, gradually becoming a roar.

They come across more soldiers, forcing them to abandon their initial route and hide behind rocks for a while. But soon the way is clear and they find themselves far enough from the Russians to feel safe talking.

"So where are these pals of yours?" Peter asks his son in a whisper.

"I told you. They're at the river."

A tributary of the Dnieper snakes through the woods.

"Who are they, anyway?" Peter asks.

"After you left, another unit of Ukrainians turned up. The guys I came with are part of it."

"So if they're soldiers, why didn't they come with you to rescue us? Why let a fifteen-year-old do it all on his own?"

"I don't know. They just said that they'd organize the escape. All I had to do was get you to the river."

"Well, I hope they haven't been caught already."

They begin to see the weaving river through the trees. The sun is coming up and purple twilight sky reflects off the water as it slides by.

"Taking me is a mistake," Khodov points out.

The knife is away from his throat for now.

"Shut up," Peter growls.

At the bottom of the hill, on a bank of the river, lies an old oak tree that's dead and gray. It is the sort of tree you can imagine Puritans hanging people from during the witch trials.

"Where are they?" Anya asks as they approach it.

"They're supposed to be here," Michael says in a curious tone.

This is when things take a turn.

The first rays of the sun reach out of the horizon. Peter spots the light glint off something inside the empty trunk of the oak.

A scope. Rested on the edge of a hollow. Pointed at them.

"Sniper!"

Muzzle flash.

All Peter can do to stop the .30-caliber armor-piercing round from decimating him is throw Khodov in the way. It hits the Scorpion's chest and rips through the atrial and ventricular septum of his heart. Essentially splitting the organ in two.

Landing in a heap in the bracken, he quickly bleeds out.

Peter, Michael and Anya throw themselves behind trees as the next shot buries itself in the mud close to Peter's foot.

"The tree, Michael," Peter shouts at his son.

Michael has a great throwing arm. In a former life perhaps he would have been a great pitcher. Earned millions playing Major League Baseball. Adored by fans. Loved as an all-American hero.

Not being shot at in a wet and cold Ukrainian forest.

The kid already has the grenade in his hand. He waits. Counts down a few seconds to make sure it goes off when it reaches. But when he goes to move, a bullet snipes across his position, hits the tree he's come out from, kicks bark up in his face. With the grenade still in his hand, he rolls quickly sideways and, realizing that it is now or never, rises from the undergrowth and tosses the bomb in a perfect arc that dips in time to see the grenade coming down on the trunk.

Eli Goldberg is scrambling out of it when it explodes right over him. The blast strips the skin off his back, revealing his spinal cord. It blows part of the tree into splinters that rain down like snow. What is left of Eli is blown into the river and swept away by the current.

The three of them trepidatiously come out from their cover.

"Who was that?" Peter asks.

Michael is frowning. "He was one of them."

"One of who?" Peter asks.

"One of the guys I came with."

That is the moment Sol Goldberg bursts from the brush and grabs ahold of Michael. In one swift moment, he places the kid between himself and the others, and presses a Glock 17 to his temple.

Cocks the hammer.

The kid recognizes who it is. "What the hell are you doing?" he exclaims.

"Shut up and throw the gun down, kid," Sol says.

"Oh so you're talking now?"

"Throw it down."

Michael drops his Malyuk into the brush.

Sol Goldberg is glaring at Peter. "You remember me?"

Peter stands with his hands out. "Eli," he says.

The former triplet winces. "It's Sol."

"What happened to the vow of silence?"

"That was his idea." He gestures at the river with a backwards nod. "I guess now I'm on my own, I get to call the shots."

"Please let my son go, Sol," Peter says gently. "I know you and your brothers. You don't kill children. You were always adamant of that when you negotiated your contracts."

"This ain't no child. This boy is more man than half these drunk fucking idiot Russians playing war. I watched him kill a man in his sleep. And he just killed my brother without breaking a sweat. No, sir, this ain't no kid I hold this gun to. This here is a demon. I should do a whole lot of people who are gonna die at his hands in the future a big old favor and snuff the little shit's life out right now."

He prepares to pull the trigger.

"Please, don't," Peter says, stepping towards him. "You want me. Then take me."

"Gladly," Sol says with a smile.

He aims the Glock at him.

A shot reverberates within the trees.

Not the shot everyone expects.

Sparks burst from the Glock as it flies out of Sol's hand.

He turns left. There are two men emerging from the brush—Yari and Mylenko. But before he has time to take this piece of information in, the kid is elbowing him, leaping forwards, and diving for the bullpup. At the same time Russian soldiers, who have heard the explosion, spot them and open fire.

It takes everyone's attention except Sol's. As the kid grabs the Malyuk and whirls around, he is right there, his AK-74M already unshouldered: the butt rushing down at Michael, cracking him in the face and knocking him clean out.

With Peter and Anya crawling for cover through the undergrowth and Mylenko and Yari occupied by the sudden arrival of the Russians, Sol Goldberg is able to grab the limp body of Michael and carry him into the river.

It is still red with his brother's blood.

Once in the freezing, rushing water, he holds the kid as though Michael were a drowning victim and he were rescuing him. In that way, he swims backstroke, aiding the current and floating away from the gunfight.

Anya and Peter are close to each other. Lying on their bellies, tight to the ground.

"We need to get to the river," Peter shouts at her.

She nods.

They sprint out of cover. Bullets whip the air around them. One of them skims the flesh of Peter's thigh as he and Anya dive off the bank. The impact of hitting the water jolts the wound and burning pain spreads along the limb. The muscle cramps up immediately—the lack of food and water telling—and before long he is unable to swim.

Michael and Sol Goldberg are nowhere to be seen.

Anya glances backwards over her shoulder and spots Peter's clumsy attempts to stay buoyant. Turning back toward the direction Sol went with Michael, she can see nothing beyond the next bend in the river.

So she goes back to Peter.

In the meantime Mylenko and Yari are pinned down in the woods. Bullets smack into the bark and bury themselves in the trees they hide behind. More and more Russian soldiers are appearing.

Yari is busy reloading the PKP, crouched within the confines of a wide spruce. Fixing a fresh ammo box to the receiver, he lifts the cover and feeds the ammunition belt into the heavy machine gun. As he snaps the cover down, he spots men coming from the rear.

"Vitory?!" he shouts.

Mylenko, who is busy firing his assault rifle at the ones in front, turns to him.

Yari is pointing.

Mylenko sees them. Wheeling around, he sends a burst of covering fire in a wide arc across the forest at the four men creeping up on them.

Yari yanks back the cocking lever of the PKP, arming it.

As he lifts the heavy machine gun up, a bullet hits the right breast plate of his body armor. It pings and hardly moves him. Merely annoys the big man as though he'd been shot by a pea shooter.

Before another bullet gets the chance to punch a dent

into his armor, he opens fire, shooting from the hip and fanning his aim across the forest, the bracken cutting up from the rapid bombardment of bullets like it's being hit by a weed-whacker.

Several men are struck. Others leap for cover or simply run away.

Happy they've all gone, Yari takes his finger off the trigger and brings the PKP a hundred and eighty degrees around to face the men firing at them from the opposite direction. But as his eyes move past the position of his commander, his heart freezes in his chest.

Mylenko is sitting at the bottom of the tree holding his neck. Blood pours from his cupped hand where the bullet has grazed the flesh.

Yari drops the heavy machine gun and runs across to him, taking a bullet in the top of his right arm as he does.

Ignoring the searing pain, he kneels beside Mylenko.

"Let me see, Vitory."

Mylenko is ghostly white. He allows the hand to come away.

Blood gushes out. The left carotid has been pierced. Yari isn't carrying a medi-kit and neither is Mylenko. Not that it would do any good if they were.

Panic erupts inside Yari. "What do I do, Vitory? What do I do?" He is practically sobbing.

Holding on to his neck, Mylenko tells him, "You run. Get to the river. Get out of here."

"I can't leave you."

"You have to."

The two men spend a few seconds staring into each other's eyes, and the reality of the situation dawns on Yari.

Mylenko is dead no matter what.

The two men take each other's shoulder and embrace one last time.

"Get me a grenade," Mylenko says when they part.

Yari nods. Unclips one from his armor.

Mylenko takes it and says, "Now run. Live to fight another day."

"It has been an honor, sir."

And with that, Yari runs.

He is hit three more times before he reaches the bank of the river and dives in. As he is swept away by the current, he hears the explosion of the grenade.

TWENTY-SEVEN

WET, COLD, HUNGRY, AND EXHAUSTED.

That is the general state of Peter and Anya as they crawl up the muddy bank of the river. At the top they take several minutes to rest on their backs, chests heaving in and out.

Peter's injured thigh throbs, though the cramps have abated.

The distant sound of men shouting to each other makes them duck back down the bank, keep tight to the ground.

"We have to move," Anya whispers.

They both get up. The wounded leg is so numb, Peter can hardly move it. Anya supports him through the wet vegetation. A light mist clings to the trees, partly concealing them.

Rapid gunfire draws their attention. It sounds close.

They reach a rocky hill where they find a lot of large boulders to use as cover. Peter and Anya press themselves into a narrow gap that runs between two especially large ones.

From there, Peter watches the forest.

"Hey," Anya whispers behind him.

She's a little further into the crevice.

"What is it?" Peter whispers back.

The soldiers sound closer. He can hear them breaking through the brush.

"Take a look," she says.

Peter twists around in the tight space. Anya has moved her body to the side. Beyond her is a hollow in the ground that passes under a huge oak tree.

"Let's see what's inside," she suggests.

Anya gets down on all fours and disappears into the gap.

It opens into a small cave. A space large enough for three people that is buried deep beneath the roots of the old tree, the entrance hidden by the rocks.

The two of them are wet through and shivering so hard their teeth chatter.

"We need to take our clothes off," Peter says. "Otherwise we risk hyperthermia. If we're naked and hold onto each other we'll share body warmth. But we need skin-to-skin contact."

Anya looks ready to cry. "I haven't been naked with a man since Roman," she breathes.

"This isn't about that, Anya. It's about survival."

"I know. I know," she says.

Both of them remove their sodden clothing and lie naked together, bodies spooned, Peter's arms wrapped around her, their temperatures beginning to rise.

After the first minute she begins to weep and he holds her even tighter. The two of them hidden beneath the world as boots march over their heads. The noisy Russians never guessing where they are.

———

MICHAEL WAKES up at the base of a tree to find Sol Goldberg sitting opposite. Glaring at him.

The kid is freezing cold and his head pounds. He goes to check his face and realizes his hands are tied behind his back.

"Why am I so wet?" Michael asks.

Sol Goldberg grins and shakes his head. "Wow. The guy whose brother you killed last night and all you got to say is why are you so wet."

"To be fair, your brother was trying to kill me."

"We only wanted your father."

"Well, you didn't get him. Not in Italy and not here. And now you're down two brothers. When are you gonna learn to let it go, man?"

Eye-twitching anger spreads over Sol Goldberg's face. He is quick. The jab comes at lightning speed and strikes Michael square in the nose, sending his head clipping back into the rough bark of the tree.

The kid gasps, wishing he could hold his face and rub the back of his head.

"You should have respect for your elders, you little punk. Now get ready to move." Sol stands up. "Because we've got somewhere we need to be."

Wincing from the blow, Michael says, "Can I ask where that is?"

"No." And with that Sol Goldberg grabs the kid roughly by the shoulder and hauls him up from the ground.

THE TWO OF them became so warm they fell to sleep.

It is an hour later when they are awoken by the sounds of movement outside the hollow. Something big is snapping the brush as it moves closer.

"It sounds like a bear," Anya whispers.

"It's big, whatever it is," Peter adds.

He rushes across to their clothing. Pulls the knife from their things, the only weapon that didn't sink to the bottom of the river. As the creature enters the narrow gap between the rocks, Peter takes a position one side of the hole.

If it's a bear, he'll aim for the back of the neck and sever the spinal column. If it's a man, he'll do the same.

The beast gets closer and closer. Its humungous shadow reaches into the cave. A shaved head emerges through the hole. A man. Peter's grip tightens around the knife. He waits for the neck to reveal itself. Goes to bring the blade down when—

"Yari!" Anya gasps, delight on her face.

"Anya?"

The big man squints in the darkness of the cave. His eyes slowly adjust. When they do, a huge smile spreads across his face.

"Anya! Man, am I happy to see you. I..." He pauses and frowns. "Why are you naked?"

She is kneeling forwards with a forearm across her breasts.

"To keep warm."

"Where's the American?"

Anya glances at Peter. Yari follows the look, his head

swiveling on its huge neck. When he sees him right there with the knife, he furrows his brow.

"We thought you were someone else," Peter says, putting the blade away.

The grin returns to Yari. "Why are *you* naked?"

"Warmth."

"Where's Mylenko?" Anya asks.

It is then that Yari's face goes grave. His bloodshot eyes look like they're about to burst. He doesn't have to say the words. The look is enough. Their commander is dead.

Anya's face fastens into a stern look, her lips screwed up, and a single tear glides down her face. "Just one more reason to kill these fuckers," she snarls bitterly.

"I didn't think anybody would be in here," Yari says next.

There isn't much color in his face.

"Looking for somewhere to hide?" Anya asks.

"No. Somewhere to treat my wounds."

It is then that the two of them notice the blood dripping from the big man. A gash to the top of an arm. Another at his hip, the fatigues ripped and saturated in blood. There are also several deep dents in his body armor. It looks like he's been peppered.

"Yari," Anya coos.

He goes even more pale. As though waiting for a moment like this to give in. His eyes roll into the back of his head and he collapses in the mouth of the hovel.

"Help me drag him inside," Anya says, coming forwards and grabbing him by the shoulders.

———

NOT EVEN THE roosters are awake when Sol and Michael arrive at the school. Finding all the doors locked, they go around the back. Sol marching the kid onwards, his AK-74M trained on Michael's back.

Sol uses an elbow to bust a windowpane. Grabbing ahold of Michael, he wraps more duct tape around his legs and lays him on the damp, dew-covered ground.

The kid doesn't move a single muscle the whole time. Just lies there watching Sol climb through the window and enter the school.

A short corridor leads him to the gym. That's where he finds the five Georgians duct-taped together, back to back, ankles, knees and wrists all wrapped in black tape, mouths gagged. Kaladze is taped to a pillar. His eyes are open. Crouching before him, Sol rips the tape from his mouth.

"Thank god you're back," bursts from the Georgian's mouth. "Untie us."

"What happened?"

Kaladze frowns. "You're talking?"

"It would appear so. Now tell me what happened."

"The two guys from Eagle Team killed the others."

"They got caught," Sol remarks dryly.

Kaladze says nothing.

"How do four men fail to kill two men in their sleep?"

The Georgian doesn't answer the question. Instead he asks, "Where's your brother?"

"Dead," Sol replies bluntly. "Where is the tablet you're using to track the Eagles?"

"It's with my kit in the classroom. Get me out of this and I'll find it for you."

Sol doesn't need or want his help. Rather than free him

he places the tape back across Kaladze's mouth. The Georgian looks confused as he watches Sol walk out the gym.

At the classroom he quickly finds Kaladze's kit and pulls out the tablet. After that he loads up on ammunition and takes the Dragunov sniper rifle that is there. Lastly, he takes a wooden chair and leaves the way he came.

Outside, he cuts the tape from Michael's legs. Sitting him up, he crouches before him and holds the tablet out. Shows the kid the screen: a digital map with markers on it. Three red dots.

"Your old man is still wearing his uniform. There's a GPS tracker in it. Same as the others. You see?"

He taps a finger on the screen. At the cluster of three dots.

"They're about an hour from here. I'm gonna set a nice little trap for your old man and wait till he steps into it."

The kid just stares at him.

Sol Goldberg stands up, grabs ahold of Michael and lifts him to his feet. Then he aims a Glock 17 at his back and orders him onwards.

"What's the chair for?" Michael asks when Sol picks it up.

"You'll soon find out."

———

YARI IS SLEEPING SOUNDLY. His snoring filling the cave.

His wide-jawed face is ghostly white and covered in beads of sweat. He is clearly in a fever. A bullet is lodged in the top of his right arm. The wound is so swollen, the pink flesh around it is going dark.

Anya is redressing his hip. A ball of flesh half the size of a golf ball is missing. As though scooped out.

"We need to properly clean and pack his hip," she says, wrapping the wound up tight. "And we need to get that bullet out of his arm."

They're both now dressed.

"I can get the bullet out," Peter suggests.

He is holding the knife up.

Anya frowns. "You can't be..."

Distant yelling surprises them and they freeze.

It's not so much the shouting per se. It's more than whoever it is is shouting Peter's code name.

He instantly grabs Yari's Glock 17 from the ground, shoving the Raider bowie knife into his belt.

Their hearts in their mouths, they listen to the creaking trees and the birds for a while until the next deep cry interrupts the natural peace and Peter is sure he heard it clearly.

"Azrael!"

It sounds maybe two hundred yards away.

"That's Goldberg," Peter whispers.

"How does he know where we are?" Anya asks.

"I think I can guess."

SOL GOLDBERG STANDS beside Michael in the woods. The kid stands atop the chair—having discovered what it is to be used for. Around his neck, and hanging from the thick branch of a tree, is a noose.

When Sol sees the two red dots begin to move toward his location on the tablet, he runs back to the sniper's den he's dug into the crater of a fallen tree, throwing himself inside and getting behind the Dragunov. Sliding back the cocking arm, a .30 Creedmoor is loaded into the chamber.

He imagines the bullet annihilating Peter's face and smiles. Laying the tablet beside the gun, he watches Michael and the forest through the scope while glancing at the screen every so often to make sure they're coming.

When the dots are close enough that he's sure they can see Michael, he rests his crosshairs on one of the chair legs and fires.

The leg burst into splinters.

Michael does well to keep balanced on the three remaining legs. In the kid's mind, if he can keep the son-of-a-bitch firing, it will give Peter more of a chance to find out where he is by spotting the muzzle flash from the Dragunov.

Another bullet hits another leg. The kid does well to trap the two-legged chair with his feet as the shock almost knocks it out from under him. The chair now wavering under his feet, rocking from side to side, the rope begins to bite into his neck, and it is as much the noose that keeps him upright as the wooden seat beneath him.

A third bullet reduces it to one leg and the chair spins under Michael until he feels it drop away and all his weight is on his neck, the cord biting into the flesh and crushing his windpipe. He closes his eyes and does his best to push away the urge to kick his feet. Knowing that it will only quicken his death.

Upset that the kid made him fire three times, Sol Goldberg keeps a vigil of the trees and the tablet. The two dots have come to a stop about a hundred yards away.

A shot comes from the woods. A single crack from a pistol.

It misses the rope by a clear yard.

Another shot. This one closer. But not much.

Goldberg adjusts his aim. The shots appear to come from the right. He checks the dots. He should be staring straight at whoever is there. A wide sitka spruce. They must be behind it. The pistol makes a sock-puppet appearance and he pulls the trigger.

His aim is off. The bullet hits the tree and doesn't make it all the way to the other side.

Goldberg cusses. He checks the tablet. Both dots are right there.

All the time Michael hangs on the end of the rope. The blood squeezed into his head. Face purple. Eyes bulging. The edges of his vision tunneling in until he's looking out from the bottom of a well. Feeling himself go numb with pins and needles.

Goldberg keeps watching the tree. Waiting for a sign of his target. Constantly checking the dots on the tablet.

"Where are you, Azrael?" he mutters under his breath.

He doesn't expect to get an answer.

It chills him to the bones when he does.

"I'm here," a voice whispers behind him.

Goldberg flips himself over onto his back, reaches for the pistol on his belt, almost gets a shot off before the foot kicks it out of his hand, and Peter is landing on top of him, and Sol is feeling the knife pass through his ribs just below the armpit and slip into his heart. The Dragunov is out of reach. All he can do is reach around and hit Peter on the back.

Peter tugs the knife out. Blood pours from the wound and drenches the floor of the fox hole. The hands thumping him get weaker with each second of blood loss, and Peter watches Sol Goldberg's life slowly drain from his eyes.

The second they go dead, he climbs off, drags the wide-eyed corpse out of the nest, and takes up Goldberg's former position behind the rifle.

Anya is sprinting toward the kid from the other direction. Michael isn't moving anymore. He just hangs there.

Peter steadies the crosshairs on the rope. His heartbeat is slow and regular. There are no nerves. He pulls in an easy breath. Holds it. Takes the shot.

Everything happens in slow motion.

The bullet flying from the Dragunov.

Anya running frantically for the kid.

Peter still holding in that breath.

The kid's dangling body.

The bullet hitting the rope.

Severing it.

Michael drops to the ground in a heap, and Peter is sprinting from the sniper nest. *Please, God. Please not the kid. Please...*

Anya reaches him first. She crouches down in the brush and lifts Michael into a seated position. She removes the noose from his neck. His throat is grazed and bruised where the rope has burned the flesh.

She checks his pulse and then his airway.

"He's got a weak pulse but he isn't breathing," she says, laying him down flat.

Peter hears her as if she's far away. A sudden, urgent fears paralyzes his whole body.

Facing the Dragunov hadn't scared him.

Killing Goldberg hadn't scared him.

Getting the shot right hadn't scared him.

But Michael dying?

It fills him with an empty horror that threatens to swallow him whole.

Anya is on top of the kid. She is giving him CPR and trying to open his airway with her fingers. She turns over her shoulder and asks Peter something, but he doesn't even hear it.

It is like he is at the bottom of an ocean.

Then all the sound comes rushing back.

Michael sits up of his own volition. As Anya rubs his back, he doubles over coughing and spluttering and Peter can hear it loud and clear.

The kid turns to him with swollen eyes.

"Dad," he croaks. Then he frowns. "Why are you naked?"

It is true. With the GPS trackers sewn into all his apparel, Peter had had to take it off in order to fool Goldberg into thinking he was with Anya behind the tree.

"You called me dad," is all Peter can say.

TWENTY-EIGHT

As well as weapons and the tablet, Sol Goldberg had retrieved a medical kit from the school. It meant they were able to give Yari the necessary treatment; removing the bullet, cleaning both wounds, redressing the hip.

Afterwards, they let the big man sleep.

"I'd also like to take look at that wound on your thigh," Anya says to Peter.

"It's only a scratch."

"It'll need stitches."

"I guess."

She has Peter take his fatigues off. The wound is covered in dry blood and dirt. It's about six inches long and half an inch wide in the middle. She cleans it with the delicate care of a mother and stitches it up.

"There," she says at the end, having bandaged it.

"Thank you," Peter says.

She lifts her eyes from the leg and meets his gaze. They stay like that a moment. Staring into each other.

A dreamlike sensation overwhelms them. Both their heads begin to move toward the other. They part lips. Close their eyes.

"Peter?"

They draw apart quickly and turn to the opening.

The kid's head is poking inside.

"What?"

"I found a kitbag out here. I think it's Yari's."

"So what?"

"So I found this in there and it's flashing."

He holds the satellite phone out to them. And there, for all to see, is a flashing green light.

Incoming call.

———

PETER AND MICHAEL stand in the woods watching Anya from afar. She's been on the telephone for some time, speaking to her superiors in Ukrainian. They are calling with urgent information.

"What's she saying?" Michael asks for the innumerable time.

"I told you. Wait until the end."

When the call does finally finish, she comes over to them. There is a brightness to her blue eyes. A flash of hope in her expression.

"They know the identities of the men that the Scorpions took," she says straight away.

"Who?"

"The man they removed from Izium is Davyd Smrnek. He's a nuclear technician. He was taken during the siege at Zaporizhzhia nuclear power plant."

"And what was his job there?" Peter asks.

"He was head technician."

"What about the other guy?"

"The man they removed from Kherson was Professor Valery Jovic. He runs a PhD program at Kherson University on nuclear science. But that's not all?"

"What is?"

"He wasn't always a professor. He used to design core reactors. That includes the one at Zaporizhzhia."

"That has to be where they're heading," Peter says. "What about the equipment they picked up at Mariupol?"

"Nobody knows for sure, but an intercepted transcript between two FSB operatives in the city around the time the shipment arrived has both men mentioning hazmat suits, control rods and a pressure vessel. All of them are tools for working on a reactor. And something else."

Her face has gone terribly grave.

"What?"

"In the intercepted conversation, the agents mentioned overriding the safety mechanisms at the plant."

Peter's eyes are wide. "You don't think that they're going there to bring the reactor to meltdown?"

"I do," Anya says. "And so do my superiors."

"Then we have to get there and stop them," Michael exclaims.

"We'll need equipment for that," Peter adds.

"It's inbound," Anya informs him. "They're sending an

attack helicopter to meet us at a rendezvous not far from here. They're bringing supplies and ordnance."

"An army, too?" Peter suggests.

"It's too dangerous. The Russians have the air. One chopper will be a squeeze, but a whole fleet, no way. Plus, intelligence believes it'll be easier if it's just a small crew."

Peter looks at the kid. "You up for this?"

"Oh yeah," Michael says with intent.

"Count me in, too," a deep voice says behind them.

They turn around to find Yari standing there, leaning against a tree.

"You need to recuperate," Anya tells him.

"No way. I'm in this till the end."

"Okay then," Peter says, turning back to the others. "Where's this rendezvous?"

TWENTY-NINE

ZAPORIZHZHIA, UKRAINE

THEY MEET THE MI-24 ATTACK HELICOPTER IN THE middle of a nearby field. Avoiding the Russian camp, it flies them north across the Dnieper. The river denotes the latest battle lines. The Russians are positioned several miles back along the southern bank, the Ukrainians several miles from the northern one.

In the rear compartment of the chopper a medic takes a look at Yari's wounds.

"You really shouldn't be going into battle," the guy tells him.

"Just bandage it up," the big man insists.

He's given a shot of Epoetin alfa. An erythropoiesis-stimulating agent (ESA) that stimulates red blood cell production in the bone marrow. After all, he may have lost as much as half a liter.

The four of them change into fresh uniforms and body

armor. Yari foregoes a new PKP. It is way too heavy and loud for the type of sneaking around they'll have to undertake at the power plant. Instead, he takes a Fort-21 bullpup and a Granatnik RGP-40 grenade launcher. Loading it with M18 smoke grenades. Michael takes a Fort-21, a Glock 17, a twelve-inch bowie knife, and several grenades. Smoke and M67 frag. Peter Takes a Fort-21, some spare mags, a knife and a Glock. A few grenades. Anya takes the same but adds her customary Dragunov SVD sniper rifle.

They apply suppressors to all the weapons—except, obviously, the Granatnik.

"Remember," Anya begins telling them through their newly acquired comms, "no explosives inside the plant."

She is looking at Michael.

"I know," the kid says. "We only fight them inside or around the reactor if we are absolutely forced to."

"Exactly," she says. "This needs to be clean and quiet."

The pilot's voice comes over the comms, telling them that they are a minute from the drop zone. Anya holds a tablet with the building plans for the Zaporizhzhia Nuclear Power Plant on the screen. The others cluster around her.

"So," she says, "as you can see there's emergency cooling channels underneath the building. They run from the three main reactors and connect to the river about a hundred yards from the main plant. They are designed to redirect the river into the reactors, allowing it to be flooded if it ever goes into meltdown."

"So if these guys," Michael interjects, "were to cause a meltdown, like we think they're planning on doing, then those channels will be filled with water. Right?"

"No."

"No?"

"No. You see in order to create a meltdown successfully —in other words, one which will cause a huge catastrophe to the whole of the region. In order to do that, they will have to override the system and stop the gates from opening in the first place. Thus allowing the meltdown to continue unabated. That's why they needed the two men. Smrnek has run the core reactor for the past twenty years and Jovic designed it. If anyone can override the system, it's them."

"And anyway," Yari pipes in. "If we're wrong and they do flood it, we'll be dead pretty quick anyway."

"Something to look forward to, then," Michael remarks dryly.

They arrive at the river about a mile southwest of the power plant and descend onto the shoreline via a winch. They are followed down by a black combat rubber raiding craft (CCRC), which self-inflates when they pull a cord.

They load themselves into the CCRC and begin gently paddling down the river. Trees and thick bushes overhang the northern bank, covering them from the air.

The Dnieper is a pretty flat waterway in this part of Ukraine. There aren't any snagging rocks or fast-flowing rapids. It is fairly quiet. This allows them to listen out.

As they close the distance between themselves and the power plant, they begin to hear the crackle of gunfire and the thud of explosions. The Ukrainian army has sent several units, including a whole tank regiment, into the western side of Zaporizhzhia to keep as many of the Russians busy as possible.

An offensive has been planned for the coming days, but

part of it is now attacking the city early to draw attention away from the power plant.

Rounding a bend of the river, they spot the pump house standing at the edge of the waterway. This will be their in; a windowless brick building about the size of a small bungalow with a flat roof. The bank running down from it has been dug out and replaced by a concrete edifice. It ends in a huge metal gate that drops into the water.

They leave the dinghy hidden in the confines of a huge elderberry bush and spread out into the woods. Taking positions behind trees, they begin watching the pump house.

Fifty yards beyond it is a tall fence that runs from the river, up the bank, before disappearing into more woodland. This is the perimeter of the power plant. As they watch, two Russian soldiers walk the fence line. They stop close to the pump house and one of them touches his ear and speaks.

"You see that?" Anya says.

She is looking through a pair of field glasses.

"Yes," Peter says. "They have comms. They're checking in with the men inside the pump house."

Right at that moment a soldier walks out of the building.

He too is touching his ear and speaking. He takes hold of a pair of field glasses that dangle from his neck.

"Get in cover!" Anya snaps.

They all tuck behind the trees. The sun is shrouded in cloud. None of them cast a shadow. As the soldier scans the river, the opposite bank, and finally the trees, they stay hidden from him.

Soon he is dropping the binoculars, touching his ear, and giving the all-clear.

The men at the fence move on.

The soldier with the field glasses then leans his shoulders against the wall and takes out a pack of smokes. Opening the cardboard box, he takes one and lights it.

"Shall I shoot him?" Michael asks.

"No," Anya replies. "There might be more inside the building. We'll need to sneak up." She turns to Peter.

He is already gone.

Reapplying the field glasses to her eyes, she spots him emerging from bushes close to the pump house. Running toward the opposite side of the building to the soldier, he vaults up the wall and gets on top of the flat roof. A foot-high lip surrounds it. He creeps up on the soldier and leans over him as the Russian gets out a cell phone.

The soldier begins speaking. "Mama," he says before entering into a conversation.

He is still close to the doorway and Peter worries that any struggle could be witnessed by anyone inside. So he waits for him to wander out of the way. Something he does when the conversation touches on the subject of what his superiors have him doing. He begins moving around the building to get out of earshot of the door.

Peter follows him like a shadow.

Earlier on Anya had asked if there was anything special he'd like brought with the chopper. He'd requested a length of wire: a garrote. The end of that steel wire is now fashioned into a noose, and he is lowering it down onto the soldier as the Russian comes to a stop at the back corner of the pump house and leans his back to the brickwork. He is telling his mother that he is okay. That at least he's eaten.

And that he's been sent with two others to guard some stupid building on the banks of the Dnieper.

Peter now knows how many there are. Three. So that's as far as the mother-son conversation gets.

The noose comes before the soldier's face, and, before he can do anything about it, it is over his head and around his neck and he is snagged.

Peter digs his boots into the lip for leverage and pulls the soldier up the wall as though he were a fisherman heaving in the biggest catch of his life. The cigarette spits out, the cell phone falls to the ground, and mama is calling, "Dimi? Dimi?"

Dimi has a lot of fight in him. He kicks and tries to pull himself up the wire, his hands slipping down it as he attempts to lift his neck off the noose.

Peter hears a cracking twig, which he knows isn't the soldier's neck, and turns sharply to the trees at the top of the bank.

Another soldier has emerged. His eyes are wide, and when his brain finally gets the message to his body, his hands grab at the AK-74 strapped to his shoulder. With both his hands full, Peter can do nothing.

The newcomer goes to rip back the cocking lever of the AK. Gets no further than halfway. A puff of pink mist floats from the exit wound on the side of his head and his knees collapse in on themselves as he falls down dead.

"Thank you, Anya," Peter whispers into his comms.

"No problem."

Seconds later, the other soldier has gone limp and Peter is lowering his corpse to the ground.

"There's one more," he whispers to the others.

He creeps to the edge that overlooks the entrance. Unclipping an M18 smoke grenade from his body armor, he tosses it through the open door. A wild hiss is followed by coughing and the remaining soldier comes stumbling out.

Peter jumps down from the roof, and before the guy can even turn around he's pistol-whipped him in the back of the head with the Glock. The blow doesn't knock the guy out, but he does drop to his knees and Peter is quick to grab his hands and zip-tie them behind his back. Then, with the Glock pressed into the Russian's neck, he growls, "How many more?"

The man glances up the bank at his two dead comrades. Trembles. Breathes, "No more."

The others emerge from the trees. Anya walks straight up to the captured soldier and places duct tape across his mouth. They then escort him back to the entrance of the pump house, white gas billowing out of the doorway.

Pulling MIRA Safety CM-7M gas masks down over their faces, they enter the building.

"Gas, gas," the soldier complains.

"Then close your eyes," Anya barks in Russian.

Inside are various large machines. A giant centrifugal pump takes up the entire back wall and there are a number of locked cabinets which contain circuit boards. A railing surrounds a large grate in the floor. It is about four feet square. They get the soldier to sit and then duct-tape him to the railing.

Outside, Peter and Yari grab the dead men and carry them into the pump house. Then they shut the door. All before the soldiers at the fence are back.

The grate is their way in. Yari has come with a battery-powered disc grinder. He goes to work on it immediately, the room filling with sparks and the sharp whining noise of the tool.

The others stand back and watch, light reflecting off the screens of their gas masks, and once he has three sides done, Michael and Peter help him peel back the grate.

Then they climb down.

It is pitch black, so they flip the GPNVG-18 quad-lens night-vision goggles down over the screen of their masks, the two compatible. The tunnel is tall enough for a man to stand, though Yari has difficulty, and is about four yards wide. An inch of stagnant water covers the floor, and the stench is quite strong. Behind them is the gate of the river— the one they don't want opened. Water trickles down it from the gaps.

Carefully they eek their way along.

Intelligence claims that Tagirov and his men have been at the facility for more than a day now. Nuclear experts have calculated that it would take around that time to set the reactor to implode. After all, a month ago UN inspectors came with a team to deactivate the core reactors. It will take at least eighteen hours to get them up and running again.

As the tunnel reaches underneath the reactors, they expect to feel the heat coming through the concrete. They expect the walls to vibrate. But the tunnel is cold and there is no sign that the power plant is running.

Next, they expect to see explosives rigged up. Being that you'll need bombs to produce a cave in.

But there is nothing. The place is clean.

"I don't get it," Yari whispers. "I thought they were going to create a meltdown."

"That's what intelligence said."

"Then why aren't they here?"

This is when they hear the rumble. They're about three hundred yards into the tunnel system. The walls now do begin vibrating and a rush of cool air comes at them as the four of them stand gazing down the tunnel through the green tint of their night-vision.

"Is that the reactors coming online?" Yari asks.

There is a faint hiss and Peter is hit with a sudden realization.

"Run!" he shouts.

Water comes crashing around a bend in the tunnel. It is a hundred yards from them as they start sprinting, the tumbling wall of water chasing after them.

A ladder hangs down from the ceiling further along. But before they get there, the wave scoops them up and carries them forwards. Peter claws at the water to get back to the surface. As his head emerges, he's right next to the ladder, and manages to grab on to one side of it, just as Yari grabs the other. As he hangs on, the big man sweeps a long arm out into the water and catches Michael, guiding him to the ladder to which the kid clings, Yari crying out as the stitches in his arm tear apart.

"The hatch is open," Peter cries at his son over the water. "Get up there."

It is then that Peter spots Anya. She is struggling with the water, her head appearing and disappearing in the tumult. She's going to pass too far from them.

"Yari," Peter shouts, "hold me out to her."

Yari hooks an arm around a rung of the ladder, links

with Peter with the other arm, and dangles him into the current.

Immediately, Peter is almost torn away from him and Yari has to use all his strength to keep hold. Anya comes past and Peter catches her, Yari pulling them in.

Climbing up the ladder, they spill out into a pitch-black room and spend some time on their backs, getting air into their lungs. They're surrounded by abandoned desks, computers, and large electronic panels with gauges and dials.

"Looks, huh, like we're in the Control Room," Anya observes.

"I thought, huh," Michael says, "they're supposed to be in here."

"They are, if they want to cause a meltdown."

"And what about the water?" Yari complains. "I thought they weren't going to flood the tunnels."

"This isn't making sense," Anya says.

"Then if they're not here," Yari says, "where are—"

All the lights come on at once, forcing them to quickly lift their night-vision.

A swarm of men file into the room. Eagle Team get to their feet and stand huddled together in the middle. A mezzanine walkway travels around the edge of the circular room. Boots clatter noisily along it.

The moment their eyes are adjusted, the four of them see that they are surrounded. From every direction there is the barrel of an AK-74M glaring at them.

"And so we meet at last," a voice resounds through the room.

They turn to the entrance and see a gaunt man walking

in, a shock of white going through his black beard, a malevolent look in his eyes.

Michael lifts his bullpup.

"I wouldn't," Tagirov says in heavily accented English, holding a hand up.

There is a key fob dangling from it.

"See for yourselves," he adds, looking up.

All four follow his eyes.

Attached to the ceiling are several incendiary devices. Not enough to blow the reactor but enough to kill them. It would appear that the fob in Tagirov's claw-like hand is the trigger.

"Now put your weapons down," the Chechen says.

"And let you kill us?" Anya retorts.

"You have two choices. Either you surrender to my men. Or you die. I don't really care which."

"And what if we surrender?" Yari booms.

"Then you will become prisoners of the Russian Federation."

"That's as good as dead."

"No. Refusing to surrender is as good as dead."

Anya throws hers down first, the others following suit, and they are quickly rounded on.

The men force them down onto their knees. They're searched for other weapons. Knives are taken. A small Makarov pistol is pulled from behind the breast plating of Yari's armor.

Tagirov comes before them, only now daring to get so close to Azrael. His dark eyes scan each of them individually, as though he is weighing them up, like a troll deciding who to eat first.

He points at Yari. One of the Scorpions takes a pistol from his belt and comes behind him.

"Hey! No!" Anya shouts.

Yari is looking around as the guy cocks the pistol.

Anya turns to Tagirov. "You said you were taking us prisoner!"

"Yes. But I'm afraid we only have room for three. And the big man takes up the most space."

Yari is smiling gently at her. "It is okay, Anya. Don't be—"

The pistol is fired into the back of his head.

"Yari," Anya sobs as his body collapses forward and hits the floor, a halo of blood spreading from him.

"Now it is bedtime," Tagirov says.

One of his men pulls out a syringe and three vials. First, he comes to Michael, and then, with the kid out cold it is Peter's turn.

As the Scorpion comes around him, the assassin's eyes are fixed to Anya. Whilst everyone's focus is on him, she discreetly lifts a hand to her mouth and slips something under her tongue.

Peter is still watching her as he passes into unconsciousness. Wondering what it was.

THIRTY

TEREK LAKE, BESLAN, RUSSIA

MIKHAIL GUTSERIEV SITS ON THE VERANDA OF THE dacha watching the mist flow down off the mountains. It creeps across the tranquil waters of the lake and gets snagged in the trees lining the banks.

The people of the town once believed that the spirts of the dead resided in those mountains. And that it was in the mornings that they came down into town in the form of the mist, believing that the ghosts would visit all their living relatives and see how their lives were getting along.

Gutseriev feels ashamed that on most mornings when his family come down to visit him, he is once more sad and lonely and growing old too fast. And that, most of all, he still hasn't gotten them justice.

Hearing the sound of a distant car engine, he lifts his stiff body out of the chair and goes inside the wood-slat cottage.

An iron wood burner takes up the center of the sitting room, and several logs burn to cinders inside.

The car pulls in front of the dacha as Gutseriev takes a seat in the far corner, where an armchair faces the doorway. Alexei walks out from the kitchen to greet the visitor. In the meantime, Gutseriev places a blanket over his lap and slips a hand underneath, reaching it into a pocket of his trousers. Grabbing the handle of what sits inside.

Outside, Alexei talks to the visitor. The man is on his own.

Good, Gutseriev thinks. *He's come as a friend.*

Alexei leads the man into the dacha and soon the apologetic expression of the bodyguard is stepping into the room. He comes to a stop by the door and stares at Gutseriev as though he were looking into the eyes of a man condemned to death.

Maybe he is.

Next into the room is a familiar face. One Gutseriev has known since they roomed together at the Soviet engineering college in Leningrad (now St. Petersburg). Godfather to his children. Best man at his wedding.

"So they sent you, did they?" Mikhail Gutseriev says.

The man's name is Victor Lebedev.

He doesn't answer Gutseriev's question. Instead he asks, "How are you, old friend?"

Gutseriev says nothing. Just stares coldly at him.

Lebedev is a small man with neatly cut brown hair that is graying at the sides. He is dressed, like always, in a pinstripe suit with a red silk tie. He gets his suits from Savile Row in London—even despite the sanctions.

"Take a seat, Victor," Gutseriev says.

Victor Lebedev looks about the room. The only other chair is a small couch positioned three yards from Gutseriev. The rest of the chairs have been dragged outside onto the veranda.

Lebedev sits hunched forwards with an uncomfortable look on his face. Like he's just sat in a pile of shit.

"I'm not looking forward to doing this," he says.

"I can see that."

"It pains me to have to relay certain things."

"Then relay them."

"How many years have we known each other, Mikhail?"

Gutseriev says nothing. Just squeezes the hand in the pocket. The blanket hiding it from view.

"Well, it's a lot," Lebedev continues. "First at the dormitory back during the days of the party. Then it was..."

All the while he prattles on, Alexei stands in the doorway. Watching the scene with a worried expression plastered on his face.

Impatient, Gutseriev snaps, "Just get on with whatever it is you've come to say, Victor."

Lebedev stops talking. He straightens himself out.

"Firstly," he says, "all your banks and shares have been frozen."

"Not all of them."

"All your wealth tied up in Russia has been, and you will be expected to give up any foreign interests."

"I've still got enough hidden away to pay the assassin."

The edges of Lebedev's mouth twitch. In an ice-cold tone of voice he informs Gutseriev, "I'm afraid not. Your assassin and his son are currently in the custody of the FSB."

Gutseriev goes cold. He feels it like a blow to the head.

"No. You're wrong. He escaped."

"Yes. And then walked straight back into a trap."

"He'll escape again."

"Not this time. This time there's no one to come and rescue him. And soon there'll be no one to rescue you either, Mikhail."

"Is that a threat?"

"No. It is a promise. I and several of your former associates and friends have done our best over the years to protect you. Now I am giving you one last favor. You will be taken from here back to St. Petersburg. There you will be held under house arrest at either your apartment at Nevsky Prospekt or your mansion in Kurortny. All your assets are hereby handed over to the state."

Gutseriev is livid. "Fuck you, Victor," he says, squeezing hard in his pocket.

"Now come on," Lebedev says, ignoring the slight. "I am to drive you to the airfield."

Lebedev goes to stand when Gutseriev says, "No."

He rises from the chair, the blanket dropping to the floor, and it is then that the Marakov finally makes its appearance.

Victor Lebedev's eyes bulge at the gun and he dumps himself back down on the couch.

"Sir, please," Alexei pleads, stepping into the room from the doorway.

"Alexei," Gutseriev says, not taking his eyes off Lebedev, "there's some rope in the cupboard under the sink. Get it and tie this bastard up."

THIRTY-ONE

DONETSK OBLAST, UKRAINE

PETER WAKES UP TWELVE HOURS LATER.

Groggy, he feels detached from the fuzzy images he sees. Like he's watching it all on television.

Scanning his environment, he finds himself seated inside an armored personnel carrier. It doesn't appear to be moving. The only other people in there with him are Michael and Anya. They're sitting opposite, still unconscious. All three of them shackled to their seats.

His neck hurts. Probably the result of traveling over rough terrain.

But where to?

He leans as far forward as he can. "Mikey? Mikey?"

The kid begins to rouse. His eyelids open slowly. He goes to touch his face and realizes he's shackled.

"I think I'm going to be sick," he says.

"Try to hold it in."

"I can't. I gotta…"

Michael lurches forward and spews the little amount that's in his stomach onto the metal walkway that runs down the center of the APC. Then he leans back, closes his eyes, and breathes slowly out his mouth, his chin shiny with vomit.

"That feels better," he says weakly.

"Oh God," Anya begins mumbling as she slowly comes to. "What's that smell?"

"It's me," the kid says. "Sorry."

Anya takes a while to compose herself. She isn't sick, but she has to sit with her eyes closed for a while. All of them are dazed and a little confused.

"We're not moving," Michael points out.

"Probably because we're already at our destination," Peter replies.

"Which is?" Anya adds.

"I don't know. I've only been awake a minute longer than you guys. The last thing I remember is being in the Control Room."

Anya's eyes suddenly brighten. She feels around her mouth with her tongue.

"It's still there," she says.

"What's still there?"

"The…"

The back door begins opening. Sunlight rushes into the carrier, burning their sore eyes. They each turn away as men rush inside.

They do it in two-men teams, picking Michael first. While one stands over him aiming an AK-74M at his chest, the other releases the shackles.

Freeing the right arm first, he snaps a handcuff over the wrist. Then, releasing the left, he orders the kid to lean forward and place both hands behind his back. That done, he secures the other wrist, before releasing his legs and marching him out.

The barrel of the AK is never more than a foot from his back.

Next it is Anya's turn, and it's not long before she is glancing over her shoulder at Peter as she disappears out the back of the APC.

He is surprised to find that only a single man comes for him. A man with blond hair thin enough to see the pink scalp underneath. His unremarkable face holds the drained, featureless expression of the intelligence operative, and he has the lifeless eyes of a rattle-snake.

Taking Michael's former seat, he relaxes back into the uncomfortable seating, fixing Peter with a devil-may-care look.

"My name is Vasily Savelyev," he says in English. "Have you heard of me?"

Peter says nothing.

"Well, I've heard of you, Azrael."

Savelyev smiles. There is something awful in it. Like it's the rendition of a smile. An alligator luring prey into the water.

"Do you know that I long thought you didn't exist?" he says. "How long I thought you were nothing but a piece of propaganda—a myth made up by the CIA to frighten us. Watch out or the bogeyman Azrael will come get you. But here you are. Sitting right before me."

He takes a pack of Yava Classics from the breast pocket

of his jacket and holds the pack of Russian cigarettes out to him.

"I don't smoke."

The pack is retracted. Savelyev places one in his mouth and lights it. Blowing smoke out through his teeth, he says, "I hear you've been sent here to get retribution. Something to do with the Beslan siege."

"And you were there," Peter puts to him. "I remember your name being mentioned."

"So you know a little about me as well, then. Well, it doesn't matter. Soon you'll be dead, my mission will be complete, and this war will be over. All the glory to Russia."

Peter thinks he knows something about the aforementioned mission.

"What were you doing in Zaporizhzhia," he asks, "if you weren't there to cause a meltdown?"

Savelyev takes a long drag of his cigarette. Says nothing.

"I know," Peter says, staring into the man's dead eyes. "You were there to take material, weren't you?"

Savelyev lets the smoke out. "So you've been paying attention."

"I only got it recently. Right before your puppet Tagirov had his men knock us out. So is that what this is? You're making a bomb out of Ukrainian material."

Savelyev grins at him. "Come," he says. "I'll show you."

The FSB commander leaves the carrier, passing two Scorpions at the door. At his signal they march up to Peter and do the same gig they did with Anya and Michael.

They escort him outside and Peter walks down the ramp onto the crest of a hill. The APC is parked on a dirt clearing surrounded by trees on one side and rocky ground on the other. In the distance is a large city that occupies an expanse of flatland. The golden spires and domes of several churches twinkle in the low sun.

As they walk him to the top of the ridge his attention is taken by an absolutely terrifying sight.

There is an M142 High Mobility Artillery Rocket System (HIMARS) set up so that it faces the city. The system is mounted on the back of a truck frame. Several men work around it. Lying across a long table nearby is a GMLRS rocket customized to carry a nuclear warhead.

Peter is taken to the others. Michael, Anya, the two scientists, and the four Georgians left from the Five-Five. All of them handcuffed and sitting in a line not far from the HIMARS. Peter is placed next to them on the ground. Three armed men watch over them.

"You like our rocket system?" Savelyev asks.

"It's the same type the Americans have been giving the Ukrainians," Peter observes.

"That's right. In fact, this one *was* given to them by the US Government. The Americans have its serial number filed away somewhere. So there'll be no denying that they gave this to Ukraine."

"You stole it," Anya says.

Savelyev glances at her. "Perhaps. But the world will be too busy with other facts to really care if we did or not."

"What other facts?" Peter asks.

"The fact that several Ukrainians—all you here—have been caught on the edge of Donetsk right after the city was hit by a dirty bomb."

Anya goes cold all over.

"Are you saying," she puts to him, frowning, "that you are going to detonate it in Donetsk?"

"Yes," Savelyev says.

Peter is nodding. He gets it the entire thing now. "Then you're going to make a pretense of capturing us, aren't you?"

"Good. What else?"

"You're going to make it look like we're the ones who set it off. Those who refuse to comply with the following mock interviews will be killed. Those willing to lie for their lives will be paraded before television cameras to admit setting the bomb off."

"That's dumb," Michael says. "There's no way it'll work. Where's the evidence?"

"Our GPS," Peter says. "They've hacked it. They're going to use it as evidence."

"How?"

Looking right at Savelyev, Peter says, "Why don't you explain that part?"

"Gladly," the FSB man says with a characteristic smirk. Turning to Michael and Anya, he tells them, "We've been tracking you all since the start of this. Your GPS tracking data—Azrael and his son, Eagle Team, and the Five-Five—will show that you have all been to the necessary places."

"Necessary for what?" Anya wants to know.

"Necessary to paint a picture."

"What picture?"

"One in which Ukraine, aided by a CIA operative, have attacked Russian-held territory with a dirty bomb."

"No way," Michael says.

"Yes way, kid. The two of you were in Mariupol. You were pictured there."

Savelyev holds out a smartphone. On the screen is a picture of Peter and Michael in the bar with Pavlov, the cowboy and the tank battalion.

"You did a deal with Colonel Sergei Razamov," Savelyev says, retracting the phone. "He and his tank battalion helped you smuggle certain equipment with you to Izium, where you met up with your Ukrainian friends. The Eagle Team. Whilst there you picked up one Davyd Smrnek. Head nuclear technician at the Zaporizhzhia power plant."

He points a finger along the line. At the end sits a rather sorry-looking man of about fifty who looks like he hasn't slept or eaten for days.

Savelyev goes on in a self-satisfied tone. "After Smrnek informed you he'd need another man for the job, a Valery Jovic PhD, you went to Kherson. Whilst there, Russian Spetsnaz unit Scorpion Team engaged you after Russian intelligence learned what you were up to. You managed to kill several of the men, including second in command Vladimir Khodov, before joining up with another Ukrainian unit the Five-Five."

"You mean your unit of double agents?"

"I mean a unit of Ukrainian soldiers ordered to accompany Eagle Team in their special mission. Ones who helped you get to Zaporizhzhia, where you infiltrated the site and had Smrnek and Jovic retrieve a substantial amount of spent uranium stored at the waste storage facility. After that, you had the two men construct a dirty bomb. This achieved, you snuck this bomb here—to the edge of Donetsk—where you used an American-supplied rocket system to attack Russia."

Peter is shaking his head. "You've known we were coming the second we stepped off that plane in Mariupol."

The grin is back on Savelyev's face. "Of course we have. We led you all the way here, Azrael. I mean, we couldn't have planned it better if we'd recruited you ourselves."

Michael sits forwards. "And what in the hell do you think you're going to achieve by this?"

"Easy," Savelyev says, turning his beady eyes on him. "If it is shown that the Ukrainians have used uranium from one of their own power plants to create a bomb, and that they have launched said bomb on Russian-held territory, then it will mean they have broken international law. It will mean they have escalated the conflict beyond the parameters the West have set out. The UN will turn their back on them. The rest of the world will shun them. NATO membership will be declined. The arms will stop arriving from Europe and America. The donations. The promises of infrastructure. There'll be a clamor for the Ukrainian president to resign and face a trial for war crimes. It will allow Russia to reply in the same terms and the next you'll know we'll be hitting Kiev with a low yield bomb. This time next year, there won't be a Ukraine left. It will all be Russia."

His rigid ghost-face is dead serious.

"Now," he adds, "enough chit-chat." He takes a radio from his coat pocket and barks into it. "Tagirov, come get your prize."

In less than a minute Tagirov and four of his men make an appearance. The leader of the Scorpions marches straight up to Peter and crouches in front of him.

"Did you like our little trap at the power plant?" he asks.

Peter just stares at him.

Tagirov smiles. "I have a surprise. Some business

associates of mine are waiting for you and your boy in the city. They are looking forward to meeting you."

He signals his men. Two of the Scorpions come forward and make their way to Peter and Michael. Anya takes her chance. She leans sideways into Peter and says, "Don't leave me without a kiss."

Peter lunges to meet her lips. The two lock in a kiss. Her tongue pushing inside his mouth.

They are soon dragged apart and Peter and Michael are loaded into the back of a Tigr four-by-four all-terrain. Four men pack themselves into the back with them. Tagirov and another get in the front.

Peter is looking out of the back of the Tigr at Anya as they drive away.

"Who do you think they're taking us to?" Michael asks.

"I don't know," Peter replies without taking his eyes off her. "But we'll soon find out."

THIRTY-TWO

TEREK LAKE, BESLAN, RUSSIA

"This is a huge mistake, Mikhail," Alexei says.

He has just finished tying up Victor Lebedev.

"Listen to your bodyguard, Mikhail," Lebedev says. "This is madness. I am your only friend right now. So listen very carefully..."

"Gag him," Gutseriev orders Alexei.

He tosses over a piece of thick cord he uses to tie back the curtains. Alexei looks down at Lebedev with an apologetic expression, shrugs as if to say sorry, and ties the cord around his mouth. It fits neatly between his teeth, cutting off any sound Lebedev may try to make.

All the time Gutseriev stands there on the other side of the room. The Marikov aimed at the government man.

Standing up from the prisoner, Alexei turns to his boss and says, "They won't let you get away with this."

"I don't care. All I want is to wait for the assassin to call."

"He isn't going to, Mikhail. Didn't you hear? He is in custody. It is all over. This man was coming here to offer you your only chance."

"I'd rather die. No, Alexei. It is you who are wrong. The assassin will make it. He will find out who the third man is. He will find out why this happened to my family."

"And if not? If he dies?"

"Then I will get the truth out of this bastard," he says, glaring at his prisoner.

THIRTY-THREE

DONETSK, UKRAINE

DONETSK IS FILLED WITH PEOPLE. THEY TRAVEL past a park where children play. Giggling and shrieking as they take turns on the swings and climbing frames. The Tigr passes a strip mall filled with shoppers. Even the Russian soldiers are still here in numbers, the Tigr crossing through several checkpoints on its way into the city center, and it appears to be just another normal day in Donetsk.

These people have no idea what is coming.

The world is about to change.

They turn onto the wide boulevard of Artema Street and head toward Teatralna Square. They pass the Donetsk State Academic Opera and Ballet Theatre. A stone building with a wide colonnade covering the entrance and supporting a large triangular entablature decorated in nymphs. The golden monument to Alexander Solovianenko the opera singer eyes them as they drive by.

They reach their destination on the edge of the square. A large rectangular building with tiny windows and Russian soldiers stationed at the entrance. Parked outside is an eight-wheeled infantry fighting vehicle (IFV).

It is some machine. A beast. Similarly shaped to a BTR-80, but much larger and meaner looking.

"What is that?" Michael asks as he gazes out the window of the Tigr.

Peter knows. Having little to no social life, he spends most of his spare time reading up on weaponry. Making sure that, as a master assassin, he is up to date on all forms of killing. There isn't a gun, bomb, poison, or attack vehicle, new or old, that he doesn't know about.

"It's a VPK-7829," he tells his son as the Tigr parks in front of it.

"What in the hell is a VPK-7829?"

Peter answers like he's reading the spec off some magazine. "It is a modular amphibious wheeled infantry fighting vehicle and armored personnel carrier. It's quite new in military terms. We're probably some of the only people to see it in the flesh. They only unveiled the prototype to Putin in 2013, and it isn't in wide service yet. Apparently the Russian Military Industrial Company that has been developing it found after preliminary trials that it wasn't very comfortable for the transportation of troops."

"And the BTR-80 is?"

Peter goes to answer but is interrupted by the back door creaking open. "Well, here goes," he says to his son.

They are marched out of the Tigr into the building. A plaque at the edge of the double doors states in Russian that this is Donetsk's main municipal building.

They are led down a wide corridor. All the doors are closed and there is not a single sound or sign that any of the rooms are occupied. The narrow passage leads to a service elevator. A soldier stands guard. As they approach, he tugs a folding metal gate to one side.

"Face the corners," the men snap, shoving them into the lift.

It goes down. Another bunker.

At the bottom a soldier rips the door open and they spill into a corridor of solid concrete. Strip lighting flickers and buzzes above their heads. They march along the passage, Tagirov leading. Their footsteps echoing. The corridor ending in a thick metal door like the type you'd get on a cell.

Another soldier opens it as they approach and they step into a large underground chamber where two gynecological chairs take up the center. Next to them is an aluminum table with various "tools" on it. Mostly medical implements. But other things, too.

The Scorpions order both to sit in the chairs. Michael looks sideways at his father.

"It's okay," Peter assures him.

The chairs have been modified with metal clasps on the arm and leg rests that are lockable with a key like a pair of handcuffs. Peter has seen this exact type once before. He now thinks he knows who the Scorpions have sold them to.

The two of them are fixed to the chairs at the wrists and ankles by the lockable clasps. Michael begins panicking. His breathing becomes rushed. Irving Berlin hums from between his teeth.

"Just keep calm," Peter tells his son.

Michael nods.

Tagirov comes before them, his men lining the walls.

"I hope Khodov didn't spoil this surprise by telling you who we'd sold you to. They were both adamant that they wanted to see the look on your face when you saw them for the first time."

Two expensively dressed men come strolling into the room. One in a blue and green tartan Vivienne Westwood suit and crocodile skin Italian loafers. The other in a gray wool Kiton double-breasted jacket and moleskin trousers. The one in the Westwood wears a pair of round tortoiseshell glasses and has a bald head. The other is taller, and has medium-length brown hair that is scraped back over his scalp.

They join Tagirov.

"Just like I promised, gentlemen," the Chechen says.

"Very good, Mr. Tagirov," the one in the glasses says.

"Now you remember the rules," Tagirov says. "You have four hours. That is when the men outside will come and get you and escort you to the airfield. You do not want to be here after that. As for the prisoners. If they are not dead by this point, a soldier will either hand you his gun to finish the job quickly or will do the job himself. You understand?"

The men agree, their eyes never leaving Peter, a mixture of hatred and excited anticipation on their ghoulish faces.

"Then I leave you to your prize," Tagirov says.

He leaves the room, his men following.

At the door he turns back on them. "And remember. There is a man outside. All you have to do is ring the bell at the door."

He is pointing to a button at its side.

"Yes yes," one of the men says, waving him away.

And with that Tagirov is gone.

All alone, the one in the glasses speaks first.

"Do you have any idea who we are?"

"You're Fred Wilson Junior, and you," Peter turns his head to face the tall one in the gray Kiton, "are John Wilson."

"That's right," John Wilson says. "We're the men whose father and baby brother you killed."

Fred Jr. leans over Peter. "You remember what you did to our father?" he asks.

He allows Peter some time to answer but Azrael says nothing.

"You remember pushing a metal rod up his nose? Well, you're gonna wish that the two of us go so easy on you and your son."

———

AS SHE WATCHES them load the rocket onto the HIMARS, Anya turns to the two scientists. "How many will it kill?"

"It is low yield," Professor Jovic answers. "The initial explosion is unlikely to cause any more than a few thousand casualties."

Anya frowns at the white-bearded old man and says sardonically, "Only a few thousand?"

"Think yourself lucky," the professor replies. "Hiroshima killed over a hundred thousand. But that's not the point of this bomb."

"What is the point?"

"The point is radioactive contamination. It is designed

to essentially spread radioactive pellets. This is what they had us creating at Zaporizhzhia from the waste uranium."

"What would exposure like that mean?"

"Anyone who is close to the blast site will be exposed to enough radiation to cause immediate serious illness. Exposed to high levels of radiation, they will develop symptoms of acute radiation syndrome; nausea, vomiting, fatigue. They could develop severe radiation burns. Depending on how high a level they're exposed to, they may die within a few days or weeks of exposure. But it is the spread of radioactive dust and smoke in the aftermath that will be the real danger to tens if not hundreds of thousands more people. If people breathe in the dust, eat contaminated food, or drink contaminated water, they could become sick and die, or, as is in many cases, develop severe forms of cancer later on. Pregnant mothers will give birth to infants with terrible defects."

Anya can't help recalling a television news item from her childhood. By the 1990s the long-term effects of Chernobyl had begun to appear. She remembers the news crew visiting a hospital ward in Kiev. It was filled with disabled children born to mothers pregnant directly after or during the disaster. She had been horrified by the images of children born with no limbs or unnaturally large heads, shrunken appendages.

Anyone who would purposely do that to people doesn't deserve to breathe air.

Not far from where she sits Savelyev watches his men finish with the rocket. It is now ready to be loaded into the HIMARS.

One of his men informs him of the fact.

"Good," he says. "Then it is time we made history."

It is then that Savelyev spots the Tigr arriving and he begins making his way toward it. As Tagirov and his men get out of the vehicle, he is there to meet them.

"You sold them, then?" he says to the commander of the Scorpions.

Tagirov smiles. Showing off his crooked teeth.

Like an old pal, Savelyev places an arm around the Chechen's shoulders and begins guiding him towards the forest.

"Come," he says. "The feast for your men is ready. Time to celebrate your success."

———

THEY START ON MICHAEL. The one with the glasses, Fred Jr., stands over him with a pair of extracting forceps. His brother John, slicked-back hair, stands the other side with a gleeful look.

A medical gag holds the kid's mouth open and a thick leather strap travels across his forehead, securing it.

Fred turns over his shoulder at Peter. Light reflects off the lenses of his spectacles making his eyes look pupilless.

"Are you ready for this?" he taunts.

He turns back to the kid. Michael's eyes are closed. Wilson goes straight for the back molar.

Peter is watching the brother. John Wilson. He stands facing Peter, watching for a reaction on his face. Peter doesn't give him any satisfaction and before long he looks away.

Now's his chance.

A line of blood begins falling from the edge of the kid's

mouth. He doesn't move, but his fingers dig into the ends of the armrests.

"Almost there," Fred Jr. hisses like a serpent.

"I wanna go next," his little brother whines.

With Michael taking all their attention, Peter recalls the lingering kiss with Anya. The hairpin she passed over with her tongue, having snuck it into her own mouth right before they were taken at the power plant. It is the same one they got off the Russians at the camp.

The metal clasps of the chair hold him at the wrists with his hands poking out. They've not secured them as tight as they should. He can still pivot his hand around so that the palm is facing upwards.

He checks the brothers. They're both watching Michael. Then he spits the pin straight at the hand and catches it.

He turns sharply to the men.

Neither has looked away from the kid.

Bending his wrist as far as it will go, he manages to poke the end of the pin into the keyhole of the clasp and begins picking the lock.

———

NOT FAR FROM THE HIMARS, within the trees of a nearby wood, the remaining Scorpions line the edges of a long picnic table eating a giant feast. The trees echoing with the sounds of smacking lips and scraping cutlery.

Savelyev has gotten a Chechen chef to cook them all the delights of their home. There is Barsh. Which is mutton stomach stuffed with ground meat, similar to Scottish haggis. Chepalgash; a sort of pie filled with cottage cheese and wild garlic. Dalnash-Chudu. Another pie. This one filled with lards and wild garlic. Smoked meats. And many, many more delicacies.

"Bless Allah," one of the Chechens says to the man next to him. "This feast is more brilliant than the one served at my wedding."

They laugh and eat.

After so many days of dried vacuum-packed rations, the men are so engrossed in their food that they fail to notice the eight members of Alpha Group, the FSB's specialist Spetsnaz unit, slowly surrounding them, spreading out in the encircling trees.

Tagirov waits until they are all in position before he stands up and taps a glass. The men stop eating and stare at him. All eyes pointed his way.

"My men," he says proudly.

"Colonel!" cries out from every mouth at the table.

It is then that the Scorpions begin noticing the Russian Spetsnaz in the trees. Nudging each other.

"My men," Tagirov announces loudly, recapturing their attention. "You have served me impeccably. A Colonel could not ask for anything more from his men than what you have given me."

"Colonel?" one of them asks, his eyes flitting between his leader and the surrounding men.

"Yes, Alik."

"Who are these men?"

"Don't worry about them," Tagirov says in a soft voice, his eyes not leaving him.

So assured in his leader, Alik leaves it at that. As do his brothers-in-arms. There is no more mention of the men in the trees.

"My brothers," Tagirov goes on, "you have served a higher purpose. You will earn our people a place at the highest table."

A cheer goes up.

"But for this," Tagirov holds a finger up, "I must ask for one last sacrifice."

They frown at each other.

"What sacrifice?" someone asks.

"Your eternal silence."

Alpha Group draw their Malyuk Vulcan bullpups and open fire. Eight sets of evenly spread muzzle flashes light up the trees in asterisks of flame. The men at the table are hit with a barrage of bullets. The shooting lasts only nine seconds and by the end the men lay sprawled over the table or in heaps underneath.

Only Tagirov remains alive. Taking one last bite of the food, he gets up and leaves as Alpha Group move in with cans of kerosene and begin dousing the bodies.

———

THE WILSON BROTHERS stand either side of Peter. Their sneering faces leaning over him. Michael is almost passed out, mumbling delirious nonsense to himself as blood leaks from his mouth. They settled on four molars before they got bored.

Peter has already gotten the first clamp off. But he needs to get rid of the second before he can even think of escape.

"Has your son ever done drugs, Mr. Black?" Fred Jr. asks in his nasal New England drawl.

Peter just glares at him.

"Because," Fred Jr. goes on, "we've also brought along a series of drugs. Torture for the mind."

He looks up at his younger sibling.

John Wilson takes the cue and disappears to the aluminum table. When he comes back, he has a medical case for holding vials. He unzips it and holds it out to his brother.

"Let's see," Fred Jr. says, a finger to the cleft of his chin. "We have some simple pharmacological drugs like insulin for a nice little shock therapy in which we put your boy into a coma and then use a defibrillator to bring him back. Over and over, with him and you begging us not to. Ooh," he adds, eyes widening at the vials lined up in the case. "There's haloperidol, an antipsychotic medication. You ever seen someone on haloperidol? They can't stay still. Like their whole body has bugs writhing around underneath the skin. They say it's like having Parkinson's disease."

"What about thorazine?" his brother suggests.

"Good idea, bro. Another antipsychotic medication that can be used to induce grogginess, sedation, and, in high doses, vegetative states. Or there's sulfazin, which induces a severe fever."

"Then there's always the classic," John says, taking a vial out and holing it label-side before Peter's eyes.

The bottle simply reads: Lysergic Acid Diethylamide (LSD).

"Ohh," Fred Jr. breathes with glee. "This isn't any normal bottle of LSD, you know. This bottle is the same type the CIA used on American Marines during Vietnam for the MK Ultra project. They had a crop duster spread it over several platoons as they camped in the jungle and then watched from helicopters as the men went crazy. I guess the CIA thought it would turn a bunch of pothead college dropouts into monsters. And it worked. Just not quite how they thought it would. Because instead of picking up their weapons and fighting the gooks, those soldiers turned them on each other. Within an hour over a hundred and fifty men were dead and the few that remained had to be locked away in asylums for the rest of their lives. You see, there was a spike in the punch. The CIA's pharmacists had mixed the exceptionally potent LSD with sodium amobarbital to cause massive loss of inhibition. I've seen the videos of men handed razorblades and told to cut their own faces. Watched as they've sliced it all off, piece by piece."

Fred Jr.'s eyes practically glow at the end of his speech. "Oh, yes," he says grimly. "Let's have some fun. Then maybe afterwards, we'll lobotomize him. Leave him to live out his days as a vegetable."

Peter doesn't bite. He just stares at him.

"Reticent as always," Fred Jr. says.

"Maybe he's just plain stupid," John adds.

"Maybe. We'll soon see how quiet he is watching his only child run a blade through his own cheek."

The chair is on a swivel. John Wilson takes ahold of Peter's shoulders and turns him 180 degrees so that he's facing Michael. He stays there, gripping his shoulders from behind.

Peter can see that he's watching his brother pull the contents of the LSD vial into a syringe.

Good. That's good. Let him watch.

Peter moves quick. Without moving his shoulders, and

thus alerting the man holding them, he releases his right hand and begins picking the lock on the left.

The hand is quickly freed. Right at the moment Fred Jr. twists around to face him.

Peter shoves the right forearm back in the clasp, keeping the left where it is. He hopes he hasn't seen.

But Fred Jr. isn't even looking at him. He's looking at his brother. Referring to the drugs, he says, "Shall we give him just a little to start the proceedings and build our way up? Or shall we inject the entire vial straight into his heart?"

"No point wasting time," the brother replies. "We've only got four hours."

Fred Jr. turns his eyes to Peter, who to all appearances looks like he is secured in the chair.

Addressing the assassin, he says, "I once watched a film of our father giving it to a girl he kept in the basement. She bit off one of her own thumbs. If he hadn't recorded it, I would have never believed such a thing was possible."

Eyes back on Michael, Fred Jr. stares into him. The kid is no longer delirious. He is staring right back at him.

His lips move ever so slightly and something hisses from his mouth. The kid smiles afterwards.

Fred Jr. frowns. "What did you say?"

The broken lips move again. Whispered words that Fred Jr. can't quite hear. He lowers an ear to the kid's mouth and when he gets real close, Michael hocks a mouthful of blood and spit that covers his face.

"Gah!" Wilson cries out as he staggers back, the gore dribbling from his glasses. "Little fucker!"

He rushes to the table, grabs up a cloth, removes the spectacles and begins wiping his face off. His brother comes away from Peter and wanders toward Fred Jr., laughing at the kid's ruse.

"You fell for the old whisper act," John Wilson says as he chuckles.

What neither of them see until it is too late is Peter bending down to his legs and releasing the thick leather straps that tie them to the chair.

By the time Fred Jr. is reapplying his wiped tortoiseshell glasses to his eyes and spotting Peter running up, there is nothing he can do. The table holds many implements of horrific destruction to the human body, but unfortunately for him, none of those things are a gun.

Observing the look on his older brother's face, John Wilson has enough time to twist halfway around when Peter grabs him by an arm, twisting it around his back, and slams him headfirst into the aluminum table. It makes a loud clattering sound. Peter immediately lifts him up by the back of the head and plows him into the table over and over until he's dumping his limp body onto the concrete floor.

FRED JR. STANDS there shaking all over. His bother's face is unrecognizable, blood pooling out of his head as he lies on the floor.

Fred has never had to fight another man in his life. Just the mention of his daddy's name had always been enough in most places he frequented. It kept him from ever having to dirty his own fists.

As Peter marches up to him, Wilson can do nothing but back off. If he had his wits about him, he'd run for the door. Ring the alarm. But the fear is too great. The man coming at him is a killer. A real one. Not some kid pulling the wings off a butterfly, but a man who can be placed in a room with other killers and come out on top.

When Fred and his friends at Harvard called themselves Alphas, they were merely kidding themselves into believing that wealth and power made you somehow better than others. But if you wanted the cold hard truth of it, this was what mattered. Stripped of all the pretense. One man on another. Kill or be killed.

And under these conditions Fred Jr. can do nothing more than back up to the wall and watch as Peter snatches the syringe from the table and marches up to him and stabs the needle straight into his chest where his heart is and pushes the plunger all the way down.

Fred Jr. cries out and drops to his knees, the syringe still poking out of him. The drugs begin to take hold immediately. His heart pumping it into his brain. His pupils dilate.

Peter leaves him on the ground in the beginnings of a major panic attack. John Wilson has the key. Peter digs it from the pocket of his pants. Then he checks for a pulse.

He's still alive.

Peter goes to the table. There's a Wagener ear hook; a four-inch-long surgical instrument used in ear surgeries to extract foreign bodies. He lifts John Wilson up by the scruff of his slicked-back hair, and pushes the thin rod all the way into the ear, not stopping until it is all the way through.

Peter leaves him, and, as Fred Jr. begins crying out and grabbing the sides of his head, he unlocks Michael. Once the straps are off his legs, he helps the kid out of the chair.

Fred Wilson Jr. begins screaming like a demented

person, making the most awful sounds. He sits up against the wall, running his hands down his face and wailing.

"You think you can stand on your own?" Peter asks Michael.

"I think so."

Peter lets him go. The kid staggers a little, uses the table to steady himself, then straightens up. Nods.

"Good," Peter says. "Pick something from the table as a weapon. It's about time we got out of here."

THIRTY-FOUR

TEREK LAKE, BESLAN, RUSSIA

GUTSERIEV WAKES WITH A START.

He has fallen asleep. He straight away checks his right hand. The Marikov is still in it. Glancing at the phone on the left armrest, he sees that no one has called.

Victor Lebedev is thankfully still in place. Sitting on the couch opposite all tied up and gagged. Staring at his former friend.

Rubbing his eyes, Gutseriev shakes himself.

Then he wonders where Alexei is.

He can hear the low bass of his man's voice. It's coming through the wall. The bodyguard must be on the veranda talking to someone.

Gutseriev lifts himself from the chair and goes to the window, pulling the curtain to one side.

Alexei is on the phone. By the look of his worried expression, he appears to be having some type of difficult conversation.

Gutseriev doesn't go straight out. He waits. Listens.

"I told you," Alexei says to whoever's on the other end of the call, "this is getting out of hand. Why did you let him come alone?"

The bodyguard is gazing out across the lake. The door creaks open behind him and he whirls around.

"Who are you speaking to, Alexei?" Gutseriev says, stepping out onto the cold veranda.

The bodyguard immediately cancels the call. Tries to shake off the obvious grimace. Attempts a smile. Doesn't pull it off.

"My sister," he says.

"The one in Rostov?"

"Yes."

The two men stare at each other for a little while. When it becomes almost unbearable, Alexei points at the cell phone in Gutseriev's hand and asks, "Has the assassin called yet?"

"No."

Alexei looks away. Toward the lake.

"This is insane," he says.

Gutseriev gazes at him. He feels weak and his vision is blurred. He's hardly eaten these past few days. For a moment he thinks he's going to faint. He stagger forwards and Alexei grabs ahold of him as he falls. Not roughly, but in the spirit of a friend. Catching the old man and guiding him to a chair.

The gun has trickled out of Gutseriev's hand and lies on the wooden floor. Alexei gets him seated and goes off. When he returns he has a banana and some medication.

"You've forgotten to take your pill again," he says softly, handing him a glass of water.

Gutseriev takes the pill, washes it down. Then he eats the banana. Breathing deeply and leaning back in the chair the whole time.

"You must come to your senses, Mikhail," Alexei says when the old man is a little better. "End this now. Allow me to untie Victor and come to St. Petersburg. Please."

Mikhail glances at the beseeching look on his bodyguard's face and then through the door of the dacha. Victor Lebedev, one of his oldest friends, sits there tied up. And for what?

Gutseriev turns back to Alexei and nods.

"Okay," he says, giving in. "Untie him and get the car ready."

THIRTY-FIVE

DONETSK OBLAST, UKRAINE

EVERYTHING IS IN PLACE. THE GMLRS ROCKET IS loaded on the HIMARS, and Savelyev's men have finished inputting the targeting coordinates and aiming it at the city.

The bomb is designed to detonate before impact so that it explodes midair and causes the widest range of fallout.

There is little more than an hour left.

Anya sits watching the Donetsk skyline below. The sun is going down and the cars have begun using their headlights. The dim yellow orbs move about the crisscrossing roads like blood cells along arteries. So much life goes on down there. Even with all the fighting around it.

"Major Petrovic?"

Anya scowls at the voice. When she turns her head from the city, she finds the grotesque Savelyev standing there with his dog Tagirov.

"Soon, Major," Savelyev says when he has her attention,

"you and the rest of these men will have an important decision to make. Do you let misplaced heroism end your lives, or do you live in peace. I promise you, take the deal. Stand trial and confess to the evidence laid before you. Give an interview explaining your mission. Then you will spend the rest of your life hidden somewhere. A nice house. All the luxuries of a good life."

"You want me to betray my country?"

Savelyev goes deadly serious. "Yes."

As he stares at her with those terrible eyes, one of the Alpha Group soldiers comes over.

"Sir?"

Savelyev turns to him. "What is it?"

"I need to speak to you urgently."

Savelyev and the man go off.

"Sir, we may have a problem," the Alpha says when they're alone.

"What is it?"

"The assassin. He's escaped."

"What?"

"I've just received word that the six men stationed at the facility have all been found dead with no sign of the assassin or his son."

"What about the Wilsons?"

"Both dead. One had a steel rod pushed through his head and the other apparently cut his own throat."

Savelyev rolls his eyes right as Tagirov strolls over. The FSB man turns sharply on him.

"You should have shot him the first chance you had," he snaps.

"What's wrong?"

"He and the son have escaped."

The Chechen's brow crinkles up and his eyes go blank.

"They were both locked into chairs," he surrounded by armed men and twenty meters of concrete. How in the hell did they escape?"

"This is Azrael," Savelyev says. "It's what he does."

"Then we need..."

A huge explosion rocks the ground beneath their feet. Behind them the armored truck with the satellite dish is a mushroom cloud of fire.

"Sir?"

Savelyev turns around to the leader of the Alpha group. The man is pointing down the hill. A dark green beast comes rolling up the valley wall toward them. He recognizes it as the new VPK-7829. Nicknamed Bumerang (boomerang).

"We need to get clear."

Several of the Alpha Group are running for their own vehicle, the BTR-80, when a Kornet-EM anti-tank missile hits its open back door and the thing is a roaring ball of flames before anyone can get near it.

That's when the BM-57 autocannon kicks in on the turret of the Bumerang. It is aimed at the hill itself, and, as the Russians run toward the woods, the ground explodes beneath their feet. Great hunks of dirt are ripped out and thrown in the air, the barrel of the cannon recoiling into the turret with each shot, the BM-57 able to shoot a hundred and twenty rounds a minute.

It makes the shooting continuous and the hill is rapidly decimated. All except the area around the HIMARS and the prisoners.

As he runs, Savelyev watches one man get hit directly by

the cannon. It vaporizes him and all that's left to mark where he was is a crater. By the time Savelyev reaches the trees, his ears are ringing and he hardly hears the explosions anymore.

The Bumerang climbs up the steep incline, the eight-by-eight wheel drive making light work of the rocky terrain, the 750 horsepower turbo-charged diesel engine roaring and the wheels churning up the hillside as the craft comes over the ridge.

It swings around and comes to a stop between the HIMARS and the trees. Thus creating a shield between the prisoners and the forest a hundred yards further on. From this position, the turret rotates so that its guns are aimed at the forest, then sends hellfire from its PKMT heavy machine gun. Bullets slice through the trees. The smart men get down on their fronts, make themselves as low as they can. Those not so smart try to run and are hit by the swarm of bullets that rips through the forest.

A door on the side of the Bumerang slides open and Peter jumps out. Anya is so relieved to see him, she is crying when he gets to her.

"I knew you'd come," she sobs as he uses the hairpin to pick the locks of her handcuffs. "Don't ask me how, but I knew."

She throws her arms around him the second they are released, pulling him into her and kissing him for real this time.

Michael is next out of the Bumerang, having been controlling the turret. They quickly release the others and soon everyone stands around the controls of the HIMARS. Anya is looking over it.

"Do you think you can disarm it?" Peter asks.

"I don't know. I've seen one before, but never used it."

"Maybe I can help," Davyd Smrnek says, coming beside her.

"Can I leave you with this?" Peter asks.

"Sure," Anya tells him.

Peter and Michael run toward the woods. Peter armed with a Beretta that he prized from the fingers of a Russian soldier whose throat he'd just cut with a scalpel. Michael holding another dead soldier's AK-74.

Heads down, they sprint into the trees. Of those that survived the Bumerang's onslaught, there are only three Alpha Group members, Savelyev and Tagirov left.

The last Scorpion is with the Alphas. They're holed up about fifty yards into a patch of weeping willow, the drooping foliage acting as partial cover. All of them watching the forest, waiting for the assassins to come.

As for the FSB man, Savelyev is stumbling randomly through the woods. The only thing on his mind is to escape the carnage. He's not a fighter. He's a schemer. It is always others who do the fighting.

The staccato echo of gunshots make him turn sharply in the direction of the sound.

Peter and Michael have engaged the three remaining members of Alpha Group. The Russians are spread out amongst the willow. Their muzzle flashes illuminating the dangling branches.

The assassins are in cover about twenty yards apart. Making hand signals. Laying plans.

Michael nods. Shoulders the AK. He stands behind a tall spruce covered in broken branches that stick out from the trunk about a foot. Launching himself up the tree, Michael uses the branches like the rungs of a ladder.

The three Russians are reloading their Malyuk Vulcans. Snapping the cartridges into the stock ends. Finished, they look at each other. Nod. Then burst from cover. Aim at the former positions of the two assassins.

Wait.

Something snaps to their left.

They turn.

The empty forest sways gently in the breeze. The men hold their breath. Listen carefully.

No one expects it to come from above.

By the time the first Alpha is spotting the kid in the tree, Michael has put a bullet through the side of his head, and he falling.

The other two react. One spins away from the willow and hurdles the tall bracken, racing for cover further along. Michael pauses a beat and drops him ten feet away. The guy sprawls onto his front, twitches once, dies.

The third man gets several bursts of the Vulcan off. Michael doesn't wait around. He's already climbed around the other side of the trunk and is in cover. The tree vibrates against his back as the bullets pound it from the other side, and he prays none of them make it through to him.

The last Alpha is so busy spraying the tree that he fails to register Peter coming right up behind him with the Beretta.

The blast to the head throws the Alpha several feet from Peter, and he slams the earth with a force at least twice his weight. He doesn't even twitch.

Peter waits. Listens.

His acute hearing focuses out the effects of the wind; the

creaking trees, the rustle of branches, the whistle of the airflow rippling in and out of the trunks. Then he hears it. A man's heavy breathing. The sound of a man clumsily breaking through bracken.

"Savelyev," Peter growls in an undertone.

Michael comes down from the tree, scavenges one of the dead Alphas for his Vulcan, tosses away the AK, joins his father.

Neither speak.

Michael hears it too.

They're off. Michael leading the chase. Peter sprinting behind. He wants to call after him. Tell the kid not so fast. To be cautious.

As they pass into a sun-exposed clearing, it becomes harder to makes things out. The sky is cloudless and the sunlight bright. Too vivid to see clearly. There is a lot of contrast between the brightness of the clearing and the dark of the forest.

It is probably why he misses what happens next.

Something charges at him. He spins around with the pistol as a forearm hammers his wrist like a steel pipe. The blow knocks Peter over. He rolls with the force, getting a spinning view of the Beretta skittering off into the vegetation.

Spinning back up on to his feet, Peter recalculates.

He is face-to-face with Ruslin Tagirov. The Chechen hasn't had the chance to find a weapon, so it will be hand-to-hand now that Peter is also unarmed. During the two weeks of preparation back in Beslan, Peter had read up on the fighting skills of one Ruslin Tagirov. After the Beslan siege, he had spent five years in hiding, never leaving the compound that he was being kept at, and it was reported that he trained for up to six hours every single day of this time.

By the time he was recruited into Ramzan Kadyrov's pro-Russian forces, he was a machine. Then, after helping to defeat his former allies, he began running his own fighting gym in Grozny. And not just that, he fought as a contender himself, winning all twelve professional fights he took part in in MMA. Retiring undefeated.

They circle each other in a tight clearing overshadowed by trees, drifting in and out of the sunlight. Tagirov is the same height as Peter but carries about twenty pounds extra of hard muscle.

They explode at each other like two cannons going off. Both strike open-hand guards, one after the other, one-two. Tagirov attacks with pencak silat, an Indonesian fighting style that incorporates every part of the body. He feints right. Smashes the left side of Peter's head with an ear smash. The assassin's eyes show mostly white as he staggers backwards, shakes himself, and the pupils roll back into view like a slot machine.

A burst of fists come at him. Peter blocks them with his forearms. A Burmese lethwei knee spear follows. Peter turns himself sideways. Pushes the knee away and clocks Tagirov with a quick headbutt. It sends the Chechen staggering backwards.

Peter waits for him to lash out defensively, then sidesteps. Turning his thumb into a dagger, he parries Tagirov's rushing fists and digs the digit into the hinge of the jaw. He feels the thumb sink pleasingly into the soft flesh at the target, but he's made a mistake. He's slipped too far inside Tagirov's reach.

Tagirov's hands blur. Peter does his best to cage his head, drawing the iron-hard bars of his forearms together, but he is getting peppered. There is no break to capitalize on. Only Peter can create one. He rotates his elbow as he lashes his forearm upwards. Knocking his opponents fist away, the tip of his ulna continues onwards and splits Tagirov's chin all the way to the bone. Blood flows from the wound, Tagirov backing off and sucking in a hard breath.

Both men are experienced fighters with the ability to pull off multi-discipline combinations. They are fighting in a multitude of languages. Filipino kali countering Brazilian jiu-jitsu. The two of them careening through the forest in a perfect dance of limbs.

Nothing else matters to either man in this moment. Nothing but the fight. Tagirov is glad that they aren't armed. That it is body against body. This is what he loves most. Hand-to-hand combat with a real opponent. If he is to die in these woods today at the hands of this assassin, he will be glad to meet Allah on such terms.

Peter feels his left brow swelling and prays it won't obstruct the eye. Tagirov's shoulders bulge beneath his shirt. He barely looks out of breath.

He charges Peter with a Japanese jun-zuki. Peter intercepts the lunging punch with a Thai front kick. The ball of his foot claws away the fist and continues into Tagirov's lower abdomen. It has little effect in itself, but it does shift the Chechen's weight forward, placing his head within reach.

Peter throws an arm clench over the Chechen's head,

locks his fingers into a lace hold across the back of Tagirov's neck, crimping the carotids of his neck with his forearms. He yanks Tagirov's face down, throws knee strikes that break through the attempted block of Tagirov's raised forearms and hammer into his cheeks, his nose. At the same time, he attempts to rock Tagirov from side to side, trying to get him off balance, rock him onto to one leg, then the other, get him down, get on top, get it finished.

No such luck.

Tagirov is a six-foot length of toned muscle. He is too strong. With Peter behind him, Tagirov bends forwards and lifts him up, bulldozes him backwards into a tree. The rough bark scrapes Peter's back and the blow knocks the wind out of him.

Peter lets go and hits the deck. Thankful that he manages to land on his feet. Tagirov rears back, ready to take advantage, to hit him with everything he has. It gives Azrael a fraction of a second of freedom. Before Tagirov can set himself, he steps forward, planting his left foot, and delivers a wing chun low front side kick with his right, pivoting to piston his heel forward, aiming at the soft tissue above Tagirov's knee. He hits it squarely, pushing the joint apart. The Chechen bellows and sags, somehow keeping his feet. For a second Peter loses his balance, and this is enough time for Tagirov to move forward, rotate his hips and drive a reverse punch into Peter's chest.

Pain explodes in the assassin's sternum, which bends inwards with the force. He's knocked off his feet. The back of his head clatters against a tree, concussion flares inside his skull, covering the world in a misty haze. The smell of the dirt is strong in his nostrils as he lies in the damp earth.

Peter blinks, sighs, snaps to it. He uses the low branches of the tree to pull himself up, a boxer climbing the ropes, right as Tagirov comes for him. The Chechen's fist skims the top of his head, missing by millimeters, as Peter reels back from him.

It is then that he spots the Beretta on the ground a few meters away. Peter throws himself down to it as Tagirov swings a muay Thai spinning back heel kick at his face that could crush his cheekbone, missing by inches.

Peter crawls along the dirt toward the gun, hands and knees sliding on the muddy ground. He can sense Tagirov coming up on him. His fingers stretch out, inches from the Beretta.

Tagirov lunges, getting ahold of Peter by the ankle, rasping his hand away from the pistol. He rips him backwards through the undergrowth, Peter's fingers clawing the dirt ground. Tagirov lets go of his ankle. The assassin goes from all fours to being flat on to his stomach.

Rotating on his hip, he hurls all his weight into a kick as Tagirov comes down on him. The foot strikes the Chechen in the throat, crushing his windpipe and sending him back.

Peter gives every last ounce of strength in his body to lifting himself from the ground and throwing himself at the Beretta. Tagirov comes back at him. Grabs him by the shoulders. Flips him around so he can finish this. Freezes.

There is a pistol pointed at him.

He and Peter lock eyes. Then Peter pulls the trigger.

The shot enters under the chin and continues all the way out the top of his skull. He goes from formidable fighter to deadweight and lands on Peter.

Peter pushes him off and gets to his feet.

In the meantime, Michael has caught up with Savelyev. Directionless, the FSB man has ended up falling into a gorge of mud and is now trying to claw his way up the opposing bank.

Michael jumps into the creek after him and Savelyev spins around.

"Stay where you are?" Michael growls, looking right at him through the optics of the Vulcan.

Savelyev raises his hands and Michael is quick. He bashes him right in the face with the buttstock, knocking the Russian out in one go.

Back at the HIMARS, the others have successfully canceled the launch sequence. When Peter and Michael rejoin them, with Savelyev balanced on Peter's shoulder, Anya runs up to him.

Peter dumps the FSB man on the ground and they wrap their arms around each other. The two kissing as Michael rolls his eyes in the background.

THIRTY-SIX

BESLAN, RUSSIA

MIKHAIL GUTSERIEV IS LOST. THE LAST THING HE did before leaving the dacha was take one last look at the tranquil green waters of the lake and cross himself. Say goodbye to his girls. To his wife. To his former world. He has one simple plan when they reach St. Petersburg: to commit suicide the first chance he gets.

At this current moment in time, he is being driven out of town to the airfield. The same one that Peter and Michael arrived at all those weeks ago inside the oligarch's Gulfstream G650.

It had been a wild fancy, the Russian now admits to himself. A whim. To think that he could get justice or even the truth in such a place as modern Russia. With its lies and counter lies. The majority just eating it up.

He gazes into the front of the car. Alexei drives and

Victor Lebedev sits in the passenger seat. Still bitter about being tied up.

Every now and then, one or the other will glance up into the rearview mirror and take a peek at him. Make sure he's still cooperating.

Gutseriev sighs and gazes out of the window.

Evil deeds that go unpunished only ever lead to more tragedy.

The words flitter through his mind, and the old man agrees.

Except that the sentence doesn't say everything. It fails to mention that often it is the innocent who are on the receiving end of the new tragedy, and that, in the end, the guilty remain unpunished.

THIRTY-SEVEN

DONETSK OBLAST, UKRAINE

MAYBE NOT TODAY.

It is Vasily Savelyev's turn to wake up inside the back of an APC drenched in ultraviolet light. The seat he's been duct-taped to vibrates underneath him as the colossal Bumerang rumbles its way north.

A shudder runs up his back like a rat.

Lying across the bench seating opposite is the remains of the GMLRS rocket. Wires poke out of the nose cone. The warhead has been removed. The four canisters of treated waste uranium pulled out of it.

He turns sharply to his right.

Two men stand there in Hazmat suits.

When they step closer, he can make out the faces behind the plastic screens. It is Peter and the engineer Davyd Smrnek. The rest are riding shotgun in the front cab of the VPK.

Savelyev glances at the canister the engineer is holding.

"I take it," Peter says, "you know what's in the canister."

Savelyev tries to grin it off. "Trying to scare me?"

It makes Peter smile. "You know me," he says. "You said so yourself. You've spent so long hearing stories about Azrael. You should know that I don't try and scare people. I kill them."

The two lock eyes. Savelyev trembles. Looks away.

"I'm going to make this very simple, Vasily Savelyev," Peter says. "You either tell me want I want to know or I'll contaminate you. The same as you were going to do to all those poor innocent people."

Savelyev turns back to him. "And what if I do tell you? You'll do it anyway. Like you said, you're a killer."

"I'm not like you. I keep my word. And just because I'm good at it, doesn't mean that I take pleasure in causing harm to others. I promise that you will be left alive and unharmed. So long as you cooperate."

"Cooperate? Huh! You mean commit treason. Betray my own country. A country I've sworn to protect."

"Protect?" Peter scoffs. "You were just minutes away from annihilating thousands of your own people. All in the name of winning new territory from a country you've invaded. You're not protecting anything if you're the aggressor."

Savelyev stares at him. A bead of sweat passes down his face.

Peter turns to Davyd Smrnek. The engineer steps closer to the FSB man. Holding the base of the canister in one of his gloved hands, Smrnek uses the other to twist the top. It makes a hissing sound and Savelyev goes cold. He holds his breath as Smrnek pulls the top off.

Green light fills the space around the canister.

"Wow," Peter says. "It actually does glow."

As Davyd Smrnek carefully places the lid down on one of the seats and begins lifting out the inner container holder the uranium pellets, he explains, "The UV excites the electrons above the ground state and gives off photons as the electrons transition back to the ground state. This gives it a lime-green glow."

Savelyev is grimacing. His Adam's apple rising and falling. His eyes fixed to the glowing isotopic rods that the engineer is now holding up.

"You feel that heat?" Smrnek says. "It may be waste material, but it's still producing plenty of energy. It'll cause serious burns if held close enough to skin. And that's not to mention the amount of radiation you'd be absorbing into you. I'd have to say that the type of exposure we're talking about here could cause serious cancerous growth."

"You hear that?" Peter says. "We could cover you in burns and tumors."

"What happens if I cooperate?" Savelyev asks.

"I told you. You'll come to no harm."

"But then what?"

"You mean once we reach the Ukrainians?"

Savelyev nods. Swallows again. He is terribly pale.

"You'll go on trial for war crimes, no doubt. All the evidence gathered from these men—the Five-Five, Mr. Smrnek here, Anya, and the professor—will be put forward to an international tribunal. More than likely on television and probably at the Hague. Unlike your version, however, they won't be lying and they won't be making statements under duress. They will be telling the truth. Showing the world how far Russia has gone down the road of self-destruction."

Savelyev's eyes bulge at him. They shine green from the uranium glass. "It won't matter," he says with the last bit of pride. "Nothing will be changed. Nobody wants war. They will make a big fuss and nothing more. We'll ride out the sanctions and the sanctimonious hypocrisy of the West. Ours is the long game."

"Be that as it may," Peter puts to him, "but you certainly won't be involved in it all any longer, Mr. Savelyev. You'll be in custody. So what do you say? A prison cell. Or a prolonged death wasting away from radiation sickness and cancer?"

Savelyev's top lip curls and he grits his teeth. Then. "What do you want to know?"

THIRTY-EIGHT

BESLAN, RUSSIA

They're on the Gulfstream G650 about to take off. Gutseriev sits alone at the back of the luxury jet drinking vodka on the rocks and feeling as low as he ever has in his sixty-eight years of life. Alexei and Victor Lebedev are at the front close to the cockpit. The flight crew consists only of the pilot and copilot. They are busy making the last of their checks before they taxi the plane out of the hangar and hit the runway.

Mikhail Gutseriev pays little attention to the preparations. As well as allowing him to use his own plane, they've let him keep his phone. Confident that Peter isn't going to call.

But they're wrong.

The phone vibrates against Gutseriev's thigh from the pocket of his pants. Glancing at the other men, whose attentions are taken, he pulls it out and checks the screen. It is an unknown number.

Gutseriev discreetly answers the call and before he speaks Peter says into his ear, "I have the answers to your questions, Mikhail. Do you want to hear them?"

"Yes," Gutseriev whispers.

As the oligarch's eyes gaze at Alexei and Lebedev, Peter tells him the terrible truth.

"Are you okay, Mikhail?" Peter asks when he's finished.

"Yes. I am. Call me back in ten minutes."

"Okay. Be careful."

"I will."

Gutseriev staring eyes fastened to the other men, he puts the phone away and gets up from his seat. He reaches to the door and before Alexei can spot him, is twisting the emergency lever and opening it.

"Hey!" the bodyguard shouts as he spots his boss lowering himself into a sitting position on the edge of the step, his legs dangling from the plane.

The oligarch turns over his shoulder. Sees that he has been spotted and drops the two meters to the hard asphalt. The shock stuns his old knees and he is limping as he rushes to the back of the car.

They had come here in his Hummer.

Alexei jumps down from the plane and chases after him.

"Mikhail, what are you doing?"

He reaches him as Gutseriev opens the trunk of the Hummer, lifts up the carpet and takes something from the well compartment underneath.

Mikhail Gutseriev twists around as Alexei lays a hand on his shoulder and before the bodyguard knows what's happening, a loud bang fills the hangar and he is staggering backwards, a terrible burning sensation in his stomach.

Alexei looks down, spots the blood oozing out the bullet hole. His legs go weak and he falls backwards onto the ground. Sitting there holding his bleeding belly, he looks up at Gutseriev.

The oligarch is holding a Sig Sauer 9mm, a thin tendril of smoke rising from the barrel. His bulging eyes are wet with tears.

"Mikhail," Alexei says weakly, his brows furrowed, "why?"

"You know why, you bastard," Gutseriev spits back at him.

"Mikhail?"

Gutseriev turns around. Victor Lebedev is standing at the open door of the G650. Gutseriev lets off three shots that spark around the doorway, sending the government man fleeing inside.

Turning back to Alexei, Gutseriev says, "Ten years you've worked with me. Ten years knowing all the time that you held the key."

The frown drops. Alexei's face loses its hardness.

"So the assassin made it," he says with a dry chuckle.

"Yes. He got the answers from Savelyev. Your boss."

Alexei sighs. Looks down at his lap. A deflated expression on his face.

Shaking his head, he says, "I'm so sorry, Mikhail."

"Liar!" Gutseriev shouts. "Fucking liar! Zoyev was there all the time—Zoyev is YOU!"

He is mad with rage and grief. His two young girls and

their mother stand with him in that hangar. They are right there watching.

"And not only that," the old man is barely able to get it out of his trembling lips. "Not only that, but you are the man... You... You..."

Tears block his vision for a moment and as he wipes an arm across his face, Alexei lunges at him. Gutseriev notices in time and sends two quick shots at him. One sparks off the concrete and the other hits him in the shoulder.

Alexei falls onto his back. Gutseriev rushes up to him, comes over him, the 9mm aimed at his head.

"You killed my children," the oligarch is finally able to say. "You shot them and then you callously came to work for me. I let you into my life. We became friends, Alexei. I told you things I've never told anyone else. And all that time you were the bastard who murdered my little girls."

Alexei is grimacing up at him. The bullet has gone through the top of his right lung. A ribbon of blood pours from the corner of his mouth.

"I am truly sorry, Mikhail," he says weakly. "Believe me when I say it. I regret killing your daughters. I regret storming that school. But I was ordered to."

Gutseriev scowls down at him. "Bastard!" he spits. "Your excuse is that you're just another braindead sheep."

"You don't understand what it is like growing up poor," Alexei splutters. "I had nothing before the military. I grew up as poor as poor can be. At times living with relatives in their three-room apartment with six adults and seven children. The only time anyone ever gave me anything was in the army and then the agency. It was my life. So when they ordered something, I did it. Just like if your father asked you."

"If my father asked me to kill a child, I would rather kill him."

"I am sorry, Mikhail. Truly sorry for what I have done to you. What I did to your girls. If it is any consolation, I have never been the same since that day. Something in me is dead and it will never come back."

"Oh yeah?" Gutseriev shouts, leaning over him. "Well, now the rest of you is going to be dead."

And with that he unloads the remaining twelve bullets of the 9mm into Iznaur Zoyev's chest. The double-agent lets out a gasping hiss and goes totally limp.

THIRTY-NINE

KIEV, UKRAINE

IT IS A WEEK LATER AND PETER STANDS IN THE cold air talking on a cell phone. Winter is coming. Frost coats the ground.

In the background is a four-bedroom house that belongs to a minister of the Ukrainian government. It has been loaned to Peter and Michael until they leave Ukraine.

As for the CIA, their wait in Kiev was fruitless. The assassin Azrael somehow got away before he could be delivered to them. President Zelenskyy has personally apologized to the Americans for the error.

"I wanted to thank you one last time," Mikhail Gutseriev says down the phone.

The Russian is currently in hiding.

"I told you, payment is enough, Mikhail. I mean, won't you need the annuity now that all your Russian assets are frozen?"

"I've been funneling money and stock out of the country for over a decade. The annuity I handed over to you and your boy is only one of several very well-paying portfolios. No, I'll get along fine. A nice retirement somewhere hot. I've lived too long in the cold."

"And you're not upset that you've had to go into hiding?"

"You always have to pay a price for the truth," the oligarch says. "But it is always a cost worth paying. The truth is more important than anything. Without it we are blind. I would rather live in brutish poverty and know the absolute truth than live in luxury and be ignorant of everything. No. Becoming a pariah is no more than the necessary cost of truth in my country."

"They will hunt you, Mikhail," Peter warns.

"And I will wait for them. No. I don't have long anyway. What do I fear of death? At least I can go knowing the truth."

"I hope it gives you solace."

"It does. It truly does. And I hope the money helps to compensate the two of you for what you have gone through."

"It's a start."

There is a second or two of silence before Gutseriev asks, "Would you have taken the job had you known what you'd go through?"

Peter doesn't reply straight away. His eyes search the frozen air. The house is in a leafy suburb. Snow-covered conifers line the edge of the garden.

"Probably not," he eventually answers. "But that's not

how the game of life works. It's best to learn from it and move on."

"So if an elderly Russian invited you to his dacha tomorrow, you would say no?"

Peter smiles. "Yes, Mikhail. I would say no."

Gutseriev waits a beat. Then. "I thank God that you said yes."

Peter turns toward the house. The kitchen window faces the backyard. Anya is washing up the dinner things while Michael dries. He watches her smile at some smart-aleck thing the kid has said. Her blue eyes sparkle. She looks up instinctively and faces Peter. Blushes that he's looking right at her. He smiles and waves. She waves back.

"But in many ways," Peter says, "I, too, am glad I said yes."

"Good. Then I am glad that our contract came to a mutually beneficial closure."

"It has."

"Then I bid you farewell, Azrael. This will be the last time we ever speak."

"Goodbye, Mikhail."

"Goodbye."

The phone call ended, Peter goes back inside. Back to the light and warmth of Anya and Michael.

FORTY

SORRENTO, ITALY

THE UKRAINIANS WERE QUICK TO PRESENT THEIR
evidence to the international community. Davyd Smrnek
and Professor Valery Jovic have given extensive interviews to
international media. The fallout of it all has seen Russia once
more condemned by the UN, but it hasn't seen an end to the
war. Russia merely denies everything. Digs in. And so it all
goes on.

Anya is back amongst it. Michael had let them have that
last weekend together alone at the house in Kiev, booking
into a local hotel.

Peter and Anya spent those two days doing practically
nothing. Just being together, watching films, eating food,
sitting in the backyard to watch the sunsets and sunrises,
sprawled out on a picnic blanket, arms around each other.
They had held each other for almost ten minutes on the last
day before she got on the train. Afterwards, he didn't run

after the carriage. He didn't even wave. All he did was stare at her through the window until the carriages slid out of the station and he was left all alone.

It would be the last time he ever saw her. Six days later Major Anya Petrovic was asleep in a military dormitory in Lviv when an S-300 antiaircraft guided missile hit the compound. Peter would find out not long after he and Michael had arrived back in Italy.

A cold feeling had come over him after the call from Ukrainian military intelligence. Like someone had thrown ice water all over him. For a moment he didn't breathe. His lungs paralyzed. The kid had asked what was up and he'd muttered automatically that it was nothing. Then he'd just snapped out of it. Shoved the memory of Anya into another compartment of his mind and slammed the drawer shut. Wiped himself clean of all emotional ties he had for her. Just like with Kate, Mother, Magda or anyone else he's lost in his life. All of it locked away in the cabinets of his mind.

Back in Sorrento now, the father and son return to their apartment for the first time in over two months. There is an odor of damp and soured milk when they walk into it.

Now winter, the cold has gotten into the house without them there to heat it. Someone has tried to break in while they've been away, but hasn't had much luck with the barred doors or ballistic-proof glass windows. You'd need a serious bulldozer to gain access to this place. Therefore, they don't find the place in disarray. Nothing stolen. Nothing trashed. Just moldy food in the fridge and dust in the air.

"I'll get the wood burner going," Peter says as Michael unloads the fridge into the garbage.

They spend the next morning cleaning the place.

Afterwards, they go for a drive through the beautiful seaside town. They drive down to the marina. Check on the *Mother-Magda*. She's still there. A little weather damaged but all good. After that they have lunch at the Piazza della Vittoria.

It is on the way back that Michael asks Peter to take a certain route home. It passes a certain apartment. On the corner, the kid asks him to stop.

"What are you gonna say to her?" Peter asks.

"I don't know. That you had urgent business back in America, but I'm all good now."

"What about your teeth?"

"I'll tell her I had dental work done in America."

"And the bruises and scars?"

"I don't know," the kid snaps irritably.

Michael gets out of the car and begins his approach to Bianca's place along the sidewalk. Peter watches him from the Ferrari. When he's halfway, the door to her apartment opens and out steps Michael's sweetheart. She has a huge smile stretching her face and looks full of her usual joie de vivre. The kid goes to rush up to her but as he does, she turns the other way and faces the approach of a dark-haired Italian coming to meet her on his Lambretta. He comes to a stop right beside her and the girl throws her arms around him.

"Gino! Gino!" she squeals.

Just like she once squealed Michael's name.

The kid comes to a stop and watches them kiss before turning around and walking away.

Peter starts the engine. With slumped shoulders the kid

returns to the car, gets in and they drive away, passing the lovebirds.

"I'm sorry, Mikey," Peter says a minute or so later.

"It's okay," the kid says. "It was me who chose the gun. Now it's me who has to live by it."

Don't miss HUNTER KILLER. The riveting sequel in the Peter Black Thriller series.

Scan the QR code below to purchase HUNTER KILLER.

Or go to: righthouse.com/hunter-killer

NOTE: flip to the very end to read an exclusive sneak peak...

DON'T MISS ANYTHING!

If you want to stay up to date on all new releases in this series, with these authors, or with any of our new deals, you can do so by joining our newsletters below.

In addition, you will immediately gain access to our entire *Right House VIP Library,* which includes many riveting Mystery and Thriller novels for your enjoyment.

righthouse.com/email

(Easy to unsubscribe. No spam. Ever.)

ALSO BY DAVID ARCHER

Up to date books can be found at:
www.righthouse.com/david-archer

ROGUE THRILLERS
Gates of Hell (Book 1)
Hell's Fury (Book 2)

JACOB HUNTER THRILLERS
The Kyiv File (Book 1)
The Bogota File (Book 2)

PETER BLACK THRILLERS
Burden of the Assassin (Book 1)
The Man Without A Face (Book 2)
Unpunished Deeds (Book 3)
Hunter Killer (Book 4)
Silent Shadows (Book 5)
The Last Run (Book 6)
Dark Corners (Book 7)
Ghost Operative (Book 8)

ALEX MASON THRILLERS
Odin (Book 1)
Ice Cold Spy (Book 2)
Mason's Law (Book 3)
Assets and Liabilities (Book 4)
Russian Roulette (Book 5)

Executive Order (Book 6)
Dead Man Talking (Book 7)
All The King's Men (Book 8)
Flashpoint (Book 9)
Brotherhood of the Goat (Book 10)
Dead Hot (Book 11)
Blood on Megiddo (Book 12)
Son of Hell (Book 13)

NOAH WOLF THRILLERS
Code Name Camelot (Book 1)
Lone Wolf (Book 2)
In Sheep's Clothing (Book 3)
Hit for Hire (Book 4)
The Wolf's Bite (Book 5)
Black Sheep (Book 6)
Balance of Power (Book 7)
Time to Hunt (Book 8)
Red Square (Book 9)
Highest Order (Book 10)
Edge of Anarchy (Book 11)
Unknown Evil (Book 12)
Black Harvest (Book 13)
World Order (Book 14)
Caged Animal (Book 15)
Deep Allegiance (Book 16)
Pack Leader (Book 17)
High Treason (Book 18)
A Wolf Among Men (Book 19)
Rogue Intelligence (Book 20)
Alpha (Book 21)

Rogue Wolf (Book 22)
Shadows of Allegiance (Book 23)
In the Grip of Darkness (Book 24)

SAM PRICHARD MYSTERIES
The Grave Man (Book 1)
Death Sung Softly (Book 2)
Love and War (Book 3)
Framed (Book 4)
The Kill List (Book 5)
Drifter: Part One (Book 6)
Drifter: Part Two (Book 7)
Drifter: Part Three (Book 8)
The Last Song (Book 9)
Ghost (Book 10)
Hidden Agenda (Book 11)

SAM AND INDIE MYSTERIES
Aces and Eights (Book 1)
Fact or Fiction (Book 2)
Close to Home (Book 3)
Brave New World (Book 4)
Innocent Conspiracy (Book 5)
Unfinished Business (Book 6)
Live Bait (Book 7)
Alter Ego (Book 8)
More Than It Seems (Book 9)
Moving On (Book 10)
Worst Nightmare (Book 11)
Chasing Ghosts (Book 12)
Serial Superstition (Book 13)

ALSO BY VINCE VOGEL

Up to date books can be found at:

www.righthouse.com/vince-vogel

PETER BLACK THRILLERS

Burden of the Assassin (Book 1)

The Man Without A Face (Book 2)

Unpunished Deeds (Book 3)

Hunter Killer (Book 4)

Silent Shadows (Book 5)

The Last Run (Book 6)

Dark Corners (Book 7)

Ghost Operative (Book 8)

JACK SHERIDAN MYSTERIES

A Cross to Bear (Book 1)

The Clay House (Book 2)

Into The Woods (Book 3)

The End is Nigh (Book 4)

A Step Into The Dark (Book 5)

Holier Than Thou (Book 6)

Streetlight City (Book 7)

An Offering for Sin (Book 8)

A Lark on the Wind (Book 9)

A Glass Darkly (Book 10)

Never Came Home (Book 11)

ALEX DORRING THRILLER

Agent 192 (Book 1)

The Hitman's Death (Book 2)

The Wrong Man (Book 3)

Who Dares Wins (Book 4)

The Highwaymen (Book 5)

The Ring (Book 6)

ABOUT US

Right House is an independent publisher created by authors for readers. We specialize in Action, Thriller, Mystery, and Crime novels.

If you enjoyed this novel, then there is a good chance you will like what else we have to offer! Please stay up to date by using any of the links below.

Join our mailing lists to stay up to date --> righthouse.com/email
Visit our website --> righthouse.com
Contact us --> contact@righthouse.com

facebook.com/righthousebooks

x.com/righthousebooks

instagram.com/righthousebooks

EXCLUSIVE SNEAK PEAK OF...

HUNTER KILLER

CHAPTER 1

BLUEMONT, VIRGINIA - 18:10 ET

"You need to run," he says into the phone. "Run right this second before they find out what you've got."

"I'll leave tonight," a man's voice replies.

It is a voice shaking with terror.

"Can't you leave any earlier?"

"Not without them suspecting something's up. Is the plan still the same?"

The best laid plans of mice and men, he thinks, quoting the poet.

Ben Knight is standing at an upstairs window of a cold, musty-smelling log cabin. Staring outside at the rows of pine that surround the place. It's a misty, moonlit night and the trees look like the silhouettes of tall, stick-thin men creeping closer and closer.

Downstairs, his wife and daughter prepare dinner, and he half listens to the sounds they make.

"No," he eventually says. "With me suspended like this, we can't trust anyone within the agency. You'll have to stay in Europe."

"They'll send everyone after me."

"I know. Give me a chance to figure something out. I might know somewhere you can hide that's off gird. Then I'll come meet you when the coast is clear."

"What about your family?"

"We're out in my folks' cabin. I've got someone coming here that'll be able to protect them. I'm waiting for her now, and once she's here, I can make my way to you. All you gotta..."

The words dry up in his throat and the blood turns to ice in his veins.

Four figures have just emerged from the trees. Four figures dressed in dark clothing. Wearing masks. Night-vision goggles. Holding battle weapons.

The power goes, the cabin thrown into darkness.

He hadn't expected them to come for him so quickly.

"Daddy?" his daughter calls upstairs.

"I'm gonna have to go," Knight whispers down the phone, his heart pounding in his chest like a jackhammer. "Bury yourself. I'll make contact as soon as I can."

"But Ben—"

Knight cancels the call. Swaps the phone for a SIG Sauer P320 he takes from the drop leg holster strapped to his right thigh.

"Sandy?" he calls out into the darkness.

"Ben?" his wife calls back.

"Take Hayley down into the basement. NOW!"

Sandy knows the tone, and it fills her with dread. She grabs her daughter from the bottom of the stairs and races away with her.

Opening the top drawer of a bedside cabinet, Knight picks up the PVS-7 night-vision goggles, the two spare magazines and the second P320 that rest inside. He'll have to duel wield for this. Four against one. Not good odds.

The sound of his wife bolting the basement hatch is quickly followed by the noise of someone busting in the front door with a sledgehammer.

Here goes.

Knight snaps the goggles down and moves quickly from the room. He has his work cut out to protect his family. But this isn't just about one man's family. This is potentially about millions of them. Because the CIA man has finally gotten substantial evidence on something he's been working at for years. Something that threatens to change the balance of power in the world.

And not in a good way.

No turning back, Ben Knight says to himself as he engages the first man from the top of the stairs.

And that's when all hell breaks loose.

CHAPTER 2

SORRENTO, ITALY - 08:07 CET

IT IS AN APRIL MORNING AND THE TWO FORMER assassins are sitting on the veranda of their little pad in Sorrento. Surrounded by sunny clifftop villas and apartment blocks, the sparkling waters of the Tyrrhenian Sea spread out below. They sit there at peace, with few worries, no one trying to kill them, and it makes them absolutely—bored.

A year since Ukraine, they have their pile—enough for an easy life and plenty to have fun. But it doesn't appear to be enough to stave off the hopeless ennui that retirement brings. During these past twelve months Peter and Michael have hiked the Himalayas from Pakistan, through India and Nepal, to Bhutan. They've climbed the peaks of Clarapurna II, K2 and the sacred mountain of Kangchenjunga; avoiding, of course, the overcrowded tourist trap that is Everest (a mountain so overclimbed that the only qualification needed for surmounting it is, most importantly, money, a strong pair of lungs, and the ability to climb stairs).

As well as that, they've been through the Amazon. Crossed the Andes. Partied in Rio. Raved in Buenos Aires. And all of it left them feeling dispirited and slightly empty. For sure, the most interesting thing that happened to them in the whole of their travels took place in Ecuador. While canoeing the Amazon, the two were set upon by a group of armed bandits that had come across their camp. That was by far the best fun they had. Those poor *bandidos* never had a clue what they'd gotten themselves into.

Nevertheless, none of it quite stirred the sense of raw adventure that their former occupation had, and the travelers returned to southern Italy with a sense of having been unfulfilled. As for the amusements of their adopted home, they weren't any better, feeling as flat as a Coke left out in the sun.

It would seem that after you've lived the life they have, it's hard to return to a normal, quiet existence, and the lack of action has become overwhelming.

This morning, the two sit on the veranda drinking their espressos and watching their smartphones. Peter is checking some investments he's recently made. Michael reads the news.

It's full of the row in the Ukraine.

The US Secretary of State and Secretary of Defense are due to meet their European counterparts in a month at the NATO Summit, with Europe preparing for the conflict to spill over.

"Man, we should still be out there," Michael says.

Peter looks up from the laptop. "You say something?"

Michael is about to tell him when he stops himself.

Since Anya, Peter hasn't liked talking about the war. In fact, the other day they were at the deli when international news came on the radio. The second the newscaster mentioned the war, he turned on his heels and walked out, the shopkeeper calling after him as he held up the abandoned order of smoked ham.

"Nothing," Michael eventually says.

The kid moves on to the next news story. It's an eye-catcher.

"Wow. You see this?"

"What?"

Michael reads the headline. "Disgraced government agent on the run after family massacred."

"Does it name him?"

"Yeah. Ben Knight."

Peter is frowning. "Ben Knight?"

"You know him?"

"Yeah."

Peter logs into the *New York Times* under a fake name. Back in his CIA days he'd performed several missions with Knight. He'd always seen him as a standup guy. An agent with a moral compass. Something that is, in the agency at least, as rare as rocking horse shit. "White Knight" was what they used to call him at the agency. That was until a week ago.

The article states that Ben Knight was suspended after evidence came to light that suggested he was colluding with a foreign government. That the White Knight may not be so white. Under investigation, it appears that the story has taken a further twist.

"I don't believe it," Peter mutters under his breath as he reads on.

Government employee Ben Knight, currently under investigation, is wanted by the FBI after his wife and thirteen-year-old daughter were found dead at their vacation home on Monday.

Police believe Knight, 50, shot his wife, Nancy, 43, and suffocated his daughter, Danielle, by placing a bag over her head, at their cabin at Lake Brittle in Bluemont, Virginia.

Detectives admit they are mystified as to the motive behind the killings. Nevertheless, speculation has been mounting as to whether this was a case of someone breaking under the strain of current legal woes.

A twenty-five-year veteran of the CIA, Knight had recently found himself under...

"It makes no sense," Peter says. "I always saw Knight as one of the good guys."

"It's the CIA, Peter," Michael retorts. "There are no good guys."

"Well at least one of the better guys, then."

———

About two o'clock they go out, dine at a local café built into one of the tall cliff faces. Their table is on a little protruding balcony overlooking the crystal waters of the sea.

After their food, they pay a visit to the local movie

theater. The picture they choose is an American superhero farce that is badly dubbed in Italian, making it worse than it actually is. Neither Peter nor Michael enjoy the film, finding the whole experience as flat as everything else.

Pouring rain greets them on the streets outside. They run back to the Ferrari, then pick their way through the rain to their place.

"Aren't you bored?" Michael suddenly asks as he drives them home.

Peter doesn't have to think about it. He answers immediately. "Of course I am."

"It's been a year. Aren't you itching for a job?"

"We don't need one," Peter cuts back curtly.

"Not financially. But don't you feel a need for it inside?"

"We've had enough of *it*. Now is the time to be normal."

"Then we need a change of scenery."

Peter gazes through the windscreen at the blurred old stone villas pitting the hills and clifftops of Sorrento.

"Maybe," he says as they turn onto their road.

Their house is a three-story villa that pokes out from a jagged corner of the clifftops. Because of its protrusion it is the only house on the street that has a complete view of the entire area. A tall wall cuts it off from the narrow road, and a gate wide enough for a car is its only feature. Due to the building backing up against sheer cliffs, there is no other access.

The gate opens electronically. Peter parks the Ferrari inside and it closes up behind them. Apart from the two of them, only one other person has access. A little old wrinkled Italian lady named Bella who comes three times a week to clean up and do the men's laundry.

They run to the shelter of the porch, and it is as Peter goes to fit the key in the front door that he stops. "You smell that?"

Michael sniffs the air. There is a faint odor of cologne. A cologne that smells nothing like anything in their own collections.

The kid nods. Makes a couple of hand signals.

Peter checks the villa's cameras on his cell phone.

They're dead.

Michael gets up on his toes. The ceiling panel of the porch isn't attached. It lifts easily and he slides a hand into the cavity—brings down two fully loaded Sig Sauer 9mms. Hands one to his father.

Next come two suppressors.

Twisting his on the end of the pistol, Peter nods sideways. At the edge of the place is a set of stone steps sunk into the hillside that takes you up to the veranda. It is the only other entrance to the place once you're past the gate.

Michael ascends the steps carefully. As he reaches the top he notices a faint yellow glow reflecting off the rocks that tower over the back of the villa.

The light is on in the living room.

With his back to the stucco and the rain beating off his head, Michael edges around the corner and along the rear of the property. Comes to a stop beside the sliding door.

Peeks.

There is a man in their house. Sitting in the middle of the room, on their couch, playing nervously with his hands. He is side on to Michael, doesn't look armed, but there could be a weapon on the other side of him.

The intruder turns sharply when the door slides open on

its runners. His eyes widen at the sight of the pistol and he lifts his hands to shoulder height.

"I'm-I'm real sorry f-for this," he stutters.

"Keep your hands where I can see them," Michael snarls.

A shadow moves across the floor from the other side of the room. When it reaches his eyeline, the man twists that way and is faced by a second gun aimed at him as Peter moves silently into the room from the hallway.

"Stay perfectly still," Peter tells him.

"I couldn't just wait outside," the man says, turning from Michael to Peter, Peter to Michael. "I didn't know if they were still following me."

"Who's *they*?" Peter asks.

"I'm not really sure myself. Please. I can explain."

"Good," Michael says cheerily, "he can explain. How about you start by explaining how you overrode our state-of-the-art security system."

A flash of pride falls over the man's expression. "Well, actually, it's not so state-of-the-art. I mean, it is for two years ago. But trust me. Not anymore for people who know their way around such things."

"And you know your way around such things?"

The pride increases. He grows bigger. "Yes. I do."

He stands up. But not for long. Dropping quickly back down when both Peter and Michael move aggressively toward him and tell him to sit.

"S-sorry," he mutters.

"What's your name?" Peter asks.

"John. John Harker."

John Harker looks like he hasn't slept for days. He's scruffy, unkempt, and his stale body odor can be smelled under the cologne. He looks to be in his late twenties. Skinny and long. Clean shaven with hair that is a big brown curly frizz. Essentially resembling some Forbes "thirty under thirty" internet entrepreneur.

"And who is John Harker?" Peter asks.

"I'm a journalist," comes the reply. "Though some may call me a hacker. I work freelance, but most of my work turns up in online publications such as *Bellingcat*."

He is steadying his voice with an effort, and his held up hands tremble.

"And what are you doing here?" Peter asks.

Instead of answering, John Harker gazes at the open sliding door.

"Is it okay if we close the door and curtains?" he asks. "I only left them open so that you could see me and see I wasn't armed. I didn't want you to think I was waiting here to do you any harm."

Keeping the Sig Sauer on him all the time, Michael side-steps to the door and pulls it shut. He then tugs on the cord to bring the blinds across before twisting a little rod that closes them.

"Is the front door locked?" the intruder asks Peter feverishly.

Peter answers that it is.

"I'm so sorry," John Harker says humbly. "I know breaking into here was really dumb. But it is all I could do. I couldn't wait for you on the street."

"How do you know who we are?" Peter wants to know.

"I'm a hacker. My life is breaking into secrets. And you, Azrael, are a secret. I heard what you did in Ukraine." He twists around to face Michael. "What both of you did. It's all over Russian intelligence channels. The Ukrainian and American ones, too."

"How did you find us?"

"I followed the money. Mikhail Gutseriev, the man you were working for in Ukraine, he set you both up with a trust fund. It was easy, really, once you got through all the false company names and crisscrossing on the accounts. Eventually, I found the purchase of this place through one of your offshore companies."

"Great," Peter groans. "That's another safe house ruined."

"Oh no," Harker disagrees. "It's pretty safe. It took me days of work to find you, Azrael."

"And what makes you so desperate to find me?"

"Because you're the only one who can protect me." His eyes grow large, like a child begging for food.

"From who?"

He looks about to cry. "I really don't know," comes out in a whisper. "Or at least not yet, anyhow."

Michael is frowning. "So you want us to protect you, but you don't know who from?"

Harker nods.

Peter stares at him. Then he flicks the safety on the pistol and lowers it. "I tell you what, Mr. Harker. We'll let you tell your story, but all I can promise is that we'll listen."

Both assassins put their weapons away.

The couch sits in the middle of the room on a sprawling Persian rug. In front of it is a square-shaped glass coffee table. A bottle of Macallan thirty-year sherry oak single malt, from which the intruder has already filled himself a stiff glass, stands on top. As Peter and Michael take seats either side of him, Harker grabs hold of the glass and finishes it in four gulps. It makes a loud crack when he sets it down.

"Sorry," he says. "I'm a mess. You see, none of this should be happening. I should have made contact with you days ago, but somehow they found me."

"Why somehow?"

He looks up from the table, turns to Peter and says, "I'm going to tell you and your son everything I know. Because I need help worse than any man ever needed it before, and you, Azrael, are the only man who can give it."

"Get on with your story," Michael says, "and then we'll let you know if we can—give it."

Harker pours himself another whiskey. He looks like he's bracing himself for some huge effort as he drains it off. Then, he begins recounting one of the most off-the-wall conspiracies either assassin has ever heard. They have to stop and ask questions throughout, but here's the gist of what he tells them:

As they'd already guessed from his accent, John Harker is an American, from, as Peter picked up earlier, Pennsylvania. Philadelphia to be exact. His father was a computer science teacher, so from an early age he's been building and programming computers. He developed a love of hacking in his teenage years. At first it had been nothing but anarchy; the love of finding a way through a locked system like a safe-cracker. But the older he got, the more his moral compass began to develop. He got into journalism and combined the two to get intel on stories. Though he followed WikiLeaks he was never a contributor, explaining that the website has no editorial responsibility, and is essentially state sponsored by certain aggressive parties. He writes a lot about international matters, the United Nations, NATO, trade deals, the movement of money from one country to the next.

"Follow the money," he tells them, "and you'll find the true motive of it all."

Two years ago he began looking into the interconnection of politicians in different states. Looked at the way they say one thing to the voter and another entirely to their foreign backer. In essence, John Harker got a little deeper down the rabbit hole than he would have liked.

"There is a group," he says, "who live within the shadows, but who control it all on puppet strings."

Michael rolls his eyes. Sensing it, Harker turns on him.

"It's true," he says. "It's a group of families. A group that have been around for generations. Who have borne witness to every single catastrophe or turning point that has faced mankind. The War of Independence. The French Revolution. World War One. The march of Communism. The Great Depression. The rise of fascism. The Korean War. Vietnam. Iraq. Afghanistan. The Financial Crisis. At each point, they've bet on disaster and won."

"That's nothing new," Michael says. "People have been profiting from a failing market since the stock market has existed."

"But what if someone is forcing that market to fail? What if they are maneuvering in the shadows and starting these wars?"

Harker claims to have come across some huge conspiracy all by accident. At first, he wondered whether he should just let it go; stop picking at the thread. But it fascinated him, so he went further. And then it unraveled completely. He got caught.

Harker speaks quickly and nervously, constantly playing with his hands. Often his statements come crashing into one another. Several times the two lose the thread of what he's saying. They gather that this "group" consists of some of the wealthiest families in the world. He mentions Rothschilds and Agnellis; and for some reason claims that surviving members of the Romanovs are involved.

He tells them that apparently the latest conflict in Ukraine is all them. That they have spent the last ten years setting the two nations against one another. He also claims that they have been twisting the knife between China and Taiwan, as well as making sure that the Koreans are on as hostile terms as possible.

When Michael asks him why they wanted the world to fall into complete chaos, Harker's initial answer is blunt and four words long.

"A new world order," he says.

Michael cracks a smile. "Really? So what—9-11 was an inside job?"

"Yes," Harker responds with a straight face.

Michael once more rolls his eyes at the stranger.

"So what about this new world order?" Peter asks.

Harker turns back to him from the kid. "From the ashes of the chaos, a new world will arise. They will use their fortunes to buy up what is left after the crumble of civilization, when whole economies will be on their knees or no longer exist, and then, once and for all, they will own every man, woman and child."

Both Peter and Michael are frowning.

"But something is coming," Harker goes on. "They have all their ducks in a row. In one month they are going to play their ace."

He stares at Peter, who asks what the "ace" is.

Harker's eyes glaze over and he shakes his head. "I'm not sure."

"You're not sure?" Michael puts to him.

"No." Harker's gaze then floats to the archway that leads into the kitchen.

"I brought a bag with me."

He goes to get up from the couch, but Peter plants a firm hand on his chest and pushes him back down.

"I'll get it," Peter says. "Where is it?"

"In the kitchen. On the countertop."

The bag is like Harker: hipster. A vintage waxed canvas roll-top rucksack. It's light. Peter guesses from the feel and weight that it contains a laptop and a few other items.

He hands it over to Harker and the journalist unbuckles it.

"This," he says, pulling out a black portable hard drive no bigger than a wallet and laying it on the glass coffee table with another sharp crack, "contains all my work from the last two years. Everything I've found. But I haven't been able to decipher all of it yet." As he adds this last statement, a look of bitter disappointment fills his face.

"What *have* you deciphered?" Peter asks.

"You read the news?"

"Vaguely."

"You know who Anthony Eustace is?"

"United States Secretary of State."

"Right. Well, from what I've gathered from my research,

Eustace is a problem for them or at least a part of it all somehow. He may have discovered some scheme of theirs, or it could be something else."

"What scheme?"

"I don't know. But a lot rests on it, so they've marked Eustace's card."

"Is that what's going to happen in a month?" Michael asks. "They're going to do something with Anthony Eustace?"

"I think so. See, they can't do it in America. Way too risky. No, it'll be done in Europe. In one month, Anthony Eustace is leading a delegation to the annual NATO summit in Rome. It's why I faked my own death. I need to survive this month."

"What about the hard drive," Peter says, "why don't you hand it over to the FBI? Let them deal with it."

Harker frowns at him. "You have a lot of faith in law enforcement."

"But how else are you going to save this Eustace guy if you won't tell them?"

"Look, the group have been around since the Holy Roman Empire. They have access to all avenues of power. These men have every important world leader on speed dial."

"And this you've gotten from the encrypted files?"

"Some of it. Other stuff I've put together from scraps. For instance there's lots of mention of the 30th of May. The final day of the summit."

"One month's time," Peter says.

"Why don't you warn the Italians?" Michael chips in.

Harker swings around to him with a grimace, like what Michael said was the dumbest thing he ever heard.

"The Italians? Really? Have you seen the current Italian government? A far-right coalition. One that was sponsored and paid for by the group. That's why I'm begging you both to let me stay here for a month so I can finish decrypting those files and find out what they're going to do."

"And then what?" Peter puts to him. "Save the day? Be the hero?"

Harker's eyes glaze over and a gentle smile curls the corner of his mouth. "Why not?" he says.

Though Michael dismisses him offhand, Peter is actually beginning to like the guy. Despite the hipster look of surf T-shirt, cargo shorts and Crocs, there is a seriousness about him. A need to get to the truth. A fire that burns in his eyes, telling Peter that in spite of his fear, he really is ready for some future battle.

And, anyway, if this is all bullshit, like Michael suspects, then he is doing a pretty good job of acting it out.

"Where did you come across all of this?" Peter asks.

"Where does anyone ever find anything these days: the internet. One of my hobbies is breaking into the financial records of the elite. You know, expose where they hide all their money. How little in tax they actually contribute. How much they invest in countries or activities that are supposed to be banned. Where they get their money from. All that."

"And that led you to this group?"

"Yes. See, I started finding a lot of crossover from different entities. Foreign governments given access to the United States through elite businesspersons. That's when I intercepted the encrypted files. Started reading communications where Eustace was discussed, and the 30th of May. That night, an hour after I finished downloading those files, a car pulled up outside my house and two men got out. They didn't knock. They just came around the back and broke in. I took the hard drive and left through a window. Luckily, I've always been paranoid. Ready to run at any time. I've seven fake passports from different countries. Several hidden bank accounts in different names. A bunch of disguises hidden in different places. I'm wearing one now."

He tugs on the curly hair and shows that his head is shaved underneath.

"It's how I got here to you guys. By zigzagging across various locations, using a different passport each time. I flew into Paris as a Canadian. Rented a car as an Australian. Flew out of Copenhagen as a Brit. Arrived in Vienna an Irishman. And so on for the past week. I was beginning to think I might have escaped. That was until yesterday."

Harker appears to shudder at the recollection, and he gulps down the remains of his whiskey.

"I was holed up in Rome. Getting ready to come down here to Sorrento and approach you. That was when I looked out the window of the apartment I was renting and saw a man standing on the other side of the road. He was staring right up at my window. Like he was watching the place."

He sits there staring nervously at Peter. Whatever it is that he's found himself embroiled in, Peter has finished weighing him up, and though he's not sure he fully believes in some "group" pulling international strings, he believes enough of it to feel that Harker is in genuine trouble with some force that is far beyond his capability to deal with.

"And you're sure you haven't been followed here?" Peter asks.

"Yes," Harker replies confidently. "The moment I saw

the man in the street, I gathered my things and left the apartment. Went to the roof and climbed out of there by the fire escape. I had already hired a boat which I kept moored on the Tiber. I used the river to reach the sea and make my way here by that way. Avoiding roads and public transport."

Peter is nodding. "Good," he says. "I'm going to trust you, Mr. Harker."

Relief floods the journalist's face. "Oh thank you," he says, twisting to face Michael as well. "Thank you."

Peter's eyes then go dark and his voice becomes a growl. "But if you make me regret that trust, you won't have to worry about some group. You will have to worry about me."

Harker swallows down a lump and nods.

CHAPTER 3

THEY MADE HIM UP A BED ON THE TOP FLOOR OF the villa; essentially an attic. It was small and more a cupboard than a room, but its windowless state was an advantage for hiding someone.

The next morning Peter awakens to the sound of Bella making a row as she enters the villa through the front door downstairs. The old Italian housekeeper has a habit of talking to herself, and often these talks turn bitter and she begins arguing. Today, it would seem, she is in a foul mood. Her husband, Giuseppe, is getting the brunt of it, and, as if he is here in person, she remonstrates with the absent spouse.

"Bella, Bella," Peter whispers as he meets her on the stairs. "I have a friend staying."

Her wrinkled brow folds like the bellows of an accordion. "*You* have a friend staying?"

In the year that she has cared for their home, Bella Tomasi has never known of anyone ever visiting Peter. The boy, yes. Girls mostly. But not the master of the house. And certainly no one staying the night.

Peter tells the old Italian a little tale about a friend of his coming to stay because he's had a breakdown and needs to get away from America.

"He needs plenty of rest and quiet," Peter explains to her. "So you must keep away from the attic."

"*Sì, Signor Swartz,*" she says, and soon the housekeeper is preparing breakfast.

It is Michael who takes it up to their guest. He finds the door to the room not just locked but wedged with a chair under the knob.

Before knocking, the kid brings an ear to the wood. The guy is tapping away at his computer. Something he's been doing since they shut him in there ten hours ago.

Eventually rapping the door with a knuckle, Michael calls out that it's breakfast. Harker stops typing, gets up. Scraping the chair away, he opens the door a crack. He takes one look at the breakfast of sausage, eggs, toast, and grimaces.

"Have you got anything vegan?" he asks.

"You like grapefruit?"

"That would be nice."

And with that he closes the door on the kid and the breakfast.

The first two days he stays with them he doesn't come out of the room. All they see of him is what they get through the gap in the door that he pokes his head out of when he takes his meals. The only sound he makes is from his fingers tapping away on the laptop—like a scratching rat above their heads.

On the third night, he creeps out from his den, comes downstairs, asks them if they have a chessboard. They do, and so begins a nightly ritual of him beating the bejesus out of them both playing chess. It is during these games that John Harker gradually comes out of his shell. Isn't so nervous around them.

Indeed, as the days gather into a week, there starts to show a restlessness in him. The refrigerator has a calendar on it. He begins marking off the days until May 30th with big red marker pen Xs.

Excepting the nightly chess tournament, he spends all his hours inside the attic on his laptop, hard at work making notes or trying to decipher the files. At these times he becomes very despondent. When Peter or Michael bring him his food, they try to enter into conversation with him. His answers are vague and come in as few words as possible, his eyes glazed over, looking like he hardly hears a thing they are saying, his mind far away in some distant meditation.

On the eighth day he becomes really edgy. He doesn't touch his laptop all day and spends the time listening out for any external noise that stands out. Then, when Peter brings him his evening meal, he asks if Bella can be trusted.

"I trust her with my son's life," Peter tells him. "Her husband, too. I know good people, and they are good people."

Twice over the next days Harker actually leaves the room with all his belongings packed inside his roll-top rucksack, ready to bolt from their abode and get out of Sorrento altogether.

Each time, Peter convinces him to stay, and, eventually,

the computer hacker apologizes and gets back inside the room.

During the nightly chess battles, Harker speaks very little, but when he does, it is to voice worry. Not for the safety of his own skin, but to the possibility of him not lasting the month until the summit. Lately, he has been working on a way of getting himself physically close to Anthony Eustace while there.

"The thing is," he says while taking Michael's bishop, "I may need your help in it."

"Isn't babysitting you enough?" the kid quips. Upset that another piece has fallen to the journalist.

"Ha-ha," Harker replies dryly.

On the eleventh day, he begins talking about his time spying on the people he believes responsible for the conspiracy. He mentions a "cuckoo" and a giant of a man who he still sees in his nightmares. There is also a man with deep-set eyes ringed in black, who he is sure is at the bottom of it somehow, but who he'd never learned the name of.

Like a lot of what he rambles on about during his days as their guest, much of it is incoherent. No sooner does he begin speaking on one subject than he's onto the next. It is almost like he's not talking to Peter or Michael but to himself. At first, they ask questions, but soon they don't bother. Because he never really gives them a straight answer, just continues to go around in circles.

After a week of being hunkered down in that cramped attic, he begins speaking about death.

"I never knew my father," he tells them. "He died when I was only six months. A car accident. One minute he was on his way back from the grocery store with Pampers. The next he's being poleaxed by a forty-ton truck with a sleeping driver behind the wheel. He was the same age as me. Twenty-seven. Just like Kurt Cobain or Jim Morrison."

"Do you fear death?" Peter asks.

He thinks about it. Looks up from the chessboard. "I don't think so."

The next day Harker is actually upbeat. They find him in the kitchen cooking them breakfast. Afterwards, they have to leave to go to their boat, the *Mother-Magda*. Harker gets nervous. It is the first time that both of them have left him alone.

"Don't worry," Peter says. "You're perfectly safe here."

"But *I* got in."

"Dude," Michael says, already a little tired at their guest's antics, "listen. We have to go check on our boat and pay our marina fees. If we don't, they get shitty. We gotta do about half an hour's work on the boat and pay a visit to the office. We'll be back in less than an hour. Promise."

The two leave him, and are back fifty minutes later.

They are chatting as they push open the living-room door. The lights are off and the blinds closed. But they can sense that someone is in the room with them.

Michael snaps the lights on. At first, they see no one. Then they spot something in the far corner which sends a cold sweat charging from their pores.

John Harker is lying sprawled on his back. His face is twisted into a look of painful horror. Blood oozes from the corners of his mouth. His chest sinks in. Someone has stomped him to death.

Scan the QR code below to purchase HUNTER KILLER.
Or go to: righthouse.com/hunter-killer